MOLLY'S REVENGE

MOLLY'S REVENGE

KAY D. RIZZO

Pacific Press® Publishing Association
Nampa, Idaho
Oshawa, Ontario, Canada
www.pacificpress.com

Cover design by Gerald Lee Monks
Cover design resources from dreamstime.com
Inside design by Aaron Troia

Copyright © 2011 by Pacific Press® Publishing Association
Printed in the United States of America

You can obtain additional copies of this book by calling toll-free
1-800-765-6955 or by visiting http://www.adventistbookcenter.com.

The author assumes full responsibility for the accuracy of all facts and
quotations as cited in this book.

ISBN 13: 978-0-8163-2490-3
ISBN 10: 0-8163-2490-5

11 12 13 14 15 • 5 4 3 2 1

Contents

7   **Chapter One:** *Changes at the Manor*

19   **Chapter Two:** *The Ax Falls*

30   **Chapter Three:** *Difficult Choices*

39   **Chapter Four:** *Shakespeare and the Cameo Brooch*

50   **Chapter Five:** *The Crossing*

57   **Chapter Six:** *An Unexpected Surprise*

64   **Chapter Seven:** *The Parting*

75   **Chapter Eight:** *Irish Need Not Apply*

87   **Chapter Nine:** *The Charade*

94   **Chapter Ten:** *Sabotage*

105 **Chapter Eleven:** *More Than an Adventure*

114 **Chapter Twelve:** *Summertime Romance*

125 **Chapter Thirteen:** *Terror by Night*

135   **Chapter Fourteen:** *Into the Unknown*

149   **Chapter Fifteen:** *Out in the Cold*

160   **Chapter Sixteen:** *Serenity Inn*

171   **Chapter Seventeen:** *A New Life*

186   **Chapter Eighteen:** *All About Tavis*

CHAPTER ONE

CHANGES AT THE MANOR

S EVENTEEN-YEAR-OLD MOLLY MAGUIRE TWIRLED across the field of Irish clover. Her green gingham skirt and layers of hand-embroidered petticoats billowed like a dandelion seed in the wind. Overhead the sun peeked through clouds; the earlier storm had moved on to the horizon. The girl lifted her face toward the sky and began to sing.

"I'll give to you a paper of pins,
And that's the way our love begins,
If you will marry me, me, me,
If you will marry me."

The breeze carried her lilting soprano voice across the fields between the Pembrooke estate and the edge of town. When a capricious gust of wind loosened the satin ribbons beneath her chin, her poke bonnet swirled high above her head. Laughing, the girl gave chase. As she did, a riot of ebony curls broke free from the confines of the whalebone combs on each side of her head, and danced about her shoulders in wild array.

Abandoning society's rules for a proper young lady, Molly executed a graceful somersault, righted herself, and quickly straightened her many layers of skirts. Only then did she hope that no one had witnessed her impulsive schoolgirl behavior. At that moment, the words to one of her father's favorite Bible verses popped unbidden into her mind. *"Rejoice in the Lord alway: and again I say, Rejoice."* Somehow the verse seemed appropriate on such a beautiful day.

Over and over, the wind played tag with Molly's bonnet, letting it land and then flit out of the pursuing girl's reach. After several attempts, she caught one of the ribbons. Holding on against a determined gust, she turned her face toward the breeze and laughed. "Aha! I win!" For that one brief moment, she felt as free as the child she'd been when she first came to live at the manor. But the moment passed. Molly sighed and stepped into the shadows hovering about the cold stone manor house.

The Pembrooke manor house cast an imposing gloom on the green fields alongside the river Shannon. As grand as the towering gray building appeared to passersby and villagers, it both fascinated and repelled the daughter of Ian Maguire, the late part-time Quaker lay preacher and full-time horse groom for the estate. The same was true of the lady of the manor.

Lady Glenola Pembrooke, a diminutive wisp of a woman, reigned supreme over the tiny hamlet and the surrounding countryside in southern Ireland. Bedecked in the latest Parisian fashions, the woman became the center of attention whenever she rode to town. As her black phaeton passed, women curtsied. Field workers and shopkeepers paused and removed their hats out of respect.

Tales of bravery during the Cromwell invasion of southern Ireland, along with numerous other legends of heroism, had reinforced the stature of the local nobility in the eyes of the community. A spooked mare, a runaway phaeton, and Molly's father's brave rescue of Lady Pembrooke had joined the family's lore. That Ian Maguire had been trampled beneath the horse's hooves only added to the vivid retelling of the yarn at the pubs and teahouse in town. Grateful for saving the life of his wife, Lord Pembrooke hired Molly's mother, Enid, to be chief cook for the manor.

Before Ian Maguire's body was cold in the ground, Lord Pembrooke had moved Widow Maguire and her twelve-year-old daughter, Molly, out of their one-room, thatched-roof cottage and into the manor house.

The estate had been in the Pembrooke family for more than three hundred years. The current Lady Pembrooke, the youngest daughter of an impoverished English baronet, came to the manor as a bride of eighteen. The aging Irish baron married the English lass, hoping the union would produce a bevy of doe-eyed daughters and rakishly handsome sons whom he could parade before friends and family in London. Alas, twenty years had passed and no children filled the empty chambers; no heirs graced the family tree that was artfully stenciled onto one of the library walls.

Instead of the sound of children's laughter, a haunting silence filled the musty rooms off of the manor's silent corridors. Giant portraits of long-dead Pembrookes lined the walls of the great room, which had been designed to hold parties and luxurious banquets. The dining salon smelled of beeswax and turpentine. Twenty-two empty black oak Jacobean carved chairs guarded the massive, highly polished mahogany dining table. The tapestry hanging over the cavernous fireplace depicted the bloody battle of 1650 against the Cromwell invasion.

"God has cursed me among women," the grand lady lamented to anyone who might listen.

When Molly and her mother joined the household staff, their benefactor's wife latched on to the twelve-year-old with the deep-set eyes the color of the waters that lapped the shores surrounding the isle. If Lady Pembrooke couldn't birth a daughter, she would turn the peasant girl into a lady of distinction and promise. The grand lady dreamed of the day she could parade Molly, as a trophy of her gracious benevolence, before her London friends. Once there, Molly would steal the heart of a titled young swain and return with him to Ireland to fill the Pembrooke manor with the babies that Lord and Lady Pembrooke could not produce.

That Molly's father had taught the girl to read and to do figures both surprised and pleased the titled woman. That the child had a unique gift with numbers pleased Lord Pembrooke, a man who could never master the simplest of mathematical concepts. On Molly's thirteenth birthday, the aging aristocrat put the girl's talents to work balancing the estate's ledgers.

By her fifteenth birthday, Molly knew more about the Pembrookes' financial affairs than did their personal solicitor, Sir Thomas Malloy. As a result, the girl worried over the trend of unwise extravagance by the lord and lady of the manor. With a famine in the land deepening, how long could such reckless spending continue?

Yet, whenever she approached Lord Pembrooke about the manor's bleak financial picture, the old man's reply was always the same. "Please, Molly, don't bother me with figures. Numbers only confuse me." As the withered old man spoke, his brow would wrinkle. Wheezing between every two words, he repeatedly reminded her, "I'll take a French cravat to tie or a piece of horseflesh to judge over tabulating a column of numbers any day."

Most days Lady Pembrooke spent a couple of hours in her private sitting room, instructing Molly about the intricacies of proper decorum for a lady entering London society. The girl learned how to glide into a room like a lady, how to flirt with one's fan, which fork to use when dining on lobster, and how to sit properly while wearing multiple layers of petticoats and a hoopskirt.

While most of the rooms in the manor were dark and shadowy, sunlight filled Lady Pembrooke's sitting room even on rainy days. Some unknown artist had scattered tiny yellow and blue flowers across the walls. Gilt-framed paintings of angelic nymphs cavorting in English gardens added to the room's charm. On shelves across from the windows, a collection of delicate Venetian glass animals sparkled in the sunlight. The delicate aroma of lemon verbena permeated the air. The lady's tight, springy curls would bounce excitedly about her face as she mangled excerpts from Bach, Beethoven, and Handel on the mahogany fortepiano.

At the end of each day's lesson, the lady would give a reading assignment from an English author such as Chaucer, Pepys, or Shakespeare for Molly to read. While Molly enjoyed reading about brave knights and ladies from England's glorious past, the art of numbers made more sense to the girl than most people and their goings-on. Her one exception was a leather-bound book of sonnets by William Shakespeare.

Because Lady Pembrooke habitually slept until noon, Molly spent her mornings in the library, working on the estate's books. As the giant grandfather clock in the hall gonged eleven, Lord Pembrooke would peek around an edge of the library's double doors and grin. "Heigh-ho, little girl," he would say. "How are ye doin'? Isn't it time ye got a wee bit of sunshine?"

Then he would hobble into the room with his silver-headed cane, always pausing in front of the massive mahogany desk to catch his breath. While no one but Molly seemed to notice, she knew that neither the man's deep, bone-wracking cough nor his wife's reckless spending could continue forever.

From Cork to Londonderry, Ireland's Second Potato Famine had struck peasants and farmers alike. While the commoners scratched for every morsel of food they could find, Lady Pembrooke dined on succulent roasts and on rich pastries. While the babies and young children in the neighboring communities grew pale and listless from the lack of proper nutrition, the lady of the manor commissioned Parisian fashion designers to create ball gowns of lace-trimmed satin. The woman imported new settees upholstered in silk brocade for the seldom-used morning room, while the lord of the manor added thoroughbred horses and luxury carriages to his stable. Lady Pembrooke lavished more on Molly's gowns than any girl could ever wear.

It wasn't that Lady Pembrooke didn't care about her people, Molly reasoned. The woman never noticed others' needs as long as hers were being met. And no one dared bring the current situation to her attention.

Not so with Molly's mother, Enid. While the head cook couldn't openly criticize her mistress's behavior, she was concerned that Molly would forget her Quaker father's values of thrift and simplicity. To instill a touch of reality in the young girl, Enid received permission from Lord Pembrooke to take food leftover from the weekend's feasts, on Monday mornings before the lady awakened, to town to the Widow's Mite, a charity organization with which Molly's father had been involved. At the soup kitchen, the mother and daughter would prepare and serve hot meals to the hungry of the community.

Enid considered this to be Molly's and her special time together. On the walk to and from the manor, the mother would remind her daughter of her father's philosophy of living.

"Love the Lord thy God with all thy heart, and with all thy soul, . . . and with all thy mind; and thy neighbour as thyself," she would say. "Jesus said this is the essence of God's law. Scripture says that 'inasmuch as ye have done it unto one of the least of these my brethren, ye have done it unto me.' What an honor it is to prepare and serve food in the name of the King of the universe, to see God's approval in three-year-old Kaitlin Conners's dimpled grin!"

Molly would recall her mother's admonitions as she ladled hot turnip soup into a wooden bowl for Doyle, the odorous town drunk with the scraggly beard. And when scruffy little boys with matted hair and runny noses threw their arms around her waist in gratitude for the food she gave them, Molly forced herself to picture each one wearing the emaciated face of Jesus as depicted in the dusty religious tomes found in the Pembrooke library.

Reaching the estate property while returning from town, Enid continued to the manor to prepare the luncheon meal for the lord and lady of the house, but the girl detoured to the stables to enjoy her favorite hour of the entire week. The stable odor revived Molly's fading memories of her father and their special times together. That she could ride Bettybelle, her favorite mount, delighted her. That she could spend time with Tavis Lloyd, the flaxen-haired young groom trained by Molly's father before his untimely death, was what she called the "dumpling in her soup."

The loss of Ian Maguire had created a bond between Molly and the young man. Tavis had come to the stables as a gangly fifteen-year-old orphan. Molly's father had taught him how to care for a stable of thoroughbreds, mentoring him to become an expert groom for the estate. And while working with the horses, Ian Maguire taught by word and by example what it meant to be a follower of the Christ, as the older man called his Savior.

After her father's death, the twelve-year-old girl trailed after the young man like an enamored pup. In her eyes, the young man was an Adonis and a medieval knight rolled into one package. And Tavis, sympathetically tolerating her adoration, paraded his knowledge of horses and life in general before her.

That Tavis had a sweetheart in town named Deidre didn't deter Molly's admiration. Thus, by default, Tavis became Molly's test subject for Lady Pembrooke's instruction in the feminine art of charm and allurement. (Years later, the girl blushed when she recalled the day she first fluttered her Spanish lace fan at him and batted her eyelashes.)

Instead of being captivated by her attempt to flirt, the boy frowned. Thinking he missed her cue, Molly batted her eyes a second time and cast him a coy, teasing smile over the ruffled fan. His scowl deepened.

"What's wrong, Molly? Do you have a blinker in your eye?"

"No!" Frustrated and humiliated, she whirled about and stomped back toward the manor. Her dramatic exit ended when her shoe became caught in her skirt hem, throwing her facedown in a mud puddle. Tavis hurried to help her to her feet. "Are you all right?"

The area of Molly's face not dripping with mud flamed a brilliant red. Fiery darts shot from her eyes. "Of course, I am all right! Why shouldn't I be?" Tears streaked down her muddy cheeks. She shook her arm free from his grasp and stalked toward the safety of the manor, leaving the confused young man scratching his head.

Similar attempts to practice on Tavis the lessons in seduction she'd learned failed just as horribly until Molly decided Lady Pembrooke's techniques might attract aristocrats in London, but they definitely did not work on horse grooms and Irish farm boys!

"Tavis? Tavis, where are you?" she called. "Is Bettybelle ready to ride?"

"I'm in here." His voice came from the tack room. "And no, I haven't had time to saddle her this morning."

Molly eyed a shiny, black English barouche with silver festoons parked at the carriage house door. She frowned. "Don't tell me Lord Pembrooke has purchased another carriage," the girl mumbled beneath her breath. "Or do we have a visitor? No one ever visits the manor unannounced."

As she passed two of the stalls on the left, a matched pair of thoroughbred Arabian horses caught her eye. Their magnificent coats, manes, and tails were freshly brushed. Molly bounded into the tack room. "What's going on? Who owns those beautiful horses?"

Tavis looked up from the silver buckles he was polishing on a harness. "Lord Pembrooke's son, the Baron and Baroness of High Wycombe." His frown deepened as he rubbed the shiny surfaces.

"Really?" Molly blinked in surprise. "I thought the Pembrookes had no children."

"They don't, at least the missus doesn't. The baron is the son from Lord Pembrooke's first marriage. The woman died in childbirth, so I've been told." Tavis placed the harness on a hook. "The baron's money came to him through his wife's lineage, not through Lord Pembrooke."

"Really? What are they like?"

"What you'd expect—London nobility." After spitting out the words in disgust, Tavis lowered his voice. "Take my word for it, little pigeon; this day will not end well. The baroness diminishes Lady Pembrooke's fancy airs to the affectations of a wealthy merchant's spouse. You better get up to the manor and change into your fancy garb before the mistress calls for you. I'm sure she'll show you off before her guests."

Molly glanced down at her green gingham skirt. *This will not do,* the girl thought. She swung her bonnet as she dashed across the barnyard toward the manor. "I hope you're wrong about an ill wind blowing," she called to Tavis over her shoulder.

In the doorway to the kitchen, Molly paused to catch her breath. A tall, thin middle-aged stranger wearing a morning coat and dark gray trousers emerged from behind the door. He ran an insolent gaze from her face down to her walking boots and back again to her tousled curls. His upper lip curled with disgust. "Molly Maguire, I presume?"

"Er, yes, sir!" The girl's hands shook as she brushed her ebony curls out of her face.

The stranger bristled. "I am not a sir!"

"Oh, sorry sir, er, I mean . . ." She blushed and shot a quick glance toward the kitchen staircase that led to the third floor and to the security of the room she shared with her mother.

The man glared down at her as he would a cockroach crawling across the floor. His left eyebrow arched. "Molly Maguire, you may refer to me as Lord Pembrooke." He studied her comely face until the girl reddened under his penetrating gaze. "So ye are the bonny lass to whom my father has entrusted the books of the manor."

"Uh, yes, sir, er, sorry, sir, er, Lord Pembrooke." She dropped her hands to the sides of her skirt and executed a nervous curtsy.

"Go to your room and change into more appropriate garb. And please, wash the perspiration from your face. I'll expect you to be in the library in a quarter hour. I need to discover the havoc you have wreaked in my father's books and how much money you've bilked from my stepmother!"

At the word *havoc,* Molly's face flushed. At the word *bilked,* her mouth dropped open and then quickly clamped shut. That she might be skimming money from the Pembrooke's till burned her to the quick. Fortunately, her parents had taught her that arguing with a person of title can only lead to trouble. "Yes, Lord Pembrooke," she mumbled.

Molly could feel the baron's icy gaze follow her up the staircase.

When she'd rounded the corner at the top of the third floor landing, the girl opened the door to her room and tossed her bonnet on to the bed. Her hands shook as she threw open the doors of the armoire in the corner of the room. At the sound of a knock on the bedroom door, the girl froze.

"Miss Molly? Miss Molly? Do you need any help?" It was Anne, Lady Pembrooke's personal maid and Molly's best friend.

Relief flooded through the girl. "Oh, yes, please come in."

A buxom fifteen-year-old with a crop of freckles and strawberry blond hair entered the room. "I thought you might. I was in the kitchen when the baron—" Anne removed a gown with a yellow and blue flowered pattern from the armoire. "Tightening your corset by yourself would be an impossible task. Also ye should tie back your hair from your face with a blue or yellow ribbon. Ye will want to emphasize your girlish innocence."

Molly bristled. "Innocence? I am innocent! I've done nothing wrong."

"I'm sorry." The girl dropped the confining garment over Molly's tangled curls. "I know that and ye know that, but Mr. Fancy Britches doesn't, so don't argue! Today is the time to use those feminine wiles Lady Pembrooke has been teaching you."

Molly planted her hands on her hips and held her breath as Anne tightened the drawstrings of her corset. "Tighter, girl, tighter!" Anne coaxed. "You are lucky you weren't here this morning. Lord Pembrooke and his hoity-toity wife have caused nothing but trouble since they arrived—shouting orders to the staff and insulting poor Lord Pembrooke for his lax operation of everything from the stables to the kitchen staff. Even milady—awakened before ten this morning, if you can believe it—has been in a worrisome snit after meeting the baron." Anne lowered a dress over Molly's head and fastened the closures at the waist.

Anne grabbed Molly's hairbrush from the bureau. "Your hair looks like you were caught in a whirlwind. Whatever did you do? Run in the rain?" The maid continued her report on the morning's harried events since the couple arrived. "When the baron learned that your mother wouldn't take the time to inventory the larder before serving lunch, he ranted and raved. Your mother apologized and asked him which he would prefer she do first—count the jars of fruit in the cellar or prepare a cheese quiche for the baron and his guests. You would have been proud of her."

Molly smirked. Even a baron withered before Enid's calm, self-controlled logic.

"Of course, he reversed his orders in favor of the meal." Anne giggled. "She's adding dumplings to a stew as we speak."

Anne drew back the top and sides of Molly's dark hair and tied them in place with a yellow ribbon. After applying a puff of powder to Molly's cheeks, the chambermaid stepped back and announced, "There! Ye look ready to greet even the grumpiest of barons."

Molly examined herself in the mirror above the bureau. The blue of her eyes appeared darker than usual, barely hiding the storm lingering somewhere in their depths. "I may look better, but I surely don't feel any better."

Anne waved a knowing finger under Molly's nose. "Have you done the best job you could with the Pembrookes' finances? Have you tried to cheat the Pembrookes out of anything that is theirs?"

Molly shook her head. "Then you mustn't let the baron intimidate you. You must go into the library with your head held high, just like Lady Pembrooke has taught you to do."

Molly gulped. "That's easier said than done."

"That's how I became milady's personal maid. I listened and learned. I know who I am; I'm good at what I do; and I never let her forget it!" Anne gave a sharp nod to punctuate her words.

Molly examined her reflection in the mirror a second time and took a deep breath. "I'll try—"

Anne's eyes flashed with irritation. "No! You won't just try; you will do it. If you don't, the baron will eat you alive. He'll blame you for any real or imagined errors he uncovers, including an out of place inkblot or a smudge in the margins. Ye must do it. Understand?"

Despite the knot growing in her stomach, Molly grinned. She'd never known Anne to display such fire.

The maid gave Molly a shove toward the door. "Get down there and prove to the man that we're not a bunch of country bumpkins!"

Molly chuckled as she straightened her spine and descended the main staircase. The girl glided down the long corridor to the library. Recalling Lady Pembrooke's instruction on the importance of making a dramatic entrance, she paused at the carved oak doors before rapping lightly.

"Come in," the baron called. His voice contained an edge of irritation.

Molly took a deep breath, squared her shoulder, and said, "Lord Pembrooke, sir?"

Seated at the massive mahogany desk where she spent most mornings, he bade her enter the room without glancing up from the open ledger. "Don't dawdle, lass! Come in! Come in!"

Molly crossed the Persian carpet and paused in front of the desk. The man glanced up from the page he'd been examining. A pince-nez attached to a brown cord pinched the tip of his long, bony nose. A deep frown creased his brow. "Ye can't see the numbers from over there, girl. Walk around the desk."

She obeyed, stopping at one side of his winged-back desk chair.

"*Tsk!* Pull up a side chair and sit down! Do I have to tell you everything? Frankly, I can't imagine how such an uneducated lass as you appear to be kept such tidy ledgers! But I must confess your records appear to be accurate." The baron babbled on about the neatness of her columns of recorded numbers while she slid one of the armless side chairs next to him and sat down. "When my father told me he had a seventeen-year-old lass keeping his books, I had heart palpitations. But I must admit I am pleasantly surprised. I only wish you could have prevented my stepmother and my dear old dad from living so extravagantly."

"That is not my job, sir, er, Lord Pembrooke."

"No, of course not." He glanced over at her for the first time, carefully noting her hair and dress. "But by the looks of your notations, ye certainly have benefitted from Lady Pembrooke's largess with numerous dresses, petticoats, shawls, cloaks, hats—"

Molly bristled. "Whatever she purchased for me was her idea. I never asked her for anything."

"Oh, I know! I know! The woman and her insane notion that she could pass off a common lass like you off as London aristocracy!" He clicked his tongue in disgust. "Besides, her purchases for you pale before the mountain of expenditures she made for herself." Again he paused to express groans of displeasure. "But then, to be fair, my father did his own damage to the family fortune as well, purchasing thoroughbred horses, and, by the looks of the carriage parked in the carriage house, a new brougham every year. Was there no one to curtail their extravagance?"

Molly stared down at her hands folded in her lap. Many times she'd brought the problem to the attention of Lord Pembrooke, only to be waved away like a worrisome child.

"And how long has he had this cough of his? By the looks of the records, he's not called the local physician to the manor in over a year."

Irked at hearing anyone criticize the kindly old man, Molly stiffened. "Milord has had a cough since his bout with pneumonia two winters ago. Otherwise the Pembrookes have been incredibly robust." Feeling awkward discussing the health of her employer and friend with a stranger, she added, "Perhaps you should talk with him regarding his health."

"Ah, do I detect a note of loyalty from you, lass?" The man readjusted his spectacles. "Of course, you are right. You are a mere servant in his house."

Mere servant? By the way the Pembrookes treated her, Molly hardly felt like a servant. But she had to admit the man was right about her station—a servant she was.

"For the sake of my father's health and for the sake of his dwindling finances, my wife and I will be making some major changes around here. But for now, you are dismissed."

Molly started in surprise. "I thought you wished to go over the books with me."

"I've seen all I need to see. You've done an exceptional job, Molly Maguire, above and beyond your station. I must confess I couldn't find even a smudge or an inkblot on any page. While your services are appreciated, from here on out, I will control the financial records of the manor. You may go."

Startled by his abrupt dismissal, she rose to her feet and gave a short curtsy. Before she reached the door, Lord Pembrooke added, "Please pass on the word to the rest of the manor staff that tonight at seven, they are to assemble in the great room. At that time, my wife and I will announce the changes we intend to make." When Molly failed to respond as quickly as the man expected, he waved her away. "Go! Go!"

CHAPTER TWO

THE AX FALLS

MOLLY STEPPED INTO THE corridor and inhaled sharply. She'd survived, just like Anne had promised. She had also maintained her ladylike demeanor as Lady Pembrooke had instructed. *Lord Pembrooke may call me a common lass, but he can't turn me into one,* she reminded herself. Remembering the baron's order to pass on the word about the dreaded meeting to the manor staff, the girl shuddered. Whatever the man had to say, she knew it wouldn't be good news for the servants.

Word swept through the estate like a midwinter rainstorm, leaving a dark cloud hovering over the staff. To avoid their questions, Molly retired to her room. With no receipts to log for Lord Pembrooke and no calls from Lady Pembrooke, the girl had little to do. She picked up the lady's copy of *Beowulf* that she'd been assigned to read and flipped through the pages. Restless and bored, Molly she sat down in the rocker beside the dormer window. Her gaze wandered to the nightstand beside the bed she and her mother shared. On top of the nightstand lay the Maguires' most treasured possession: a tattered and worn copy of the English Breeches Bible. The girl smiled, remembering when her father told her the history of the book.

"The version was called the Breeches Bible," he had explained, "because of the text in Genesis in which the translator used the word *breeches* instead of *fig leaves* to tell how Adam and Eve cover their nakedness. This book was passed down to your grandfather from his grandfather, and for several generations past."

After Molly's father died, Enid read aloud from it each night before she extinguished the flame in the oil lamp beside the bed. Many times the girl was so tired after a long day that she wished her mother would forget the nightly ritual.

Molly so wished she could talk with her mother about the day's events. A sense of panic arose inside of her. She felt so alone. The girl picked up the Book and flipped through the pages.

"Let's see, where is the text Mama read about having perfect peace?" But try as she might, Molly couldn't find the promise Enid so often claimed.

Knowing her mother would be busy until the seven o'clock meeting, she thought of Tavis. No, he'd been busy caring for the additional horses in the stable. As for Lady Pembrooke, the great lady was sure to be occupied with her guests.

"Stop fretting," Molly scolded herself aloud. "The baron and his wife will return to London soon, and life around here will, once again, return to normal."

Outside the window, clouds gathered in the sky. A cold drizzly rain began to fall. The hours dragged by. Each hour she heard the grandfather clock gong on the second-floor landing. She tried reading Spenser's *The Faerie Queene* but couldn't concentrate. Abandoning *The Faerie Queen,* Molly thumbed through a book of poems by Christopher Marlowe but quickly tossed it aside.

Molly wandered down the stairs to the kitchen, where she found the staff abuzz like bees in an overturned hive. Knowing she was in the way, the girl set out in search of Anne. She slipped back up the kitchen stairs to the third floor and knocked on the door of the chambermaids' quarters. There was no answer.

"*Hmm,* perhaps she's helping milady." The girl descended the main staircase to the family quarters on the second floor just as Anne rushed out of Lady Pembrooke's dressing room. The little maid's face was riddled with anxiety. Her arms filled with Lady Pembrooke's gowns, Anne rushed past Molly toward the kitchen stairs, which also descended to the laundry and sewing room.

"Anne, what is happening?"

"Sorry. I can't talk now," Anne called over her shoulder. "Milady has me repairing and packing her traveling clothes."

"Why?"

"She and milord are going to London! And by the sound of it, I am going along as well."

"What?" Molly squealed. "For how long?"

The maid shrugged. "By the amount of outfits she has me packing, I would say, at least, throughout the winter."

Molly stared dumbfounded as Anne disappeared down the staircase. "London?"

For years, Lady Pembrooke had been preparing to present Molly at a debutante ball in London. *Will I be going too?* Molly wondered. Her heart skipped a beat. *And what about Mama?*

When the double doors to Lady Pembrooke's private suite opened, two chambermaids, their arms also filled with milady's fancy ball gowns, rushed past Molly toward the rear staircase. Both had been crying. As Molly put her ear to Lady Pembrooke's bedroom door, she could hear the woman shouting at her other chambermaids. Molly backed away. She hated being on the receiving end of one of the woman's tirades.

Farther down the hall, the doors to Lord Pembrooke's bedroom suite opened. Two of his male servants emerged, also burdened with several of the man's morning coats and riding apparel. Arnold, the lord's personal valet, appeared; his voice was edged with more stress than Molly had ever before heard. "And take care of the creases in those trousers. You know how milord hates double creases!"

If there was anyone at the Pembrooke manor the girl could trust, it was the milord's valet. Since Lady Pembrooke brought the girl to the manor, the short, rotund man had been like a grandfather to Molly.

"Mr. Arnold, what is happening?" she asked.

The man shook his head sadly. "Sorry, dear, I don't have time to explain. You'll know soon enough." He closed the door in her face.

"Explain? Explain what?" The girl threw her hands up in frustration. "That's it. I'm going to ask Tavis! Busy or not, he always knows what is happening." She rushed to her room, grabbed her cloak and bonnet, dashed down the kitchen stairs, and went out the door. Dodging mud puddles, she hurried toward the stables. Inside the barn, she shook the raindrops off of her bonnet. "Tavis! Tavis! Where are you?"

"I'm in Brownie's stall," he called.

Molly ran the length of the stable. "Tavis, what is happening around here?"

"I'm not sure," he admitted. Curry brush in hand, the young man peered over the back of the sleek animal. "All I know is Mr. Grimes, the head groom, ordered me to prepare the horses for inspection, which usually means a buyer is expected."

"Sell the horses? All of them?"

Tavis shrugged. "Whatever is happening must be big. Grimes has the other hands mucking out the stalls and scrubbing down the tack room."

Molly's face drained of color. Her voice became loud and shrill. "They wouldn't sell Bettybelle, would they?"

Again, he shrugged. "I don't know. I'm just doing as I am told to do."

"Oh, I can't let this happen!" If anyone could stop them from selling Bettybelle, she realized it was Lady Pembrooke! The girl gathered her skirts in her hands and dashed back to the manor.

Molly flew into the kitchen, where she found her mother kneading the next day's batch of bread. Enid's eyes were filled with tears.

"Mama! Whatever is happening?"

Molly's mother glanced down at her daughter's muddy feet. "Wipe your feet, child. You'll dirty Mistress Murray's freshly washed floor." The woman pounded the lump of dough with her fist. "All I know is Effie, the parlor maid, told Shawna, the serving girl, that one of the chambermaids told Marybeth and the other the seamstresses that Lord and Lady Pembrooke are closing the manor and moving to London with the baron and his wife."

Molly took a step back as if she'd been punched. "What? What will happen to the manor staff? To you—to me?"

"I suppose we'll discover that at the seven o'clock meeting." Enid folded the dough and continued kneading it.

"Maybe I should ask Lady Pembrooke directly."

Molly's mother blew a strand of hair from her face and shook her head. "Milady's taken to her bed with a case of the vapors."

By the strained expression on Enid's face, Molly knew her mother was as worried as she was.

Whatever will become of us? the girl wondered. *Will we leave our beloved Ireland to live in London?* With all of milady's talk of presenting

Molly to London's high society, the girl had always thought of it as just talk, a fantasy game they played on rainy afternoons. Molly never truly imagined living anywhere but at the manor.

Before the hall clock gonged seven times, the manor's staff gathered outside the great room's doors as ordered. Molly and Tavis exchanged worried glances. The butler Bronson arranged them in the order of the importance of their station. At precisely seven, they filed into the great room and lined up against the nearest wall. Bronson was the last to enter. He slid the great room doors closed behind him and turned to face the Pembrookes.

On the far side of the room, the baron and baroness sat on Lady Pembrooke's forest-green velvet settee. To the left of the baron, Lord and Lady Pembrooke posed like wax mannequins on padded straight-backed chairs. Only Lady Pembrooke's puffy, red eyes and the linen handkerchief knotted in her fist revealed her emotions. When Molly caught her eye, the woman shook her head slightly and mouthed, "I'm so sorry, my dear."

The baroness tilted her nose higher into the air and looked away when she intercepted the message between the lady of the manor and the young girl. Stone-faced, Lord Pembrooke stared at a portrait of his great-grandfather hung high over the double doors. The old gentleman would have stayed immobile had he not broken into a bout of coughing. Molly winced, knowing each deep cough racked his body with pain. Arnold rushed to his employer's side and handed him a clean handkerchief, medicated with a potion of camphor and peppermint.

As Lord Pembrooke's coughing subsided, he leaned back against the chair and closed his eyes. The man's shoulders slumped forward, as if the kindly old man had surrendered to the dictates of his determined son.

The baron cleared his throat and shot a condescending glance toward his father. "As each of you know, over the last couple of years, my father's health has been failing. He is no longer capable of governing the manor properly. My wife and I believe closing the manor and transporting my father and his wife to London will best serve the family estate."

The staff held their collective breaths as he continued, "Lord and Lady Pembrooke wish to thank you for your outstanding loyalty and service. You have each performed your duties admirably. However,

since my wife and I"—he paused and cast his wife a quick glance—
"have an efficiently operating staff in both our home in London and our
summer estate, we cannot possibly assimilate every one of you into our
household."

Molly slowly released her breath as Enid squeezed the girl's upper
arm.

"We have decided my father's valet, Arnold, will go with us, as will
as my stepmother's personal maid, Anne. In the meantime, Bronson
will stay here to close up the manor and sell off the animals. We've
agreed to pay him a small stipend that will allow him to retire at his
home in Cork."

Lady Pembrooke uttered a sudden uncontrolled cry, and then quickly
clamped her handkerchief over her mouth and nose. Several of the
kitchen staff wept into their handkerchiefs as well, as did a number of
the chambermaids.

"I realize that this is a bad time for anyone to be seeking new employment in Ireland, what with the famine and all, but I assure you, this
move cannot be helped. However, we have come up with a possible al-
ternative that might ease your situations." The baron studied the toe of
his left boot for several seconds before continuing. "My wife's brother
owns a tobacco plantation in Virginia. He has agreed to pay your way
to America in return for two years of service. That's more generous than
the customary seven-year contract for indentured servants. Considering
Ireland's current conditions, you might want to consider accepting his
munificent offer."

Slavery. As the ugly word popped into Molly's head, her eyes welled
with tears. She'd heard horror stories from the families of those who'd
fled to the new land. She shot a quick glance toward her mother. Not
only would they be leaving their beautiful Ireland forever, but they'd be
leaving as short-term slaves. Staring straight ahead at a spot above the
heads of the Pembrookes, the woman slid her arm around her daughter's waist.

"I know this sounds harsh, and I wish there were another way, but
alas, there is none." The baron spoke with less confidence in his tone. "I
will expect your decisions whether or not you will accept our offer by
Friday. You are dismissed. Good night."

In their tiny room at the top of the stairs, Enid and Molly prepared for bed in silence. The girl hung her everyday cotton dress in the armoire alongside the fancy evening gowns of lace, velvet, and satin that Lady Pembrooke had commissioned for Molly to wear on their dream journey to London. With London but a fading dream, she wondered where she'd ever wear such delicate garments either in Ireland or in a faraway Virginia plantation.

Enid opened her Bible to Psalm 91. Molly had heard her mother read the passage so often she could recite it: "He that dwelleth in the secret place of the most High shall abide under the shadow of the Almighty. I will say of the LORD, He is my refuge and my fortress: my God; in him will I trust."

The woman paused. A tear dropped on to the page. Even during the days following her father's funeral, the girl had never seen her mother cry.

Molly sat down beside her and slipped an arm around her mother's shoulders. In an almost imperceptible voice, Enid whispered, "Would you please continue reading the passage for me?"

Surprised, Molly took the Bible from her mother's hands. The print blurred before her eyes. Clearing her throat, the girl read, "Surely he shall deliver thee from the snare of the fowler, and from the noisome pestilence. He shall cover thee with his feathers, and under his wings shalt thou trust: his truth shall be thy shield and buckler."

Molly swallowed hard before she could continue. "Thou shalt not be afraid for the terror by night; nor for the arrow that flieth by day; nor for the pestilence that walketh in darkness; nor for the destruction that wasteth at noonday."

Enid dotted her eyes with a handkerchief. "Skip to verse eleven, please."

Molly nodded. "For he shall give his angels charge over thee, to keep thee in all thy ways. They shall—"

"Go to verse fourteen." The older woman's voice broke.

"Yes, Mama." By now Molly's tears made it almost impossible for her to read the words. "Because he hath set his love upon me, therefore will I deliver him; I will set him on high, because he hath known my name."

Even as Molly read the passage, her heart doubted its truth. From what the girl could tell, she and her mother were on their own. "After all we've done for Lord and Lady Pembrooke, we've been thrown to the dogs," she muttered. "And no empty promises from a Bible will change that."

The older woman shook her head. "Oh, no, child. Your father lived by these promises. This particular passage was his favorite. The words have sustained me these last few years as well."

"And a lot of good it did him. Where is he now? And you?" Molly spat out her words.

"Honey, I understand your anger. Many times since your father died, I've felt just as angry."

Molly grunted. "*Hmmph!* Maybe God's mad at you, too, and that's why this is happening to us."

Her mother gave her a sad little smile. "I don't think so. King David, an author of the book of Psalms, got much angrier at God than you or I ever have. And God called him a man after His own heart." The woman continued, "Despite how it looks right now, God promises never to leave us, never to forsake us. And 'never' is a long, long time. In the book of Jeremiah, the prophet said that God loves us with an everlasting love and that He has a unique plan for each of our lives." A strange peace washed across Enid's face as she spoke, easing the heavy worry lines on her forehead. "My problem is, while God may know His plan for us, I do not. And tonight, my faith in God weakened. Please forgive me."

Color flooded Molly's face. "Mama! You have every right to be angry at God. We're being abandoned at a time when our neighbors are dying from a lack of food. We've been given the choice either to starve in Ireland or to sell ourselves into slavery to an unknown, unseen overlord for the next two years!" Her eyes flashed; her heart pounded. "And yes, I'm furious. I'm furious at the Pembrookes—every last one of them! I'm furious at the English government for sitting by and watching the people of Ireland starve! But I'm mostly mad at God for putting us in this situation!"

"Darling, God didn't—"

The girl violently shook her head and covered her ears. "Mama! I don't want to hear it! You and Daddy have been faithful to Him. Even after Daddy died, you continued feeding the starving people of this community. Just who is God going to get to do that now? And if we stay here, how will we eat?"

For a moment, the older woman stared down at her fingers clutching her moist handkerchief, then she looked pleadingly into her daughter's face. "Molly, please pray with me. We need God's strength and His wisdom to know what to do. He's promised that if we acknowledge Him in all our ways, He will lead us down the path we should follow."

"But, Mama—"

"Please?"

"I'm sorry, Mama, but my faith in your God isn't as strong as yours."

Molly arose from the bed, slipped her blue flannel nightgown over her head, and began buttoning the row of buttons on the bodice. "Maybe if your God hadn't taken my father from me, I would be stronger too!"

"My God? He's your God too. Honey, you are His darling daughter, no matter how angry you might be right now. And as frustrated as I am with the Pembrookes right now, I'm certainly not blaming God." Enid gave a short laugh, "The Old Testament warns against putting one's trust in princes. I imagine our situation could include lords and barons as well. As your daddy always said, 'People will often let you down, but God never does.' "

Not pacified by her mother's admonitions, the girl climbed into her side of the bed, turned her face to the wall, and pulled the quilts up to her chin until only an array of tangled black curls on the white pillow-slip could be seen.

When the older woman reached across the bed and touched her daughter's shoulder, Molly pulled away. "Honey, if we ever needed to trust God, it's now. He's promised to supply all our needs—not a few, not half, but all. I must believe He will keep His word, or I think I would wither and die." The woman's voice had dropped to a whisper.

Biting her tongue, Molly wavered between the desire to maintain her pout or to throw her arms around her mother and sob. But the girl knew she was no longer a five-year-old crying over her lost kitten. No amount of tears or comforting hugs could change their situation.

Her mother refused to give up. "You never knew it, but it was your father's dream to immigrate to the New World. He called it a place where a pauper could become a king. *Hmm,* I'm thirty-eight years old. That's not so old. Perhaps I will be allowed to live out his dream."

Molly rolled over in time to see her mother gaze up toward the wood-beam ceiling. The girl had never heard her father talk of migrating anywhere.

The older woman's lips widened. "Yes, this might be the answer for both of us. You will go to London and become a lady of quality, and I can go to America." Enid continued, "I believe that if we ask Lady Pembrooke, she will take you with her."

Molly lowered the quilts away from her face. "You would go across the ocean without me?"

"Darling, like it or not, you are almost a woman now. In the next few years, you will fall in love with a handsome young man and marry him. You will have a passel of babies. It will be your duty to cleave unto him. That's the way of life." Enid laid the Bible on the nightstand beside the bed and extinguished the flame in the oil lamp. "This may be God's way of providing us both with a future."

Molly lay speechless. She'd never imagined that her mother would leave her in England. A sliver of light from the cloud-covered moon outside their window illuminated the foot of the bed. "Mama, I don't want to be away from you."

"Nor I, you; but I do want what's best for you. In Ireland, we have no future. We have no family, no employment, not even a roof over our heads. Our home where we lived before your father's death was rented from Lord Pembrooke, remember?" Molly felt her mother's hand resting on her shoulder.

"Tonight we should both pray about it. Tomorrow morning we can decide what is best for both of us. But know one thing for certain, my dear: God promises to provide for us, whether or not we believe His promises. And He always keeps His word."

Silent tears moistened Molly's pillowslip. After a few minutes, the ropes supporting the feather mattress creaked as her mother climbed out of the bed and dropped to her knees on the cold wooden floor. The girl dropped off to sleep to the familiar rhythmic squeak of the rocker by the window.

Hours later, an overcast light filled the room. Opening her eyes, Molly reached out and felt the other side of the bed. It was empty. As she had every morning for the past several years, Enid had risen early to prepare breakfast for the lord of the manor and his guests.

Molly yawned and stretched. She would wash up, dress, eat a light breakfast, and then go to the library to record the latest transactions in the lord's ledgers. Suddenly, yesterday's events popped to the front of her mind.

"Oh, no!" She leaped from the bed. *What if Mama has already talked with Lady Pembrooke? What if our fates have already been decided?*

She poured water from the white porcelain water pitcher into the tin washbasin, splashed her face, and dried it with the hand towel. Snatching a cotton camisole from the dresser drawer, she slipped it over her head, followed by several petticoats. Without thought, she chose a lavender dress from the armoire and dropped it over her head. Her hands trembled as she tightened a black cinch belt around her waist. After quickly brushing through her hair, Molly gathered her hair into a bun at the nape of her neck and fastened it in place with a set of whalebone combs.

Oh, Mama, please don't speak with Lady Pembrooke about your plan yet. Looking in the wall mirror, she noted the heightened color in her cheeks. *I need you, Mama. I don't want to live in London if you're not with me.*

Molly dashed down the back stairs into the kitchen. "Mama?"

Her mother stood at the stove, stirring a pan of white gravy. "What is it, child? Where are your shoes?"

The girl looked down at her bare feet; her face reddened. She'd forgotten to don her stockings and shoes.

"Go back upstairs and dress your feet, child. You'll catch a death of a cold."

"You haven't spoken to Lady Pembrooke yet, have you?"

Enid smiled and pointed toward the stairs. "Go! Finish dressing. We'll talk after you have eaten your breakfast."

"But you haven't—"

"Go! Now!" The woman warned. "We'll talk later."

Reluctantly, Molly obeyed.

CHAPTER THREE

DIFFICULT CHOICES

MOLLY'S WORLD SEEMED TO have swirled out of control. Molly's mother had arranged for Lady Pembrooke to take Molly to London, in spite of Molly's protests. The girl watched as her mother packed the large steamer trunk Lady Pembrooke had given for the young woman's use. A smaller, more modest trunk rested beside the armoire, the trunk that would hold her mother's less generous wardrobe.

"Please, Mama, please don't make me go," the girl begged even though she knew whatever the Pembrookes decreed would happen.

Enid paused and straightened, her eyes revealing her grief. "Molly, dear, can't you see that this is best for us both? You were always intended to go to London with Lady Pembrooke. As much as I will miss you, I want what is best for my girl. Whether you go to London and I stayed in Ireland or I went to the New World, the results would be the same. We'd be apart. Can't you see that?"

"I could go to America with you, Mama." Tears streamed down the girl's face. "I promise I'll work hard; I am strong."

The older woman took her daughter by the shoulders and stared into the girl's ocean-blue eyes. "You have no idea how difficult the life of an indentured servant can be. Whether your contract is for seven years or for two, you are a slave during that time. You, as a young single woman, would be particularly vulnerable to the prurient whims of your owner. I am older, less likely to attract attention."

"But Tavis says many indentured servants die aboard ship on their way to America," she pleaded.

"He's right, yet he's chosen to leave Ireland nonetheless." The older woman gave her daughter's shoulders a gentle shake. "Again, honey, I am strong. I will be fine, I promise."

"You can't make that promise!" Molly shook free of her mother's grasp and strode across the bedroom.

"No, I can't. I do not know the future. Neither do you. I can only trust that God will be with me to the ends of the earth." Enid picked up the Bible from the nightstand. "And right now, the Commonwealth of Virginia certainly seems to qualify as the ends of the earth."

"Oh, Mama," the girl wailed and flung herself into her mother's arms. "We will never see each other again!"

"We don't know that, darling." Enid dropped the Bible onto the bed and drew her daughter into her arms. Gently, the mother rocked the girl as she would rock a child. "We'll always love each other. I'll always carry you in my heart. And wherever I am, that will always be your home."

"I hate the Pembrookes! And nothing you can say will change my mind!"

"Oh, little one, don't say that. *Hate* is a very strong word. I admit we have a right to be angry, but to hate? It's a poison that eats its host from the inside out."

A knock sounded on their bedroom door, interrupting their conversation. Molly turned toward the window to hide her tears while her mother hurried to answer it. "Yes, Fiona?"

Fiona, the head parlor maid, stepped into the room. "Begging your pardon, Mistress Maguire, but the younger Lord Pembrooke is asking to speak with Molly in the library."

Molly turned in surprise. "Me?"

"Yes, miss." The middle-aged maid bobbed a curtsy. "Right away, in fact."

Enid grabbed a comb from the bureau and tossed it to her daughter. "Here, do something with your hair!"

The girl frowned. "I wonder whatever the baron wants of me. He made it mighty clear the day he reviewed the ledgers that I would no longer be needed."

"I don't know, darling. Who can read the mind of nobility?"

Molly yanked the comb through her long locks while her mother poured water in the porcelain washbasin. "Here! Splash water on your face. Your eyes are red and puffy."

The cool water on her face felt refreshing. Molly adjusted the bodice to her dress, retied the strings to her cinch belt, and pasted a smile on her face. "There! I think I'm ready to go to the lion's den." The staff had given the baron the nickname of the Lion of Pembrooke for his gruff ways.

"Go! Go," her mother urged. "The baron hates to be kept waiting. *Aargh!* He goes absolutely doolally when his morning porridge isn't served the moment he enters the dining hall."

Molly's skirts whirled about her legs as she rushed out of the door and into the third-floor corridor. "Pray for me, Mama," she called.

The girl flew down the two flights of stairs and along the corridor to the library door. Before she could knock, the door slid open.

The lean, ramrod-straight baron scowled down at her! "I didn't call you to have you dillydally in the hallway."

"Yes, sir, er, Lord Pembrooke." She bobbed an appropriate curtsy.

The baron stepped back and allowed her to enter the room. "In the next few weeks, neighboring aristocracy will be visiting, and, as much as I hate it, I must endure their presence in order to sell off the family holdings. With my time employed elsewhere, I need you to once again take over the books, to record each of the transactions I'm making in the sale of the estate goods."

He strode across the room and adjusted a lone book that protruded farther than the others on one of the shelves. The man then flipped his handkerchief as if to remove a speck of dust missed by the parlor maid that morning. "You will find the ledger and the receipts on the desk. Rest assured, I will be looking over your shoulder regularly to be certain you don't fail to record any sales."

Molly's eyes flashed, but she gritted her teeth to remain polite. "I will do my best to please, Lord Pembrooke."

A slight grin teased the corners of his lips. "So my stepmother's pretty little Irish lass has fire behind those deep-blue eyes! Aye, I like a woman with passion in her soul, even if she's merely half a woman."

Molly straightened to her full five-foot four-inch height and glared at the baron's insolent gaze. "Half a woman or not, I will record your sales and tally your sums accurately and in a timely manner as I have always done for your father!"

The baron's expression switched from arrogance to a leer. Remembering her mother's warnings about controlling her temper around aristocracy, the girl stifled a fresh wave of anger welling up inside her. Though Molly had never before seen that particular glint in any other man's eyes, a wave of fear coursed through her body.

"Carry on." Without another word, the baron strode from the room. As the door slid shut behind him, Molly leaned against desk. Her stomach churned; her heart raced; her legs felt weak. She stumbled around the edge of the desk and dropped into the massive leather desk chair. Opening the ledger, she forced herself to forget the strange encounter and concentrate on the task of recording the sales receipts in the appropriate columns.

The afternoon passed quickly. Molly started when she found a sales receipt for her favorite Bettybelle. After recovering from the shock, the girl resumed her task with a renewed determination. When the clock in the hall gonged four, she glanced up from the books in surprise.

Day after day, Molly recorded the required transactions. Day after day, more and more animals and equipment were carted away. And each day the baron dropped by the library to check her work. That he would stand so close beside her that she could count his nose hairs bothered her. She'd become quite adept at leaping to her feet and stepping to one side to let him sit at the desk chair.

The girl hated having so little time to visit Tavis in the stables, though she knew he had no time to spend with her. The baron also had canceled her Monday mornings excursions to town with her mother.

A half hour before teatime one afternoon, Molly was intent on the last of the newest receipts in the ledger when the library door slid open and the baron entered. Dressed in a red silk smoking jacket over a ruffled shirt and dark trousers, he sauntered across the room to the desk. The insolent smile on his face alerted her to the fact that he was up to no good. The girl placed her pen in its holder, slid her chair back, and rose to her feet. Noting that the baron angled toward the left, she stepped to the right.

"What's the matter, little lass? Afraid of me?" He poised himself on the opposite side of the desk. Molly froze. She had heard the rumors about how the baron made untoward advances to the younger chambermaids and scullery maids.

She lifted her chin defiantly. "Yes, I am fearful. Every woman in the manor has warned me to watch out for you." The look of surprise in his eyes pleased her.

"I'm sure that my reputation is exaggerated in the minds of these ignorant wenches."

"Not really, Lord Pembrooke." Molly held her ground. "By the way, those young women are not as ignorant to the ways of a cad as you might think."

"A cad, am I?" A grin teased at the corners of his mouth. "You are a saucy minx, aren't you? I like that." Suddenly, he darted to the right. She headed left but not before he trapped one hand. "Come, my pretty one. Don't play so hard to get."

Molly yanked to free her hand but to no avail. Her skirts pressed against her ankles as he pinned her with his body against the bookcase behind the desk.

"Let me go!" Terrified, she squirmed and pushed against his chest with her free hand.

A guttural laugh rumbled through his body as he pressed himself against her. As Molly fought to escape, he untied the strings of her cinch belt. The belt fell to the floor. "You are a little spitfire. Will we ever have fun once I get you under my own roof in London!"

Molly shoved against his chest but her 115 pounds was no match for the baron's 180. "Let me go!" she demanded but to no avail.

The baron pressed his face against her neck and planted a trail of kisses from her left ear, down her shoulders. As his lips neared the gathered neckline of her blouse, he whispered, "*Aww, give me just one little kiss, a promissory note for good times to come.*"

Molly fought to swallow the bile rising in her throat. She gagged at the smell of the baron's whiskey-laced breath. Tears stung her eyes. A silent prayer came to her lips. "Please, dear Jesus, if Your promises are true, help me to escape this animal."

The man's free hand clutched her about the waist. With the other hand, he fumbled at the buttons at the lace-edged neckline of her blouse.

Molly swiveled her head from side to side. It seemed his lips were everywhere. "Please, Lord Pembrooke, don't do this! Let me go!" she shouted.

When the library door behind them slid open, the baron froze. Molly heard a woman's hysterical shouts. "Owen Pembrooke, unhand that child!"

The baroness swept across the library like a tornado. The man had barely released Molly from his grasp when the woman caught one of the girl's wrists and yanked her away. "You may go!" she snarled at Molly. "I'll deal with you later."

The girl's cheeks flamed as she stumbled to make good her escape. Upon reaching the corridor, Molly leaned her head against the wall to catch her breath. From the corridor, she could clearly hear the baroness's shrill voice. Molly believed the entire population of the manor heard the woman's voice.

"How dare you, you bounder! You rotter! You will not humiliate me in this manner. I won't allow it. Remember, I hold the purse strings. Did you think I wouldn't find out what you've been up to since we came to Ireland? You, of all people, should know that tongues wag in both English and Irish manors. One word from me and my solicitor will cut your allowance to a pittance. You won't only be begging for feminine favors from the scullery maids but also begging for your daily bread!"

Humiliated, Molly fled down the kitchen stairs. The girl wanted to hide—hide from the baron, hide from his wife, hide from her mother—hide from anyone who might have overheard the baroness' rant. As she ran past one of the chambermaids, the girl shot Molly a knowing look.

Not knowing where else to hide, Molly ran toward the stables where Bettybelle had been housed before the mare had been sold to the vicar of Waterville. She dashed into the empty stall, curled up in the back corner, buried her face in her arms, and sobbed. Molly tried to review everything she'd ever said or done that might have encouraged the baron to force himself upon her. If she had flirted with the baron, it was unintentional. Tavis was the only male with whom she'd ever attempted to flirt.

The comforting warmth of the stable and the familiar smells of horses and hay soothed her. "Daddy," she sobbed aloud, "I miss you so much."

Molly tried to recall her father's face. Instead, the baron's leering grin blocked her memory. She realized that this time she'd been lucky—this time she'd escaped. But what about when she found herself alone with him in London? The baron had threatened, "Sooner or later." The girl wrapped her arms about legs and buried her face in her knees.

Molly didn't know how long she remained there but the afternoon sun coming in through the window was low in the western sky when the shadow of a man fell across her. Terrified that the baron had tracked her to the stables, she skittered farther into the corner of the stall.

"Molly? What are you doing out here?" It was Tavis.

Relieved, the girl threw herself into Tavis's arms and buried her face in his chest. Startled, he grasped her quaking shoulders and took a step back to look into her eyes. "Molly? Have you been crying? Are you all right?"

"No," she wailed, shaking her head from side to side. "I'm not all right. I'm far from being all right!"

"It can't be all that bad, can it? Tell me what happened," he coaxed.

Tavis's frown deepened as she spoke. "The baron . . . the baron . . . he . . . he . . . tried to . . ." she sobbed, her words broken by uncontrolled hiccups.

Tavis's body tensed. His grip on her shoulders tightened to the point of pain. "He tried to what?"

"He cornered me in the library. I couldn't get away! He pressed me against the bookshelves. I tried to escape. I really did." She begged him to understand. If Tavis didn't believe her, if he thought she was to blame, she didn't know what she'd do.

Tavis drew the quaking girl into his arms. "What happened is not your fault, little pigeon. Tell me again exactly what happened."

Little pigeon? Little pigeon had been her father's pet nickname for her. No one had called her that since he had died.

"Wait. There are too many ears listening here in the stable. Come where we can talk in private," he urged.

Once isolated in the tack room, Molly repeated him everything, including the baron's remark about what would happen once she went to live in London. Tavis's eyes filled with fury. "You stay here! I'm going to—"

Molly grabbed his arm. "No! You can't do anything. He's a baron. He'll have you thrown into jail, if he doesn't just kill you first."

The young groom shook his arm free of her grasp. She reached for him a second time.

"Think, Tavis! Think! You know I'm right. You can't help me if you're dead or in prison."

The young man heaved a heavy sigh. His head dropped in defeat. "I don't like it, but you're right. Trust me; it will only get worse, regardless of the baroness's threats. And eventually she'll take his side and blame you."

Molly hadn't thought of that possibility. "Me? But I didn't do anything."

Tavis stuck his hands into his pockets and shrugged. "That's a betrayed wife's way of saving face—blaming the other woman."

A new panic rose in Molly's thoughts. "What can I do?"

"First, tell your mother. Then, I think you should reconsider going to live in London. As enticing as Lady Pembrooke's invitation may be, it's not worth destroying your soul. The baron will not quit until he gets what he wants, and then he'll toss you aside. And as far as the law is concerned, a member of the nobility can do whatever he wishes with commoners."

Molly stared down at her hands. Tavis took a step toward the girl and caught her hands in his. Slowly tracing a forefinger over her smaller, delicate hand, he confided, "This is one reason I am going to America. From what I hear, if I work hard, I can escape my old station in life. I can become whatever I want to be in the new world."

"Anything?"

"That's right." His eyes glistened with hope. "I'd like to learn a trade such as blacksmithing and eventually own a livery stable."

Molly blinked in surprise. She'd never before heard the young man speak of his dreams. "And Deidre, is she going with you?"

Tavis slowly shook his head. "No. First, I have no way to earn passage money for her. And, second, she cannot bring herself to leave her family." He sighed. The sparkle in his eyes faded. "I don't blame her. It's easy for me. I don't have a family. If I did, I might feel the same way."

Molly glanced down at the strong, callused hands surrounding hers. "Will you save your money and eventually send for her?"

He shook his head. "No. I can't ask her to wait for me. Her dreams are to be a wife and have a bevy of babies. That is a noble calling for a woman. And the truth be known, I don't think it matters to her whether or not I'm their father and her husband."

"I'm sorry."

"Thanks. Rumor has it Sean O'Riley has already come a-courting." He dropped her hands. "Now you need to find your mother and tell her what happened."

Molly sniffed and nodded. Back at the manor, the girl had barely entered the kitchen when Anne told her she'd been summoned to the baroness' sitting room.

CHAPTER FOUR

SHAKESPEARE AND THE CAMEO BROOCH

SQUARING HER SHOULDERS FOR what Molly feared would be a night-mare, the girl knocked on the room's partially opened door. From inside, the baroness screeched, "Well, answer it, you stupid cow!"

Seconds later, the baroness's personal maid opened the door and stepped back to allow Molly to enter. Molly could see the girl had been weeping.

"You asked to see me?" Molly noted redness around the baroness's eyes. She, too, had been crying.

"Don't just stand there, come in!" The woman dabbed at her nose with a linen handkerchief. "As you obviously know, I saw you in my husband's arms. When I asked, he told me you've been flirting with him every day, and he finally succumbed to your advances."

"Uh—" Molly gasped. Tavis had been right. She would be the one at fault in the baroness's eyes.

"I won't have it, do you hear me, young lady? I won't have it!" The woman grew in volume. "While I admit I don't believe his story, I can't risk this happening again—especially not in London under my own roof. Obviously, if I must choose between my husband and my mother-in-law's pet project, you must be the one to go."

Like a lightning bolt, the realization hit Molly. If she could no lon-ger go to London with the Pembrookes, she would have to go to Amer-ica with her mother. The girl struggled to control her sudden urge to laugh.

"In the meantime, until we leave for London, I expect you to avoid both the library and my husband at all costs. Do we understand one another?"

Molly nodded with more enthusiasm than she had intended. As the girl stepped into the hall, laughter bubbled out of her. Strangely, somewhere in the dark recesses of her mind, she heard her father's voice saying, "All things work together for good to them that love God."

As she skipped up the stairs to her bedroom, the girl giggled. "Maybe all things do work together for good after all. Maybe God *is* answering my prayers."

The baron encountered no problem arranging for Molly to join the indentured servant transfer. The baroness made sure of that. The day of the aristocrats' scheduled departure for London, Lady Pembrooke called Molly to her private sitting room, the room the grand lady had seldom left since the arrival of her stepson and his wife. The girl found the woman reclining on her gold-brocade chaise longue. The lines around the woman's eyes and mouth had deepened. Her pale porcelain skin appeared almost transparent. "Come in, my dear, come in."

Lady Pembrooke gestured for Molly to enter the once orderly room. Brightly colored garments tumbled out of the partially packed travel trunks. The shelves that had held the lady's Venetian figurine collection were empty. Crates containing the woman's favorite books, once at home in the tall, mahogany bookcase beside her beloved fortepiano, were stacked in the back corner. The familiar aroma of lemon verbena had been replaced by the odor of disturbed dust.

Molly curtsied and walked toward the woman she'd come to love and admire. "You asked to see me?"

"Yes, Molly. I am sorry things turned out like this. I had such high hopes . . . I am going to miss you so. Worse yet, I'm afraid I've done you a grave disservice by training you to live above your station in life. For the last five years, you've been the light of my life. I truly think of you as the daughter I never had." She paused and dabbed at her eyes with a lace-edged handkerchief. "Please forgive me for letting you go." The woman gazed up into the girl's face, pleading for understanding.

Tears glistened in Molly's eyes. "Of course, I forgive you. Just assure me that you believe I did not, in any way, encourage Lord Pembrooke's attention."

"Of course, I believe you! My chambermaids keep me informed on the goings-on around here. In his short time in Ireland, my stepson has accosted every young female within a five-mile radius of the Pembrooke estate!" The woman clicked her tongue in disgust. "If I were Lady Pembrooke, I would have shoved him out the door long ago! But alas, things are as they are! However, before I leave, I have some mementos I want to give you."

Molly immediately recognized the leather-bound book the lady pressed into her hand. Embossed on the cover were the words *Sonnets by William Shakespeare.*

"I-I-I cannot take this, Lady Pembrooke," the girl stammered. "You love this book as much as I do."

"But not as much as I love you, my dear." The grand lady's curls danced as the woman vigorously shook her head. "Besides, if I keep it, Lady Pembrooke will eventually claim it for herself. And it will comfort me knowing it is in your possession." Then Lady Pembrooke reached beneath the pillow at her side, withdrew a small black-velvet pouch, and handed it to Molly. "Here, slip this into your pocket. And don't tell anyone, especially my daughter-in-law, about my parting gifts to you. That woman would likely accuse you of theft! Go ahead. Look at it."

With great care, Molly loosened the silken ties and opened the pouch. The girl gasped when a black cameo brooch, surrounded by diamonds and encased in silver filigree, tumbled into her hand.

"Oh my!" So many times she'd admired the exquisitely carved profile of a nameless aristocratic lady. Lady Pembrooke often wore the brooch at the neck of her favorite gray-and-white gown.

"Molly, every time you look at this brooch, I want you to remember that no matter where you go or whatever situation in which you might find yourself, you are a lovely lady of true value."

"I can't take this from you. Isn't this the brooch Lord Pembrooke gave to you on your wedding day?"

"Serves him right, siring a son like Lord Pembrooke!" The woman's fingers cupped Molly's hands. "I'd planned to give it to my oldest daughter. Since you are the only daughter I will ever have, my dear, and the only woman I know who is worthy of wearing this fine piece of jewelry, I want you to have it. Please don't deny me my most treasured wish." Lady Pembrooke touched her lips to the back of Molly's hand. "Go! Go, Molly Maguire. Go with God."

Molly stumbled from the lady's chamber. The girl dropped the brooch and the silk-lined pouch into her pinafore pocket alongside the tiny volume of Shakespearean sonnets. Upstairs in her room, Molly slit the lining at the bottom of her trunk and slid her treasures in the slit. Tears moistened the trunk's rough cotton lining as she carefully sewed shut the tear she'd made for her treasures. She realized that the end had come to the pampered life she'd enjoyed at the Pembrooke manor. *What will the future hold?* she wondered.

Later that morning, Lord Pembrooke slipped a silver coin into Molly's pocket. "When you marry, my child, wear this in your shoe for good luck." He wagged his finger in her face and whispered, "But don't tell anyone I gave you this."

Molly gazed at the shiny object in her hand. She'd never before held such a valuable coin. All she could do is whisper, "Thank you, milord."

The man planted a kiss on her forehead. "Please, Molly, if you can, remember me with fondness."

* * * * *

After the family had departed from the manor, the talk among the staff was the probable fate of those who'd chosen to remain in Ireland. Morgan O'Toole, the groundskeeper, and his wife, Gertie O'Toole, a parlor maid, chose to move in with his impoverished mother in Donegal. The estate's carriage driver Chauncey, who found temporary employment at a neighboring estate, warned Enid, "Ye cannot imagine the hardships ye will need to endure during the crossing. Me uncle Ian wrote me mum from a city called Boston. His ship hit one storm after another during the crossing. During the storms, no one could cook for fear of starting a fire on board. So all he had to eat were dried crackers. Uncle Ian would put the rock-hard crackers in a canvas bag and pulverize them with an iron skillet. Then he would mix the powdered crackers with a small amount of water to make porridge. That would be his daily ration of food."

During Molly's and her mother's last visit to the soup kitchen in town, the local priest warned the women of the unsanitary conditions on board a ship. And for drama, he described in detail the possibility of being shipwrecked on the high seas. If that didn't curdle Molly's and her mother's blood, he told tales of Indian attacks that grew with each retelling.

"You'll never see Ireland again," Cordelia, the town's midwife lamented. "Mark my words, ye are travelin' aboard a 'coffin ship.' "

The days before they were scheduled to leave for America flew by faster than Molly ever imagined possible. The girl helped Enid close up the kitchen. Her only escape was an occasional visit to the stables, where she would beg Tavis to remind her of the good things about migrating to the new land.

Early on the morning of the emigrants' departure, the remaining staff members stood in a chilling drizzle and silently watched as Molly and the others crawled under an oil-coated canvas tarp on the back of an open farm wagon. A second wagon followed, carrying their belongings and crates of enough food to sustain them during the ocean voyage. Tears filled Molly's eyes as she watched Tavis bid Deidre goodbye. Without a second glance, he climbed into the wagon and dropped the canvas.

Silence filled the farm wagon as the draft horses lumbered through the iron gates of the estate and onto the county road. Lifting one corner of the tarp, Molly strained to catch one last glimpse of Pembrooke manor and of the wee cottage where she'd lived as a child before her father's death.

Sandwiched between Enid and Tavis, Molly smiled as her mother softly sang the girl's favorite Irish lullaby.

"I'll give to you a paper of pins
And that's the way our love begins,
If you will marry me, me, me,
If you will marry me."

The damp, cold drizzle of the bleak spring day faded as other voices joined her. Before long, they were singing old familiar favorites usually sung at funeral wakes and in taverns. Despite the chill, laughter passed around the circle as the people shared personal experiences of their lives at the manor.

"See, Molly," Tavis teased, "Going to America is not going to be so bad after all." The girl had to admit that her friend might be right.

Silence descended as the overcast sky faded into night, except for the occasional whimper of a young child or the quiet grunt of someone shifting about to find a comfortable position.

"Are you sure that, once you're a free man again, Deidre will not reconsider emigrating to America?"

"Not likely." In the darkness beneath the tarp, she heard the catch in his voice. "She'll never leave her mum."

Molly understood that. The girl couldn't imagine how she would have felt if she'd gone to London without Enid. The very thought was unbearable.

Daylight peaked out behind the clouds by the time the wagons halted beside the Irish Sea. As Molly climbed out of the wagon and her eyes adjusted to the sunlight, she started in surprise. The girl had never before seen so many humans assembled together in one place.

Being shoved and accosted by the mass of people, all scrambling to reach their own destinations, the fourteen servants from the Pembrooke household snaked their way through the crowd. Tavis skillfully led them toward the giant yellow-and-green sign hanging above the ticket office of the City of Dublin Steam Packet Company.

"Are all of these people going to America?" Molly shouted at Tavis.

"Many are," Tavis called over his shoulder. "But be careful and protect your purses, ladies."

"Trust no one!" Lord Pembrooke had warned them before he left the estate. "Dublin's streets are filled with grifters and petty thieves who make a living by robbing inexperienced travelers of their passage money."

"Don't worry," Molly's mother assured him. "We're ready for that." Before leaving the manor, Molly and the other three women in the group each pinned a small cotton sack of cash inside their camisoles.

"It would take a brazen thief to steal our money!" the older woman laughed in satisfaction.

However, no amount of warning could have prepared Molly for the chaotic frenzy of Dublin's crowded streets. She shuddered at the anxious and unhappy faces she passed. For an Irish lass who had found each day to be a cause for joy, this was disconcerting.

"Fortunately, we do not need to carry an abundance of cash," Tavis reminded the fourteen under his care. "Lord Pembrooke's solicitor has prepaid for our passage both on the steam-run ship to Liverpool and on the sailing ship to Norfolk, Virginia. Our trunks and our crates of food have already been loaded on board. All we need to do is identify ourselves to the ticket agent, and we're ready to sail."

By the time their entourage cleared the ticket booth and headed toward the waiting steamship, the rains had returned in earnest, not as a gentle Irish mist but as a bone-chilling downpour.

"Hurry!" Tavis shouted, pointing ahead toward the waiting ship. "Let's make a dash for it." He grasped Molly's hand and broke into a fast trot, weaving the way through the throng. A burly giant of a man with deep, angry red scars on his forehead and left cheek halted them at the foot of the gangplank.

"Not so fast, boy!" The guard, his beard and mustache dripping with rainwater, slammed the length of his club across Tavis's chest. "The cattle board first."

"Cattle?" Molly couldn't believe cows and sheep would take precedence over humans.

"Cattle!" The sailor swiped at an accumulation of moisture on his forehead and pointed toward the main street where people scrambled out of the path of scores of *moo*ing cattle and *baa*ing sheep being herded toward the gangplank. The shouts of the cattlemen punctuated the thundering hooves tramping over the wooden dock.

"Isn't there somewhere these ladies can go to escape the rain? A cabin on board, perhaps?" Tavis asked the guard.

The guard gave a loud guffaw. "Ain't no cabins on this vessel, boy."

From farther back in the line, one of the hands from the manor called, "What about letting us go down below in steerage?"

The sailor guarding the entrance snorted in derision. "That's where we pen the animals during the voyage. We can't have the people and the cattle occupying the same space. Wouldn't be healthy for the animals. Trust me, the livestock is worth more to the ship's owners than a few wet and wheezing Irishmen!"

After the livestock had been placed in the hold, a convoy of farm wagons filled with sacks of food arrived, accompanied by a contingent of longshoremen, with swords hanging from their belts. The wagons rolled past the miserable emigrants. Molly, her fingers stiff from the cold, struggled to tighten the ribbons of her drooping bonnet under her chin.

"Look, Mama." Molly pointed toward a shriveled old man limping toward them and leaning on a woman and a teenage boy. "Do you think that man will survive the crossing? He already looks like he's at death's door. And have you noticed that these people's lips and mouths are green?"

Enid nodded. "Probably all they've had to eat for some time is grass. If we had chosen to stay in Ireland, we might have been in similar desperation. Isn't God wonderful, the way He's supplied our needs?"

Somehow, the girl didn't feel comforted by her mother's remarks. She wondered if they would ever find themselves eating grass in order to survive. Molly watched load after load of food being carried on board past the starving children. Compulsively, the girl tabulated the quantity of produce being shipped to England on the paddleboat: 147 sides of bacon, 135 barrels of pork, 300 bags of flour, and 542 boxes of eggs.

Finally, the last of the produce had been stashed below deck, and the motley line of passengers was allowed to board the steamship. Quickly, Tavis found a corner near the wheelhouse, partially protected from the rain.

"Come over here, folks. We need to press together to stay warm."

"Stay warm?" Molly's teeth chattered from the chill. "I may never be warm again!"

"Here." He gathered Molly and her mother to his side and sat down with his back against the wall. The rest of their group pressed together as well. Other travelers followed their lead until the deck was littered with small clumps of humanity sharing body warmth. From time to time, the men on the outer ring rotated into the center of the group to get warm. Molly estimated that more than five hundred persons were on board.

By the time the paddleboat docked in Liverpool, the rain had stopped. Even the heartiest of the travelers was bedraggled and miserable. But the sight of the wharf brought a smile to Molly's face.

As their small group of travelers stepped onto the dock, they were immediately engulfed in a horde of bustling humanity. Wet, soggy, and shoved one direction and then the other, Molly had to fight the desire to claw her way free of the tangle of bodies. Spotting a boarded-up doorway, the group clustered together while deciding their next move.

Tavis stood on an overturned wooden box to scan the port. "It looks as if our ship hasn't docked yet. We need to find lodging until we are allowed to board. Lord Pembrooke told me to avoid the neighborhoods around Regent Street and Denison Street. He recommended we stay at the Red Rooster Hotel and Bar. A night's stay costs a little more there than at some of the other places—but it will be much safer, especially for you ladies."

"Then let's find it," one of the men shouted. "So far his advice has been right on the penny."

"It will cost each of us four pence a night," Tavis warned. "And don't expect private or clean quarters."

Ellie, a fourteen-year-old orphaned chambermaid, sniffled, "I'm so cold. I just want to go home!"

The older man who'd cared for the animals at the estate, encouraged her, "Buck up! This is the only home ye got now, little lass."

Enid slipped her arm around Ellie's quaking shoulders. "Don't worry, Ellie. If we stick together, we can survive anything."

"Yes," Tavis agreed. "We will protect one another. Besides, we can endure anything for one night, right? Once the ship docks, we can board twenty-four hours before it's time to sail. In the meantime, we men will form a buffer around the women like we did on the paddleboat."

Above the door to the Red Rooster Hotel and Bar, a gold sign with blue lettering and a painting of a red-and-brown rooster swung on two chains. Inside, the odors of whiskey, old wood, soggy woolen clothing, and human sweat accosted the travelers' senses. Molly trailed after Tavis and Enid through a labyrinth of booths and tables occupied by ogling males in various stages of inebriation. The girl closed her ears to the rude catcalls as she passed.

Once they paid for their night's lodging, the innkeeper led them down a narrow flight of stairs to a chilly, dank, windowless cellar. A single oil lamp swung from an iron hook in the ceiling. Moisture shone on the moss-covered gray stone walls and on the faces of several family groups who already occupied the heavy log bunks nearest to the light. A flimsy blanket lay folded at the foot of each bunk.

"Let's lay claim to those beds over there on the left," the former groom suggested. The man led the way to an almost completely darkened section of the cellar. "Here we'll have more room since most of the people will crowd around the lantern."

After claiming their sleeping berths, the travelers agreed to take turns leaving the basement to allow for time outside in the fresh air. When her turn came, Molly chose to stay in the cellar rather than endure the embarrassment of traipsing through the bar a second and third time. Enid sat down on the wooden bunk beside her daughter, when suddenly the person on a neighboring cot groaned and doubled over with pain. Concerned, Enid reached out to the stranger. "What? What's wrong?"

Perspiration beaded on the older woman's forehead. Through clenched teeth, she replied, "Just the same old pain in my right side. It never lasts long. I'll be all right, honey. Don't worry. I haven't come this far to give up now."

Questions plagued Molly despite the scripture promise her mother quoted aloud for all to hear. "Lo, I am with you alway, even unto the end of the world" did little to comfort the frightened girl. As Molly lay in the darkness, she wondered if any of them would survive the hazardous crossing. And once in America, could they endure their two-year contract to ever again be free?

When Molly awoke, the room was totally dark. Disoriented, she tried to roll out of bed, but her legs were tangled in the flimsy blanket. "Mama?" she whispered.

"I'm right beside you, Molly darling."

"Where are we?"

"In the cellar of the Red Rooster. Remember?"

Relieved, the girl lay back against the wooden bunk. Around her the other travelers began to stir. *The ship! Today is the day we sail for America,* she told herself.

A typically overcast English sky greeted the travelers as they emerged from the cellar accommodations. News that their sailing ship, the *Peregrine,* had docked, arrived by a runner as Molly and her mother finished their breakfast—a piece of black bread and a cup of tea—in the common area of the inn.

"Come on," Tavis urged. "We need to get on board as soon as possible." Though Lord Pembrooke had reserved cabin accommodations on board the ship for them, they'd all heard tales of travelers waiting until the last minute to board and having to scramble up the sides of the ship after the gangplank had been removed. Some of the more athletic latecomers made it on board; others, not so fit, fell into the water and drowned.

At the dock gates, Molly was surprised to find a large number of spectators already gathered. Ships leaving for America were the most exciting events in most of these people's dreary lives. As she passed through the cordial throng, they wished her a safe journey and prosperity in her new land. A few smiled wistfully.

As the sailors removed the gangplank and the ship inched out of the narrow berth, a man burst from the crowd and leaped toward the moving vessel. Two constables chasing him stopped running inches from the edge of the pier, one shaking his fist. Molly held her breath as the man grasped, with one hand, a rough-hewn board on the side of the ocean-going vessel. She breathlessly watched as the man, wearing a giant canvas sack on his back, climbed inch by inch up the side of the ship. The crowd cheered when the man's hand finally grasped the railing and four of the male passengers hauled him on board.

She wondered who the stranger might be and why the constables had pursued him, until a queasy feeling in her stomach deadened her curiosity. Molly grasped the wooden railing and closed her eyes.

CHAPTER FIVE

THE CROSSING

LIKE A TOY SAILBOAT in a child's bathwater, the *Peregrine* tossed about in the rough current of the Irish Sea. As the last point of land disappeared into the mist, Molly realized she would never again see her beloved Ireland. Lost in thought, the girl started when Enid touched her shoulder.

"Shall we unpack a few things while we get our sea legs? We women will need to fix a meal for our group before the seas get much rougher. Otherwise, we'll not have hot food to eat tonight."

Inching slowly along the rolling ship's corridor, Molly followed her mother to their assigned quarters. As crowded as the tiny cabin was for eight occupants, the interior of the room was brighter and cleaner than the cellar at the inn where they'd stayed the previous night. The berths were wooden bunks built into the ship's timbers, with a passage down the middle. There was no bedding or mattresses. The blankets they'd brought with them would be their only source for warmth and modesty.

The other women watched as Enid, with hands on hips, inspected the space. "If we are to avoid lice and ship fever we must keep this area clean. Fortunately, I brought along extra bars of lye soap."

Enid strode to the washstand and poured cold water into the basin. Grabbing a rag from under the stand, she began to scrub the bunks. Layers of dirt and scum coated the rag. Molly and the other women pitched in on the project.

"As angry as I was at Lord Pembrooke"—her mother talked while she attacked the surface of the second bunk—"I must confess, so far he's taken good care of us. Imagine if we'd had to dicker with the shipping agent for our passage and then wrestle our trunks on board like the folk traveling alone."

Perched on an upper bunk, Molly grinned down at her mother. "You never told me you were angry at Lord Pembrooke. I thought I was the only one furious with him."

Enid chuckled. "Are you serious? I was so angry I could have fed him to an evil leprechaun! To be honest, I was angry at milord and milady as well."

"Once the baron and baroness arrived from England, Lord and Lady Pembrooke couldn't have done much for us." Molly scrubbed the wall behind the bunk.

"Actually, I think it is Lord Pembrooke whom we can thank for insisting we be treated well. I couldn't see the baroness caring one way or the other about what happened to us." The woman carefully laid the Bible on her bunk.

"But, Mama, isn't it against yours and daddy's religion to be angry at others?" Molly teased.

"Our religion? Anger isn't about religion, child. It's who you are inside. There's nothing wrong with a bit of healthy anger, especially for an Irish mama!" Enid huffed. "What you do with your anger is what's important. Eventually, you have to let it go. If you harbor anger in your heart, it will control you."

Molly thought for a moment. "I don't care! As long as I live," she vowed, "I will despise the baron and baroness for what they did to us."

"Fury burns bright in one so young," her mother smiled sadly. "But I pray we will both eventually let go of all our hate. Jesus said, 'Forgive us our debts, as we forgive our debtors.' I need forgiveness every day for my sins, so if I expect to be forgiven I must forgive others. And that includes the Pembrookes."

Molly snorted, "Why does it matter? They'll never know because we will never see them again."

"True, they won't. But forgiveness is a gift the forgiver gives to himself, not to the one being forgiven."

While Enid checked their supply of water, barley, rye, and peas piled in one corner next to a large tin of rock-hard water biscuits called blahs, Molly peered out of the small porthole over her bunk. "*Hmm,* isn't it strange that it feels as if we were heading back the way we came?"

"That's because we are." The woman laughed, "The first mate told me that the available winds dictate the ship's route."

Molly turned about in surprise. "When did you meet the first mate?"

Her mother continued counting the containers. "While you were waving at the people on shore, the first mate advised me to bring some of our foodstuffs into our cabin because no one cooks during rough seas. The food kept in our cabin will be better protected against mold, maggots, and weevils."

Eeugh! The girl grimaced.

Enid chuckled. "Get used to it, darling. Before we land, we will eat more than one meal enriched by tiny vermin."

At the thought of weevils and maggots, Molly gulped. A wave of nausea blurred her vision. She held onto the wooden bunk and swallowed several times.

"Are you all right?" Her mother touched her arm. "You look a little green. If you think you might be sick, use the chamber pot by the door."

The girl buried her head in the stack of clothing her mother had placed on the bunk. "I won't be sick! I won't be sick!" she repeated several times until the urge to vomit subsided.

Enid wrapped her shawl about her shoulders. "The first mate suggested I join the evening cooking line quickly. With more than two hundred passengers preparing their meals in the cooking shanty, it will take some time. Pray, honey, that the weather doesn't get rough— or no one will be able to prepare food until the seas calm once more."

The thought of any food made the girl want to retch. she couldn't imagine ever wanting to eat anything ever again.

Her mother bent over the girl and caressed her moist forehead. "Are you sure you'll be all right down here alone? Fresh air might help. Come up on deck."

Molly waved her mother away. "Go! Go!" The girl closed her eyes and gritted her teeth. "I will not vomit! I will not vomit!" With every roll of the ship, she felt the urge to lurch toward the chamber pot. Any attempt to maintain any dignity faded as the roll of the waves intensified.

As she rolled about on her bunk, the term *coffin ship* popped into her mind. The thought of dying sounded strangely appealing. Molly didn't know how long she'd lain on her bunk when a knock sounded on the hatch.

"Who's there?" she moaned.

"It's me—Tavis. May I come in?"

Her hands flew to her tangled hair. "No!" She lifted her body up on one elbow. Tavis's worried face peered around the door.

"Your mama says you are feeling sick. I've brought someone to help you feel more comfortable—Doctor Sheridan."

Tavis entered the cluttered cabin, followed by a short, wiry man with red hair, freckles, and snapping blue eyes that dared Molly not to smile.

"Molly, I'd like you to meet Doctor Sheridan."

"Me name is Seamus, Seamus Sheridan from Cork." The stranger appeared to be in his midtwenties. He touched her forehead. "No fever. That's good. Tavis moisten a cloth and hand it to me."

Molly closed her eyes and allowed the physician to wash the sweat from her face.

"Mistress Molly, I have a mug of hot tea for you to drink that might settle your stomach."

She shook her head from side to side. "No, I don't want—"

"Don't be difficult, lass. It's a mixture of chamomile and peppermint. Tavis, could you lift her for me?"

Tavis lifted the girl to a sitting position. Molly leaned limply against him.

The doctor held a flask to her lips. "Now be a sweet little lass and take a sip."

When she tried to obey, half of the potion dribbled down her face and onto the bodice of her garment.

"Good girl. Let's try that again," the doctor insisted. One tiny sip after another, she ingested the tea as ordered. When Molly had emptied the flask, Tavis laid her back on the bunk.

"Don't worry, Mistress Molly, you'll be feeling chipper in a few minutes. And once you get your sea legs, you'll be a good as gold, I promise."

"Thank you, Doctor Sheridan," she mumbled.

"And now Tavis and I will let you take a short nap. When you get hungry, your mother has a fine porridge for you and some salty crackers. They will help settle your stomach as well."

Porridge? Crackers? Molly groaned. The mere mention of food set her stomach churning.

"If you come up on deck and feel the crisp ocean breeze blowing through those lovely curls of yours, you will feel better much faster, I promise." The doctor's eye twinkled.

As the two men exited the cabin, Molly flung her right arm across her eyes. *On deck?* she thought. *Surely, I couldn't feel any worse up there than I do down here.*

The tea she'd drunk sloshed about in her stomach as she slid off the bunk. Molly held onto the lid of her mother's open trunk to steady herself. After changing out of her wrinkled garments into a blouse and pinafore, she ran a comb through her tangled curls and popped a matching bonnet on her head. "There!" she announced to the empty cabin. "That's as good as I can manage, I'm afraid."

The girl stepped into a dark corridor. She stumbled up a flight of steps onto the deck. The warm afternoon sun caressed her cheeks as she staggered toward the railing. *Where's Mama?* she wondered. Molly spotted her mother fixing supper in the cooking shanty."

Smoke billowed from the twelve-by-sixteen-foot lean-to. A bin filled with sand, four feet wide and eighteen inches high, stretched along the back wall. Perched atop a triangular frame of iron, cooking kettles were heated by small wood fires. With about two hundred passengers on board, the lines were long. Keeping a place in line would become part of the daily routine. The men in the group agreed to save places in line for the women if they would prepare enough food for them, as well.

Because she knew the crossing would be long and the food tasteless, Molly's mother had sewn small fabric bags of herbs and spices onto her petticoats. A little salt here, a dash of pepper there, and a sprig of dried parsley did wonders for the blandest of stews. As a result, the aromas coming from her pot of stew drew the hungry and the curious to the shanty. And being the compassionate person she was, Enid managed to make extra stew for any child who hadn't have enough to eat. As Enid dispensed nutritious food, she also dispensed tasty promises from the Word of God.

"Jesus said, 'Blessed are the meek: for they shall inherit the earth.' He also said, 'I am the way, the truth, and the life.' "

The news of the generous cook and her tasty dishes spread throughout the vessel until the ship's crew were bringing their uncooked food for her to "doctor." With provisions being exchanged for tasty, hot meals, the usually boring diet became more varied. Molly and many of the other female travelers were drafted to help.

At night, as the exhausted girl fell asleep, she would dream, "Molly, stir that stew! Be careful not to scorch the cabbage."

Enjoying Enid's tasty soups and stews, the women on board asked her to teach them ways to improve the taste of their cooking.

One night as the two exhausted women settled in to bed, Molly whispered to her mother, "Do you think all your preaching makes a difference to these people? They listen only in exchange for the food."

The creaking of the ship's timbers and the *moo*ing of the cattle in the hold below them blended with the gentle snoring of the other women sharing their cabin.

"Molly, my love, I don't know whether my actions will make a difference for these people, but I know I'm doing what my Savior did. He fed the hungry and shared the truths of eternity with anyone who would listen. That's good enough for me."

"Yes, but He could bless the food and, *poof,* it was ready to eat. What you're doing is hard work!"

Her mother chuckled. "Having to prepare the food allows more time for me to tell them how much God loves them."

Molly shook her head. She didn't understand. "Look at you. You're exhausted each night. I just can't see what you're getting in return."

Again Enid laughed. "More than you can imagine. Just like back home, when I give someone a bowl of hot food and a smile, I am not only helping a fellow passenger, I'm helping in the name of Jesus. That is reward enough."

Molly considered her mother's words. Before dropping to sleep, the girl asked, "Mama, what do you think of Doctor Sheridan?"

"Why do you ask?"

"Oh, I don't know. I think he's kind of sweet on me."

"Molly, I know what it's like to be young. But remember, you agreed to serve two years in the new country as an indentured servant. You vowed you would complete your service before considering marriage."

"Mother! I'm not going to marry the man. I just want to know what you think of him. And I will be eighteen by the time we land in America."

"Yes, you will, my dear. I admit the good doctor has no lack of Irish charm. He could sweet-talk the blush off a rose."

"Everyone on board loves Seamus."

"So it's Seamus now, is it?"

"He asked me to call him by his given name. Is it proper, Mama?"

"I suppose that some of the rules of proper etiquette for young ladies in polite society on land might be relaxed on board ship."

"Good, because I do like him. And you must admit those freckles across his nose are kind of cute."

"Remember, dear, beauty is as beauty does." The woman yawned. "You and I need to get some sleep. Tomorrow's another busy day."

"Good night, Mama. Seamus," Molly whispered in the darkness. "Seamus is a good Irish name."

CHAPTER SIX

AN UNEXPECTED SURPRISE

WHILE THE OTHER EMIGRANTS found boredom and home-sickness the biggest of battles to fight, Molly blossomed under the attention of the ever-popular doctor. Whenever someone aboard the ship fell ill, Doctor Sheridan supplied a flask of tea guaranteed to make the most stubborn of fevers abate.

Between helping her mother prepare soup and stew in the shanty kitchen and being escorted around the perimeter of the ship by moon-light, Molly seldom spoke with Tavis except at mealtimes.

The day before they landed was Molly's eighteenth birthday. The entire day had passed without anyone wishing her a happy birthday. Feeling more than a little piqued, she emptied the last of the soup for the evening meal into a large pitcher.

"Here, let me help." Tavis took the pitcher from her hands.

"It's for that family over there," she snapped, pointing to her right.

The man glanced at her in surprise. "Is something wrong?"

"No! Should there be?" She set a kettle to one side, where several women were doing the dishes.

"I would think, since it is your eighteenth birthday, you'd be in a more pleasant mood. It isn't every day a lass turns eighteen."

She cocked her head to one side, her tone riddled with accusation. "So you remembered?"

"Of course, I did. Come, I have a surprise for you." He led her to the common area on deck and shouted above the voices of the milling crowd, "Play it, O'Riley!"

Paddy O'Riley, the former groundskeeper at the manor, removed a harmonica from his shirt pocket and began playing the old Elizabethan favorite "Greensleeves." Everyone began to sing.

Molly blushed and glanced toward Enid and smiled. A grinning Seamus stood to one side. After the well-wishers concluded singing the twentieth verse, Tavis announced, "Happy eighteenth birthday, Molly Maguire." He then quoted the lines from Shakespeare's *The Merry Wives of Windsor,* "Let the sky rain potatoes; Let it thunder to the tune of Greensleeves."

The ship skimmed full sail through smooth seas as everyone wished the girl happy birthday, everyone except Doctor Seamus Sheridan. Paddy lifted his harmonica to his lips and began playing the lively Irish ballad "The Girl I Left Behind." Sailors grabbed the nearest females about their waists and began to dance the traditional Irish jig. The other emigrants joined in. When Paddy tired and dropped his harmonica into his pocket, people wandered off to their quarters to sleep.

Stars twinkled overhead as Molly ambled over to the ship's railing and gazed into the night. Captivated by the luminescent water in the moonlight, she stared into the deep. *How different this birthday is compared to my seventeenth,* she thought.

On her last birthday, Molly's mother made her a personal-sized, chocolate-potato cake, a recipe that had come down through her father's family. Lady Pembrooke gave her a red satin gown. Because of the restricted space in her travel trunk, the girl gave the dress to Anne before she left the manor.

"Looks like a devilish leprechaun spread fairy dust across the water, doesn't it?" Seamus whispered into her ear. She started in surprise. "*Ooh!* Don't be fearful, little darling. I will never hurt you." He slipped an arm about her slight waist and drew her to his side. Her heart sank as she spotted Tavis disappear around the ship's mainmast.

"A perfect night for romance, isn't it?" Seamus asked. "It's as if we are living in our own garden of magic."

"Aye, my mother is right. You are an Irish charmer, Seamus Sheridan," she teased.

"Perhaps ye mother has poisoned your mind against me?" He

leaned closer. Unfamiliar sensations rushed through her as his warm breath caressed her neck.

Molly clicked her tongue. "Of course not. Why would she? You have every female aboard ship yearning for your smile."

Tilting her chin toward him, he gazed into her eyes. "Tell me, Molly Maguire, do you yearn for my smile, as well?"

With him standing so close, the girl couldn't think straight. Her lips went dry; her mouth felt like she'd swallowed a ball of cotton. Molly wanted to cry, "Yes! Yes!"

But instead, Lady Pembrooke's advice on how to flirt with a gentleman popped into her mind. Before she could stop herself, but not before she shot him a saucy grin, she retorted, "Are you, Doctor Seamus Sheridan, trifling with me?"

The doctor stepped back. His hand dropped from her waist. He gave her a strange look. "Why no, Mistress Maguire. I never trifle with a maiden's heart."

His answer left her speechless. The magical moment in the moonlight faded. Worse yet, Molly couldn't remember what coy answer Lady Pembrooke would have given to fit the occasion. She would have melted into the ship's floorboards if she could. Instead, the girl mumbled, "I am certainly glad to hear that, kind sir."

When she felt a tap on her shoulder, the girl glanced over her shoulder to find Paddy O'Riley had returned. "Hey, Molly, ye got a favorite ye'd like me to play."

The girl could have kissed the scruffy, bearded groundskeeper for his timely arrival. "Do ye know 'Black Is the Color of My True Love's Hair'? When I was a little girl, my father used to sing it to me before I went to sleep at night."

"What kind of Irishman would I be not to know that ditty?" The wiry old man began a soulful rendition of the traditional Irish ballad.

Molly's eyes misted when she saw her mother standing on the far side of the deck. The shadows of the night almost hid the woman's pensive gaze.

"Excuse me for a moment, Seamus." Molly hurried to her mother's side. Without asking, the girl knew what memories were going through her mother's mind. Ireland seemed so very far away.

Controlled pandemonium reigned the hour before the *Peregrine* docked in Norfolk Harbor. Molly had barely stuffed her last petticoat into her trunk when two men arrived to carry the trunk topside. She paused to take one last look at the tiny stateroom that had been her home for the passage. The girl tied the bow of her gray-felt poke bonnet under her chin, slung her gray shawl around her shoulders, and climbed the steps to the main deck.

Molly stood on her tiptoes to see over the heads of the excited travelers, hoping to spot her mother.

"Here, let me help." Tavis sided up to her and placed one hand in the middle of her back and grabbed her arm with the other. Slowly, they weaved their way through the eager travelers. As crossings went, Molly knew theirs had been relatively uneventful. No one had died during the journey and needed to be buried at sea. Thanks to Doctor Sheridan, most didn't suffer from any of the horrid diseases that usually accompanied such a journey. She also knew that her mother's good cooking and the lack of violent storms were responsible for their success.

Following the evening of her eighteenth birthday, Seamus had treated her differently. While he still attended to her needs and wishes, he behaved with more deference. As for Tavis, he was kept busy caring for the needs of all fourteen former Pembrooke staff members.

Molly gazed at the approaching Norfolk waterfront. As the boat docked, dozens of runners swarmed the ship, offering their services at finding the immigrants housing for an outrageous fee. One burly man with a grizzled beard and a shiny gold front tooth grabbed the leather handle on one side of Molly's trunk. Having been warned this could happen, the girl grabbed the opposite handle. A tug-of-war ensued.

"Help! Let go! Somebody help me!" The determined girl closed her eyes and leaned back. She tried to dig the heels of her black leather boots into the wooden deck. All the while, the thief was hollering back a string of curses. With his superior strength, he hauled the trunk and Molly several feet closer to the gangplank. The same was happening with other women in her group.

Suddenly, the force on the opposite end of the trunk let go, sending Molly tumbling backward and revealing numerous layers of petticoats under her black-and-red plaid skirt. She lay there, stunned for a moment, and then opened her eyes to find Tavis reaching down to help her to her feet. With her face suffused with color and her bonnet askew, Molly spat out her words. "That rapscallion tried to take my trunk—and I wasn't about to let him!"

A laughing Tavis straightened her bonnet. "That was quite a tug-of-war, you had, little girl."

"You think that's funny?" Her lower lip protruded defiantly. "You need to know I would have won except my feet slipped on the wet decking!"

He laughed again as he retied the ties of the bonnet under her chin. "You are quite a warrior, my lass."

"You're making fun of me!"

"No, no, never! I mean it! You are one lion of a woman."

Lord Pembrooke's brother-in-law's attorney waited on shore for the fifteen exhausted travelers and their belongings. When they staggered down the gangplank, he read their names from the black leather-bound notebook in his right hand. The attorney knew the right officials, for in no time, he'd whisked them through the immigration process.

To Molly, the attorney was her new hero. The middle-aged man cut a dashing figure in his black cut-away frock coat, with wide, satin lapels and velvet collar, his smoke-gray trousers, and a burgundy silk brocade vest. A pair of gold-rimmed spectacles perched on his nose. His beaver-skin stovepipe hat made him appear to be seven feet tall. The man could have stepped out of one of Lady Pembrooke's *Godey's Lady's Books*.

After leading the Irish immigrants beyond the iron fences that surrounded the immigration building, the man introduced himself. "My name is Attorney Angus Adams. Master Edmund Taylor, the gentleman who owns your indentured servant papers, has instructed me to tell each of you where you will serve out your two-year assignments."

Fifteen pairs of eyes and ears focused on the attorney. Molly shot a quick glance toward her mother. Enid shook her head and grasped her daughter's hand more tightly.

"Obviously, Master Taylor cannot employ every one of you at his tobacco plantation in Richmond, so he has sold your contracts to other landowners and merchants in the state."

The immigrants gasped in surprise. They'd never considered the possibility they wouldn't be working together. He waited for their protests to die down before proceeding with his announcement.

"As I read your name, please step forward to be informed of your assignment."

Tavis's hand shot into the air. "Lord Pembrooke never mentioned we would be separated and sent to different places."

The attorney peered over his spectacles at the young man. "What's your name, sir?"

"Tavis, Tavis Lloyd."

Hmm. The man scanned his notebook. "Lloyd . . . Lloyd. Here it is, Tavis Lloyd." He looked at Tavis and smiled. "Lord Pembrooke put a lot of trust in you, young man. I understand you were to act as the leader of the group, right?"

"Yes, sir." By the set of Tavis's jaw, Molly knew her friend was upset.

"You, son, have been assigned to Master Taylor's employ near Richmond. Let's see." He studied the list for a moment. "Both you and, uh, Joseph Potter, will serve your two-year contract at Master Taylor's."

One by one, Attorney Adams read off the names. The longer he read, the more nervous Molly became and the tighter she held onto her mother's hand. Some would be going to work at a plantation in western Virginia; others were assigned to business places in and around Norfolk. Dazed, the group huddled together for support. Finally, the attorney read, "Enid Maguire?"

The woman timidly lifted one hand in the air.

"Mistress Maguire, for the next two years, you will be serving as a cook at the Taylor plantation." He adjusted his glasses. "My man Percy has arranged each of your transportations to your new homes. He and his men are waiting for you in the carriage lot to the left of this building." Closing his notebook, the attorney gazed at the faces of America's newest immigrants. "There! That should complete our business."

Molly raised her hand. "Sir, what about me? I'm Molly Maguire."

The man looked at Molly's diminutive size and blinked in surprise. "You're the little lass who is gifted with numbers, right?"

The girl nodded. "Yes, sir."

"I didn't read your name Miss Maguire because you will be working as a clerk in my law office here in Norfolk. You come highly recommended by the Pembrookes for your trustworthiness; but when I purchased your contract, I never dreamed you'd be so, er, youthful." He tugged nervously at his collar. "Obviously, I will have to make a place for you to work in a back office as it would be unseemly for a young female to work side by side with my male law clerks."

Molly's mother's hand shot into the air. "Sir! I am Mistress Molly's mother. Please, how far is the Taylor Plantation from Norfolk?"

The attorney cleared his throat. His gaze darted from Molly's face to her mother's. Sweat beaded on his forehead. "Mistress Maguire, did you read the contract you signed? When you and your daughter entered two years of servanthood, you also signed over any familial rights during that time."

Enid shot a confused glance toward Tavis. The young man shrugged. But Molly would not be deterred. "Could you answer my mother's question? Just how far away from me will my mother be?"

"Er, about ninety miles, as the crow flies." He tugged nervously at his starched collar.

"Ninety miles?" The girl gasped and turned to her mother. "Do we have any recourse?"

The attorney shook his head sadly.

Molly turned toward her mother. "Mama, do something."

Tears streamed down the older woman's cheeks. Taking her daughter's face in her hands, she whispered, "Two years will go by quickly, little one; and then, we'll be together once again. You'll see."

CHAPTER SEVEN

THE PARTING

BEFORE ENID CLIMBED INTO the farm wagon that would carry her to the faraway Richmond, she opened her trunk and found the Maguire family Bible. "Here, darling. Your father would have wanted you to have this."

Molly looked down at the leather-bound Book in astonishment. "No, Mama! You read from it every day. I don't even know if I believe what it says."

Enid patted her daughter's hand. "Which is exactly why I want you to have it. I have put many of its promises to memory, which I will take with me wherever I go. You have not. You're going to need the courage it will give you."

Tears spilled down the girl's cheeks as she shook her head. "No, it's not right. It's not right."

But Enid was firm. "All I ask is that you promise to read a portion of it every night before going to bed. Will you do that for me?"

Reluctantly, Molly nodded. "I'll do it, though I don't promise I'll believe it."

A glint of humor sparkled in her mother's eyes. "As long as you keep your word, God will take care of His part of the bargain."

The girl knitted her brow. "What do you mean?"

"Nothing about which you need to be concerned, my little one." She planted a gentle kiss on her daughter's forehead.

"Wait. There's something I've not told you." Molly opened her trunk and pawed through her clothing to the bottom and pulled out the velvet sack that contained the silver coin. "Here. I want you to have this."

The woman stared in disbelief. "Where under God's heaven did you find this?" she hissed.

"Lord Pembrooke gave it to me before we left Ireland. He said that one day I might need it, but I want you to have it." Molly closed her mother's fingers over the coin.

"No! No! I can't take it. Living here in the city, you may need it more than I."

Molly shook her head. "I won't accept your gift if you don't accept mine. Consider the coin to be a promise that in two years we will be together again."

"Are you ready to leave, Mistress Maguire?" Tavis strode toward the two women, his eyes revealing his reluctance to separate mother and daughter. "The wagon bound for Richmond is loaded."

Their parting was imminent. Enid drew her daughter into her arms and whispered her favorite Bible text in the girl's ear. "Remember the Good Book says, 'Have I not seen the righteous forsaken, nor his seed begging bread.' I know that I can trust you to our Father's tender care."

The girl clung to her mother. "I can't do this. I will never forgive Lord Pembrooke for this!"

"If you don't forgive, Lord Pembrooke will always control you by your letting him control your thoughts and attitudes. Remember, the best revenge is forgiveness—because forgiveness sets you free."

Molly glowered.

"Be strong, my child. Do your father proud." Enid brushed a stray curl from Molly's face. "Trust the promises in your father's Bible."

Turning to Tavis, Molly changed the subject. "Promise me you will take good care of my mother."

"I will, little pigeon. I will. But what about you? Who will take care of you?" He glanced down at the Bible resting in her hands.

The girl straightened her shoulders and sniffed, "I will be fine. As you can see, Mama gave me my father's Bible."

The young groom planted a tender kiss on the girl's forehead. "Don't worry. I promise to bring your mother back to you safe and sound." Taking Enid Maguire's arm, he helped her into the waiting wagon.

Molly hugged the leather-bound Book to her chest and stared after the wagon carrying the only people in the whole world she knew and loved until the vehicle rounded a bend and was no longer in sight.

"Mistress Maguire?" A stranger from behind her left shoulder spoke her name. She turned and stared into the first chocolate brown face she'd ever beheld. Molly eyed the man's wrinkled hands. Would the color rub off onto her if he touched her? She didn't know. She returned her gaze to the man's face.

Above the topographical map of wrinkles around his eyes and cheeks, a shock of white hair protruded out from under a dark brown soft-brimmed hat. The man's well-worn clothes, though neat and clean, spoke of years of use. He touched the brim of his hat and bowed slightly. "My name is Percy. I am to take you to Attorney Adams's law offices." He smiled, revealing an uneven picket fence of white teeth.

Percy's deep brown eyes sparkled. "I have already loaded your trunk onto the buggy. So if you are ready to go . . ." He glanced at the Bible clutched in her hands. "Good Book," he said. "It contains secret powers."

"Secret powers?"

"Aye. But you have to read it to find them." Taking her by the elbow, the man guided her to a shiny black phaeton by the curb. Harnessed to the phaeton, a pair of matching sorrels that were eager to run, snorted in the afternoon air. Percy helped Molly into the cab, closed the door, and climbed up the steps into the driver's seat.

Alone in the carriage, the young woman watched busy shipping docks and then rows of shops and small businesses. A giant tooth hung over the door of one office. *A dentist,* she thought. Swinging above the door of the next shop was a giant stein of beer. The girl smiled to herself. "Some things never change." Ireland had neighborhood pubs on every street. Because few people could read, the objects painted on the signs made it easier to identify the different shops or businesses.

Molly's father, a teetotaler, never failed to lecture the young girl on the evils of alcohol. "Been the ruin of more than one Irishman," he would say. "If the drunkard doesn't spend the family's food money on alcohol, he'll get killed in a barroom donnybrook." And from what she'd observed growing up in Ireland, the girl agreed.

Within five minutes, the horses halted in front of a red-brick, three-story building with dark-green shutters at the windows. Beside the door, a large wooden sign read, "Adams & Wadsworth, Attorneys-at law." Above the door hung a judge's gavel.

Molly took a deep breath. *So this is to be my new home,* she thought, clutching the Book for security and also to stop the trembling of her hands.

"Master Adams wants to speak with you. I will take your trunk to your room." Percy's gaze was one of sympathy and understanding. "Don't be afraid, Mistress Maguire. Master Adams is a fair employer. If you give him an honest day's work, he will treat you well."

Molly allowed him to lead her into the building. Particles of dust floated in the rays of light coming through the windows. Along opposite walls, leather-bound law books tumbled with one another on the stacks of wooden shelves. Beyond a gated banister, the faces of four law clerks peered over their elevated oak desks. Before her eyes completely adjusted to the darkness, the attorney she'd met at the docks burst through the first of the three closed doors along the rear wall.

"Mistress Maguire, good day. Glad to see that you arrived safely. I am sure it was difficult to say goodbye to your mother, but, under the circumstances, it can't be helped."

Molly noted the man's graying temples and determined him to be close to the age of her deceased father. "Mistress Molly, I'd like to introduce you to Mister Kerr. He's from New York City."

The pair of round wire-rimmed glasses on the end of his nose threatened to fall off as the balding, middle-aged man bobbed a respectful greeting.

"And this is Samuels, a native, blue-blood Virginian." Obviously proud of his heritage, the man tilted his head to one side in a half bow.

"Mister Simms is our youngest clerk. He dreams of running for public office one day." The man with sandy hair and a slight mustache blushed and nodded.

"And last, but not least, my head law clerk, Ridgley. Ridgley

graduated from the University of Virginia, number two in his class."
The gaunt, clean-shaven man in his late twenties arched one insolent
eyebrow and glared at Molly.

She smiled, but he didn't respond.

Master Adams noted the exchange. "Oh, don't mind Ridgley. He's
merely protecting his domain against the threat of an all-out female
invasion he is sure will come if men don't hold the line, whatever that
line may be."

"Female invasion?" Molly didn't understand.

"In the Commonwealth of Virginia, it is not customary for a gen-
tlewoman such as yourself to be employed outside the hearth and
home. Old Ridgley believes a woman is good enough to cook his vit-
tles, bake his bread, and wash his shirts. But keep his books? Absolutely not! But don't worry. It may take time, but the clerks will grow
accustomed to your presence—including Ridgley. The man is loyal to
a fault."

The lawyer curled the ends of his mustache and chuckled. "Because
I know it would be awkward for you to work in the outer office with
my clerks, you will perform your duties from the library." He strode
across the room and opened the middle of the three oak doors. Inside,
he gestured toward a scarred oak desk surrounded by shelf after shelf
of leather-bound books. "Your task is to maintain my financial records. No bringing my law clerks tea or crumpets or any other domes-
tic assignment they might ask you to do for them. Is that clear?"

"Yes, sir." The blended aromas of old parchment, mineral oil,
leather, and pipe tobacco reminded Molly of the Pembrooke library.
She felt a sense of security in the familiar surroundings. The matching
leather-upholstered winged-back chairs stood on each side of a massive stone fireplace. Attorney Adams pointed to a giant portrait of a
well-dressed man in a gilt frame above the fireplace. "That is Horatio
Wadsworth, the founder of this law firm and my first wife's father. I
choose to operate alone, except for my four clerks out front."

Molly gazed at the subject of the painting's strong jaw and his
knitted brow.

"I hired you because of Papa Horatio. He was a man advanced for
his time. He trained his daughter Temperance, my beloved wife, to
work beside him here in this very library. I met her working as his law

clerk. I must confess that is my main concern with you that one of these eager young bucks will woo you away from me before your contract is completed."

Molly gave her head a violent shake. "Oh, that won't happen; I assure you."

Again the man laughed. "Ah, for one so young to be so certain. Unfortunately, when it comes to the heart, there's many a slip twixt the cup and the lip."

Molly cast him a quick glance. "Is that a quote from Shakespeare?"

It was Attorney Adams turn to be surprised. "You are familiar with the Bard?"

"Aye. Lady Pembrooke taught me many things, one of which was to appreciate fine English literature."

"What a delightful surprise. Actually the quote isn't from Shakespeare. It's an old English proverb. Beyond your love for literature, how did you learn of your gift with numbers?"

"Before my father died, he discovered I had a natural bent toward mathematics. He's the one who taught me how to read as well. Fortunately, the Pembrookes encouraged me to develop both interests. Most numerical problems I solve faster in my head than I can write them down." She chuckled nervously.

"If you enjoy reading books as well as you balance them, I can see we are going to get along famously!"

He led her to a set of double French doors. Beyond the doors was a proper English garden. Pink, orange, and white primroses bordered the red-brick pathways that meandered through the small space. Molly sighed with pleasure when she recognized the wild array of lavender, daisies, and dahlias, staple flowers in Lady Pembrooke's lovely parlor garden.

In front of the stone wall along the rear of the property, a wooden bridge spanned a tiny pond. Hedges of sculpted boxwood and several arching dogwood trees added height and interest to the delightful space.

"This is my wife Julia's pride and joy, and her only interest in life," he explained. "She won't speak to you. Julia hasn't spoken to anyone since our only son Joshua died of consumption, four years ago. He was eight." A wave of sorrow washed across the attorney's brow.

"You are welcome to walk out there whenever you need a break from computing numbers. But I warn you, do not pick any blossoms! Even dead ones! Or my wife may skewer you on the nearest petard or, perhaps, on the tip of her trowel." The man chuckled. "However, when you do meet her, nod graciously, greet her politely, and move on. She'd doesn't like to be disturbed."

The man continued, "My number one rule for you is, you will, at no time, leave the premises unattended. Should you need to go anywhere, Percy will accompany you. Norfolk is a sea town. It isn't safe for a decent young woman to roam the streets alone. Rule number two: never, never ever invite a gentleman to your room! For that matter, I would advise you to remain free of romantic entanglements until you've completed your service."

Molly's face reddened. "Sir, I have no intention—"

Again the attorney chuckled and moved on. "When I learned your contract was available, I was eager to hire you. Over the years, I've observed that female Irish employees are industrious, cheerful, and honest. They work hard and live by a strict moral code." He glanced at the Bible she held against her chest and frowned. "Do you happen to be a Roman Catholic? Virginians don't take kindly to Papists."

"No, sir. My mother and father were Quakers, but I'm not sure what I am."

"Good! I like your honesty already. Now, let's return to the library where I will enumerate your other duties." Once inside, the lawyer lit the four wall sconces and a lantern on the corner of the desk. "You are to keep my books in order, take care of my billing, and record all incoming receipts. Can you do that?"

"Absolutely, sir."

"And please, stop calling me 'sir.' Henceforth, I will refer to you as Mistress Molly and you will refer to me as Master Adams. My wife, of course, will be addressed as Mistress Julia."

He went on. "Percy is known only as Percy. The man is not a slave. He is a free man, who works for me and is my friend. Percy comes and goes as he pleases. His granddaughter's name is Fern. We employ her as a chambermaid. I think you two will get along famously."

Molly nodded.

"Before you begin the task of unscrambling the mess my former accountant made of my books, you may go to your room, freshen up, and unpack your belongings, after which Fern will escort you to Mae-Mae's kitchen. And mark my word; it is Mae-Mae's kitchen. Even I tread lightly around that formidable lady." He rolled his eyes toward the ceiling and grimaced.

"After you have had time to review the books, I expect a full report as to the numerical mayhem my former clerk may have caused." With that, Master Adams exited out of the library. Before the door closed behind him, he turned toward Molly. "I will be with clients throughout the rest of the afternoon. However, should you need anything, my office is to your right. The closed office on the left is the conference room."

Molly ambled along the shelves of books, most of which were books of jurisprudence. Many were written in foreign languages. Several were about constitutional laws of countries around the world. The girl was pleased to find a smattering of books containing English literature. Crossing the room, she ran her hand across the shiny oak desktop. It was then that she remembered Master Adams's instructions to get her own belongings settled first. Molly climbed the stairs to the third floor.

A girl with a darker coloring than Percy met her in the hallway. "May I help you unpack, ma'am?"

"Please call me Molly. I understand your name is Fern. What a lovely name." She followed the girl into a small bedroom with a dormer window looking out on the garden. Molly laid her Bible on a small nightstand and plopped down on the edge of the puffy feather bed.

"*Ooh!*" she sighed. She fell back against the multicolored quilt atop the mattress. It had been weeks since she'd slept in a real bed.

When she opened her eyes, Molly was surprised to find the girl still in the room. She could tell by the excitement in the young servant's eyes that the girl was reluctant to leave.

Molly pointed to the trunk. "I suppose you can unpack my things and hang my dresses in the wardrobe if you'd like."

"Yessum." Fern sprang into action, removing one elegant gown after another out of the trunk. The girl even swooned over the dresses Molly considered to be her everyday clothing. Fern held up a deep blue-velvet confection with white-lace edging at the neckline. "These are *sooo* beautiful, Mistress Molly. Were you a princess in Ireland?"

Again Molly realized that Lady Pembrooke had treated her as a daughter and as nobility. "No, no," she answered. "Just very blessed." She cocked her head to one side and asked, "How old are you, Fern?"

"Almost sixteen," the servant girl replied. "How old are you, ma'am?"

Remembering how carefree her life had been at Fern's age, Molly sighed. "I turned eighteen on my way across the ocean."

"Really?" The girl's dark eyes sparkled with excitement. "When I turn sixteen, I will marry Norwood Washington."

"How do you know that? Has he asked for your hand in marriage?"

"Oh, no, the arrangements were made when we were children. Norwood is the son of a freed slave as well. He is a doorman at the Regent Inn here in Norfolk." Pride glowed in the young girl's eyes.

"I thought Percy was your grandfather."

"He is. My father died two years ago in a hunting accident, but my grandfather will honor the agreement."

"Have you met Norwood?" Molly asked.

"Oh, no. We will officially meet on my sixteenth birthday. We will court for three months and then wed." Fern seemed pleased with the marital arrangement that had been made for her by others.

"What if you don't like Norwood? What will you do then?"

Fern hugged herself and closed her eyes dreamily. "Oh, I know I will like him, and in time, I will learn to love him."

A surprising wave of homesickness washed over Molly. She felt tired and frightfully alone. While the girl couldn't see beyond the next two years of employment, Fern knew the plans for her life not only for the next two years but for several years thereafter. Suddenly exhausted, she asked, "Fern, could you give me a few minutes to rest? I think I need to lie down before lunch."

The servant girl gave her a wide grin. "Certainly."

Molly rubbed her hand across her brow.

"Do you have a headache? I can get a headache potion for you from Mae-Mae."

Molly smiled. "No, I'll be fine if I can close my eyes for a few minutes. Come for me in a half hour, please. Thank you."

THE PARTING

The servant girl slipped out of the room and closed the door. Molly rolled over to face the wall. The events of the last few months had finally caught up with her. As she gazed at the wall's rough whitewashed surface, Molly wanted to cry, scream, vent her pain and her frustrations in every possible way, but she had no tears left.

Anger against the Pembrookes, especially the younger Lord Pembrooke; anger against the wealthy plantation owner who separated her and her mother; anger against Attorney Adams for purchasing her contract—bitter, acidic anger seethed within her. Her head ached, her stomach churned, and her spirit fought against the injustice of her life.

She wondered about her mother at the Richmond plantation. Would the folks there treat her well? When would she ever see her again? By the time Fern returned, Molly had fallen asleep.

"Wake up, Mistress Molly, wake up. Mae-Mae's stew is ready to eat. She made dumplings!" the girl confided as they tripped down the stairs to the large, open kitchen.

A fire in the eight-foot-wide rock fireplace produced a cheery glow in the otherwise dark room. Beside the hearth, a kitchen rocker with a multicolored throw tossed across the seat sat empty. In the middle of the room, six Windsor-style chairs surrounded a solid maple table. Hefty iron pots and herbs drying on strings hung from the ceiling's massive wooden beams. Red bricks in a herringbone pattern covered the floor. Beyond the two six-paned leaded glass windows, she could see glimpses of deep green ivy growing on the wall.

Molly hadn't eaten since leaving the ship. When she inhaled the succulent aroma of the hot, bubbling vegetable stew, her stomach growled. She suspected both Mae-Mae and Fern heard the rumble.

The cook, a generously rounded woman with cheeks and nose as red as apples, gestured toward the nearest chair. Her gray hair peeked out from under her white, lace-edged morning cap.

"My, aren't you a wisp of a lass—nothing to ye! A strong east wind come up and you'd blow out to sea." The woman tapped the back of the chair and laughed. "Sit! Eat! I can't have you passing out from hunger in my kitchen. Be warned! I'm going to make it my mission to put some meat on those bones of yours, young lady." The woman strode over to the stove and ladled steaming hot stew and three dumplings into a gray-and-white ceramic bowl. She then placed the bowl in front of Molly, along with a silver soupspoon. "Eat, child, eat!" Mae-Mae ordered, filling a second bowl with the steaming, hot liquid. "You, too, Fern."

Molly delicately lifted the large silver spoon to her lips. Suddenly, Mae-Mae shouted, "Wait! You didn't bless it! At my table, we always bless our food before we eat it."

Fern bowed her head as Mae-Mae, her eyes squeezed shut, offered a short, to-the-point prayer. "Father God, bless this food prepared by your humble servant."

Molly peered out of the corner of her eye at the strange woman who ran the Adamses' kitchen.

The older woman opened one eye. "And, Lord, teach these girls proper gratitude for their food and for all of Thy bounteous blessings. Amen."

Molly shot a quick glance toward Fern. The younger girl grinned and ate her first mouthful of soup. Mae-Mae waddled over to the brick warming oven and returned with four slices of homemade bread. "Would ye like raspberry jam on your bread?"

"Oh, yes, ma'am," Molly nodded as she scooped a second spoonful of stew into her mouth.

Hmmph! The woman snorted. "Please call me Mae-Mae."

CHAPTER EIGHT

IRISH NEED NOT APPLY

A

S THE DAYS PASSED, Molly quickly adjusted to the Adamses' routine. In fact, she almost enjoyed it. It was only at night, when alone in her room and reading her parents' Bible, that she remembered how very lonely and how bitter she felt toward the people who'd injured her in the past. Her resentment intensified when she found ranting newspaper articles about the invading Irish horde. One morning she'd had all she could take.

Master Adams started in surprise when Molly stormed into his office and slammed the door. "What is it, Mistress Molly?" he asked.

"I can't believe what I read in this newspaper! It's one thing to see signs for job opportunities that read, 'No Irish need apply.' But this? It's despicable." She tossed an edition of the *Norfolk Chronicle* onto the desk in front of him. "Did you see today's editorial? 'The Irish fill our prisons and our poorhouses. Scratch a convict or a pauper and chances are, you will tickle the skin of an Irishman. Putting them on a boat and sending them home would end crime in this country.' "

Aching for a fight, Molly glared at her employer. Her ocean-blue eyes glinted with displeasure. "Why do Americans hate Irish people so much? They scorn our brogue, our peasant clothes, and our customs, as if we had a choice where we were born. It's not that my people want to be poor; but without work, they are forced to live in basements and hovels that lack life's basic necessities. Last week, the Norfolk newspaper reported that eighty percent of infants born to Irish immigrants die before the age of two."

"And how many died in Ireland during that time due to the potato famine?" Master Adams calmly asked.

Miffed, Molly clicked her tongue in disgust. The girl considered Attorney Adams to be a fair and intelligent man—someone with whom she could freely debate events and politics without fear of censure. "But America is supposed to be the land of opportunity—the Golden Door, right?"

"And it is. But as a nation, she is young." The attorney smiled and tapped his fingers on the arm of his winged-back chair. "Besides, regardless of their nationality, people fear the unfamiliar, that which they do not understand." His voice took on a professorial edge, as if addressing a classroom of law students. "They cluster together like frightened geese on a frozen pond. Any stranger is immediately suspicious. This tendency has been true since the first European colony was established on America's shores, and it will probably continue long after you and I have been assimilated into the culture."

"Does that make it right? What's the cure? Is the Irish immigrant's only hope to become more American than the Americans?" Molly snarled.

"A wise suggestion, my dear. In time, America's fledgling society will refocus its prejudices on other nationalities who immigrate here and, alas, new fears will emerge."

"But it's so unfair!" she wailed.

"However, Mistress Molly, you must admit that it is easier for Irish immigrants to blend into America's culture than for someone like Percy or Fern. The Irish immigrants can update their clothes, hide their customs, and lose their brogues far easier than Fern can change her skin color. Also you came to America of your own free will, while the colored people were kidnapped by ruthless slave traders, sold on an auction block like livestock, and forced to live in deplorable conditions, not for a two-year or a seven-year contract, but for life."

Unable to think of a quick retort, Molly bristled and stormed out the garden door. She wandered along the red-brick garden pathway and considered Attorney Adams's words. He was right. Percy or Fern could never blend into the culture. Wherever they went, their skin color would immediately be recognized as of a different race. "Life isn't fair! Why do I get so angry about things over which I have no control?" Closing her eyes, she rested in the quiet seclusion until Mistress Julia, carrying on her arm a covered wicker basket, stepped out of the house and silently walked across the garden and slipped through the wooden gate at the rear of the property. Five minutes later, the tiny woman returned through the gate without the basket.

During Molly's first few weeks at work in the law firm, she straightened out the tangle of numbers in Master Adams's ledgers. It was evident to her that the clerk who'd previously kept the books knew little about accounting or even basic mathematics. The numbers entered were smudged and disorderly. The stack of unrecorded invoices she found in the bottom drawer of the desk were many months old.

No wonder Master Adams purchased my contract, she thought. *The poor man is swamped with unpaid bills, both coming and going from his office. If he weren't a lawyer, someone would have taken him to court by now!*

In no time, the young woman had completed her main task and wanted more work with which to occupy her days. Being a wise and frugal man, Attorney Adams asked her to organize his vast library. This task took longer than necessary because she often got lost reading an interesting book.

This additional assignment didn't keep the energetic young woman busy for long. So the attorney tried again. Knowing that Mae-Mae disliked shopping, Master Adams suggested that Molly, accompanied by Percy, do the grocery shopping at the farmers' market. While the freed slave was known and well respected by the stall vendors, to have him carry any cash made him prey to the hoodlums who hung out near the docks. With Molly carrying the cash, these troublemakers would fear retribution from the good citizens of the community if they treated a white woman in such a manner.

During the drive through the Irish shantytown, Molly tried to close her eyes to the poverty. This was the section of the city near the wharf where Irish immigrants who'd been hoodwinked out of their savings were forced to huddle together in dank cellars and tenement houses for survival. The girl knew if her father were alive and in Norfolk, this was where he would be—helping to relieve the people's hunger and their illiteracy. She could almost imagine seeing her mother or her father standing in doorways, holding a scrawny toddler in his or her arms.

However, Molly could almost block out the horrors of the shanty-town when Fern was allowed to accompany her on the afternoon excursions. Poor Percy had the difficult task of corralling the two young women as they laughed and dillydallied through the open-air market stands along the wharf. But the man's ever-watchful presence served to dampen the inclinations of potential swains or lechers who might have tried to accost the girls.

On one Friday morning foray, Molly had purchased the peas, carrots, and summer squash Mae-Mae requested for the evening fare. All that was left to buy was the fish. She and Fern were examining a counter of freshly caught fish when Molly noticed that Percy was no longer in sight. "Did you see where your grandfather went?" she asked Fern.

Fern lifted a dismissive hand. "Oh, don't worry. Grandpa can't be far away."

Molly scanned the nearby faces a second time. "Well, I surely don't see him anywhere. You don't think he might be in danger, do you?"

Fern picked up a freshwater bass by the tail and studied it. "No, I'm sure he's fine. What do you think of this fish? It would round out the stewpot, wouldn't it?"

"I would think you'd be more concerned about your missing grandfather than about some widemouth bass for tonight's stewpot!"

The mild-mannered girl's eyes flashed with irritation. "Molly, Grandpa's just fine. You must trust me about this. He's probably carrying out Master Adams's business."

Molly blinked in surprise.

The fishwife behind the counter interrupted, "Girlie, do you want to buy the fish or not?" The woman, her hair matted and the bodice of her flour-sack dress muddied, spotted the silver coins in Molly's hand and shot her a toothless grin.

"Yes, yes, of course." After unsuccessfully dickering with the woman, Molly handed her the money. The woman wrapped the fish in an old newspaper and handed the package to Fern, who stuffed the fish in her shopping basket and then ambled over to a stall selling baked goods. "If we have any leftover money, we should buy a surprise for

Mistress Julia. She's been feeling a bit under the weather lately. And she adores gingersnaps."

Molly shot Fern a quizzical glance. "How can you tell she's not feeling well? She never speaks a word."

Fern smiled. "She doesn't have to speak. I just know."

With their purchases made, the girls hurried back to the Adamses' carriage, where they found Percy polishing the brass decorations on the far side of the carriage. As they approached, a man dressed in the garb of a ship's captain snatched a small burlap sack, bulging with coins, from under the driver's seat on the carriage, nodded abruptly toward Fern's grandfather, and disappeared into a nearby wooded area.

"Who was that?" Molly whispered to Fern as Percy rounded the carriage.

"It doesn't concern you. You ask too many questions!" The girl handed their purchases to her grandfather and climbed into the vehicle.

"Well, you don't need to be snappish!" Molly allowed Percy to help her into the carriage.

"And you don't need to be so nosey!" Fern avoided glancing toward Molly.

Tears rose in Molly's eyes. She didn't understand what she'd done to offend her friend. Molly turned her face away. That's when she spotted a brightly painted wagon, much like the Gypsy wagons she'd seen as a child in Ireland.

The Adams carriage had barely stopped in front of the law offices when Molly hopped down and hurried inside. Ridgley, the head law clerk rose to his feet, expanded his suspenders with his thumbs, tilted his head to one side, and sent her an insolent glare. "Where have you been? Master Adams has been looking for you. Master Chagall, a very important client of Master Adams, I might add, stopped by to pay his bill. I couldn't help him. Finances aren't my forte, are they?"

Molly shot him a simpering smile. "I am so sorry, Ridgley. I didn't know writing out a simple receipt for the gentleman was above your position."

"Don't get cheeky with me, little lass," he warned. "I can make your life miserable should I so desire."

The level of ire in her own tone startled the girl. Up until now, she'd kept her dislike of the man under control. She paused, her hand on the doorknob to her office and smiled sweetly. "Oh? Isn't that what you've been doing since the first day I entered this office? And now, if you will excuse me."

The man glowered, lowered his body onto his wooden desk chair, and hid his face behind a legal brief.

Once inside the library, Molly leaned against the door and took a deep breath. "This has been one absolutely horrid day!" she announced to the books on the shelves behind her desk. "Molly, my girl, one of these days that mouth of yours will get you in deep trouble."

As she dropped to her knees behind the desk, she buried her face in her gloved hands. "Oh Mama, I need you so badly," she cried aloud. "You always helped me keep my temper in check by quoting a promise or two from the Book. You know I try to read it every day like I promised, but the words on a page, no matter how profound they may be, don't get through. God, please help me control my emotions before I do or say something irreparable."

At a sudden knock at the door, she jumped up from behind the desk and smoothed the wrinkles out of her skirts.

"Some young man is asking to see you, Mistress Molly." Ridgley's voice oozed with condescension.

"A man? Now?" She blinked in surprise. Her hands flew to the bonnet still askew on her head. "Who would come asking for me? I don't know anyone outside of the law offices."

Knowing the rules about entertaining members of the opposite sex in the office, Ridgley smirked at her discomfort. She struggled to regain her composure.

"Thank you, Ridgely. Show him in please." Whoever it was she didn't want to create a spectacle by greeting him in the outer office. Snagging her bonnet from her head, she removed a linen mobcap from the top drawer of her desk and placed it on her head. She'd barely tucked the last stray curl under the cap when in strode Tavis Lloyd.

"Tavis!" Molly squealed and ran into his arms. Behind him all four law clerks peered around the edge of the open door. Embarrassed by her spontaneous display of affection, she quickly straightened. "What are you doing here? I thought you were in Richmond. Did Mama come with you? Is she all right?"

"Hey, Molly girl. Everything is fine. Your mama sends her love as well as a packet of letters for you." He handed her a small stack of letters tied together with a coarse cord from a flour sack. Molly's eyes filled with tears as she gazed at her mother's familiar handwriting.

"Thank you. Thank you," she whispered.

"She said to tell you she is fine. Life on the Taylor plantation is nothing like Pembrooke manor, but she's getting accustomed to the differences."

"I'm so glad! I've been terribly worried about her. But, wait! What are you doing in Norfolk?"

"Master Taylor has assigned me the task of overseeing the shipments of tobacco from the plantation to Norfolk. In fact, I will be traveling to town at least four more times before winter. He and Master Adams have business together."

"Four more times? Wonderful! Next time you come, I'll have a packet of letters written for Mama."

Her childhood friend's face was leaner than she remembered. He looked less like the boy she'd known and more like a man she'd never met.

"Master Taylor must think a lot of you to give you so much responsibility," she observed.

"Yes, it has worked out well for me. I like the travel, especially now that I will be able to see you."

"I would like that as well." She blushed and dropped her gaze to her hands folded at her waist.

"By the way, on the way into town, I ran into Seamus. You remember Doctor Sheridan? He's bought horses and a large covered wagon in which he lives as he travels from place to place, selling ointments and healing elixirs. I'm surprised he hasn't stopped to see you before now."

Molly frowned. "No, I've not seen him."

When someone behind them cleared his throat, she glanced over Tavis's shoulder. "Oh, Master Adams, I'd like you to meet my childhood friend from Ireland. Tavis, let me introduce you to Attorney Adams, my employer."

The two men shook hands as Molly babbled nervously about how he brought letters from her mother. Master Adams exchanged a knowing glance between the two.

"Yes, I remember you, Tavis Lloyd. You're the exceptional young man whose papers I tried to secure, but my friend Master Taylor refused to sell. Come! Join me for a cup of tea by the fire. Molly, would you have Mae-Mae bring us a fresh pot of tea and maybe a few of her gingersnaps as well?" He waved Tavis toward the wing-backed chairs on each side of the fireplace.

"Oh, yes! Yes, Master Adams." The girl almost danced from the room. Molly delivered the request to Mae-Mae and hurried back, hoping to eavesdrop on their conversation.

"By the way, how is my old friend, Edmund? He sent word that you'd be stopping by. Did you have a safe trip?"

"Yes, sir. No complications. The cargo arrived safely at its destination." Tavis reached into his vest pocket, pulled out a note, and handed it to Master Adams.

The attorney scanned the note and stuffed it in his vest pocket. "Thank you. Good news. I'll see that this reaches the powers that be."

"Master Taylor wanted to know what you've heard about the Dred Scott affair. Has anything been decided?"

Molly's ears perked up at the mention of the Dred Scott case. Working in the law office, the girl had heard everyone talking about the case as it worked its way through the courts. Though he'd never discussed the case with her, many times Master Adams had discussed with his guests and his law clerks about the unfairness of it all.

"Personally, I think it's looking good for the Scotts," Master Adams told Tavis. "As you know, they have a fair judge and, I believe, a strong case."

"Yes, that's what Master Taylor believes as well." Tavis nodded, his hands folded under his chin.

Molly enjoyed hearing the familiar deep baritone roll of Tavis's brogue. She realized how terribly lonely she had been since leaving the ship. She smiled to herself. The day, which had begun so miserably, had certainly taken a delightful turn for the better.

Remembering her errand, Molly rushed back to the kitchen and insisted Mae-Mae allow her to carry the silver tray with a porcelain tea service, steaming hot tea, and a plate of gingersnaps to the two men. When she reached to open the door, she heard her name. The girl paused to listen further.

"I've known her for her entire life. I believe we can safely trust her," Tavis said.

"But you don't know for certain."

"No, but I do know Molly, and I knew Molly's father. Being a practicing Quaker, he fought for fairness and justice for all of God's children. If he were here in America, he would be in the thick of it. Molly is cut from the same cloth."

"A bit nosey are we?" Mae-Mae stepped up behind Molly. "Hardly befitting of a proper lady."

"A bit," the girl admitted. It was the second time in one day she had been accused of nosiness.

"It's all right," Mae-Mae admitted. She lowered her voice. "There are times we ladies must resort to eavesdropping to keep informed about the goings on around here. And trust me, there is much on which to eavesdrop in this household. But I would have thought you already knew that. Now, go in there and serve the tea before it cools."

Molly nodded and pushed open the door with her shoulder.

"Molly, come in." Master Adams waved her into the room. "We were just talking about you."

"About me?" She set the tray on a small side table between the two men and blushed. Her hands shook as she poured the hot liquid into the first teacup. "Master Adams, would you like one teaspoon of sugar or two?"

"I'll take care of the tea, my dear." He waved her back from the tea table. "Please sit down."

She glanced about for a place to sit and for the first time noticed one of the cane-back side chairs from in front of her desk had been placed between the two winged-back chairs. Obedient and more than a little curious, she did as told. Careful to smooth her skirts, she folded her hands primly in her lap.

"Mistress Molly," Master Adams began, "over the past several months since you've been in my employ, you've proven yourself to be trustworthy and typically tight-lipped, even when goaded by Ridgley. What we are about to share with you no one else can know. People's lives are at stake. Do you promise that what we say will never leave this room?"

Molly nodded, her eyes wide with concern.

"Tell her, Master Tavis."

Tavis reached into his vest pocket and withdrew a folded envelope. "This is from your mother. Open it and read it."

Molly unfolded the envelope and broke the wax seal on the back. Her mother's familiar penmanship brought tears to the young woman's eyes. She swallowed hard and began reading.

> Dearest Molly,
>
> I am writing this letter to authenticate what Tavis and Master Adams are about to tell you. I realize that what they are asking of you can be dangerous and frightening, but I also know you are more than able to perform the task. However, if you do not wish to get involved, I will respect your decision and your discretion in the matter.
>
> Lovingly, your mother,
> Enid Maguire

The young woman glanced inquiringly first at Tavis and then at Master Adams. "I don't understand."

"Molly, your mother and I have joined an organization that helps runaway slaves to escape," Tavis explained. "It's unofficially referred to as the Underground Railroad."

"Forgive me, Master Adams, but aren't you an attorney, an officer of the courts of Virginia? Didn't you take an oath to uphold the law?"

The man reddened. "Yes, my dear, I did. And it pains me to break it, but I believe that, in this case, God's law overrides man's."

"Oh, sorry, sir." Like an errant schoolgirl, she stared down at her hands.

"No, you did nothing wrong. You asked an important question, one I pondered for some time before I agreed to get involved. Anyway, let Tavis continue."

"When runaways are delivered to the plantation, your mother hides them and feeds them until a conductor comes to move them to the next safe house and the next, until they reach Norfolk. Once there, Percy smuggles them to one of the cooperating ship captains in port, who then transports them north to Canada." Tavis paused and searched Molly's face for a reaction. "Doctor Sheridan is also a conductor, but along another route. I am a scout. My job is to warn the station masters of incoming cargo."

Molly's head pounded from too much information. "I don't understand. What does this have to do with me?"

"I'm getting to that," Tavis continued. "Last week one of our main conductors was killed by bounty hunters. As a result, that route is now unsafe for shipment. My job is to repair the rails between here and Richmond. That is the real reason I will be traveling to Norfolk so often."

"I still don't understand." The girl couldn't believe that her mother could be involved in an illegal activity. But when she remembered her mother's passion to feed the hungry and care for the downtrodden, then it made sense. "So what do you want me to do? Hide runaway slaves here in the law offices?"

Master Adams laughed. "Hardly. My wife does a fine job of that. We need you to supply an excuse for Tavis's frequent visits to Norfolk."

"Me?"

"Yes, he will ostensibly be courting you." Master Adams cast her a benign smile. "He will squire you around the city while his cargo is being safely transferred out of the country. Fern or Mae-Mae will chaperone. Of course, you need to remember that this is only pretend—and not a real courtship."

The attorney continued, "As your legal guardian, I must point out that the physical danger for you, Molly, will be minimal because you won't personally come into contact with runaways. As I see it, the greater danger will be to your hearts; neither of you is in a position financially or socially to participate in a proper courtship at this time."

He eyed Tavis thoughtfully. "I don't need to remind you that you both have eighteen months left on your contracts, which, of course, I expect you to honor. As for you, Molly, your responsibilities as my accountant and librarian will continue."

As Molly licked her suddenly parched lips, her mind raced over the events of the last few days. *These new facts explain what happened today at the market. No wonder Fern told me to mind my own business,* she thought. *And this could also explain the strange shadows I sometimes see in the garden at night.*

"Well?" Master Adams said, breaking the silence.

There will be no need to pretend, she thought. *Can't the insightful Master Adams tell I am already emotionally attached to Tavis Lloyd?*

"Would it be so distasteful being courted by me?" Tavis teased. "On a temporary basis, of course."

"No!" She blinked in surprise. "Not at all."

A shiver ran the length of her spine. Could she protect herself against the inevitable heartache when their little charade ended?

"As long as Tavis and I are totally honest with each other. There can be no deception between us!" She studied Tavis's eyes as she spoke.

A wave of sadness washed across his face. "When have I ever been anything but honest with you, little pigeon?"

"Never, but in an effort to protect me from the truth, I can see the possibility arising." She glanced toward Master Adams. "That applies to you as well—total honesty! No secrets are to be kept from me to protect me."

"Absolutely! Then you agree to the plan?" The man's face grew animated. "You will be helping so many people to gain their freedom. It is so rewarding. You'll see."

CHAPTER NINE

THE CHARADE

THE PLAN WAS SIMPLE. A letter carrier would deliver a note to Molly of Tavis's upcoming visit. While the coded message would appear to include only the time and day of his arrival, it would also alert Percy to the time, day, drop point, and number of runaways to be transported to whatever conspiring ship captain was in port at the time.

On a cold, drizzly autumn morning, Tavis's first note arrived. A chilling draft skittered along the floorboards between the garden door and the outer office. Molly huddled behind her massive desk and blew her nose into a man-sized linen handkerchief Mae-Mae had given her at breakfast.

Following a sequence of sneezes, the girl wrapped her woolen shawl tightly about her shoulders and slipped into the kitchen for a cup of hot peppermint tea.

The older woman welcomed Molly's interruption. "Would you also like a couple of lemon sugar cookies? Freshly baked this morning." Like a mother bear, the woman lived to care for her cubs. From the first moment the frightened and lonely Irish girl arrived at the Adamses' household and had stepped into the woman's warm and cozy kitchen, Mae-Mae had included Molly in an overprotective circle of love.

"Why don't you bring your work in here? It's much warmer than in that drafty old library," the woman insisted.

Molly laughed. "And just how much work would you get done chatting with me all afternoon? And don't say we wouldn't talk. Admit it, I'm Irish; I talk too much. And you, you can't help yourself."

Mae-Mae threw back her head and laughed. "I suppose you're right. I don't have any one nationality to blame for my gift of gab, but I can gab with the best of 'em." The woman filed a porcelain teapot with the steeped tea, placed it and a teacup on a tray, and handed it to Molly. "You go ahead. I'll be along with cookies, cream, and sugar in a minute."

Knowing that arguing with the woman would be useless, Molly hurried back to the library. The instant she entered the library, Molly sensed someone had been in there during her absence. She cast a judicious gaze about the room. Her pen was leaning to the left instead of toward the right of the ink well. The main ledger was slightly askew. Her chair had been pushed to one side. Several times during the previous weeks she'd had suspicions that someone had moved the ledgers on her desk. Before she analyzed the situation further, a knock sounded on the door to the outer office.

"Come in," she called.

The door opened. Ridgley entered, strode to her desk, and handed her a small envelope. "This note just came for you, milady."

"You may call me Mistress Molly, sir." She took the envelope from his hands and examined the wax stamp on the back. "The seal appears to have been broken and re-sealed. Would you know anything about that?"

"*Hmm.* I'm sure you're mistaken. Surely no one around here would do such a dastardly deed as read your personal mail." The man's sarcastic sneer infuriated her.

Molly snatched the envelope from his grasp. What should she do, make a fuss or let it go? Before opening the envelope, she shot an insolent glare at Ridgley. "Will there be anything else, Ridgley? If not, you may be excused."

A flash of anger darted across his face. He opened his mouth to speak but quickly changed his mind. "Very well!"

Molly watched him leave the room. She'd purposely infuriated him by reminding him of his place in the hierarchy of the law firm. That this little immigrant from Ireland answered only to the attorney stuck in the man's craw, as her mother would have said.

Once the door closed behind him, the girl removed the seal on the envelope and opened the folded sheet of paper.

My dear Mistress Molly:

It has been a fortnight since I last visited with you at Attorney Adams's establishment. I thoroughly enjoyed our delightful conversation and eagerly anticipate further communication once again. I will be in Norfolk on the fifteenth of this month on business. I would be delighted if you would do me the honor of taking afternoon tea with me at the Upton's English Teahouse and Garden. If the sun is shining, perhaps we can complete our afternoon with a rowboat ride on the Elizabeth River.

Your lovingly devoted servant,

Tavis Lloyd

Molly pressed the note against her breast, closed her eyes, and sighed. If only she could keep it as her first love note and treasure it. She'd secret it away at the bottom of her trunk along with her copy of Shakespearean sonnets and her precious brooch. But alas, as real as she wanted it to be, she knew it was but a ruse that she had to pass on to Percy.

All thought of recording the stack of receipts that had arrived in the morning mail were abandoned in preparation for Tavis's visit. Since she and Fern had become a part of the same conspiracy, their friendship had deepened.

"Do you think it might rain this afternoon?" Molly asked as she peered out of her third-floor dormer window. "The sky is clear now, but that would mean nothing if we were living in Ireland. In Ireland, the weather can change from sunny to stormy in a heartbeat."

Behind her Fern opened the wardrobe door and gazed at the bright array of lovely afternoon frocks. "I think you should wear your robin-egg-blue dress with the Chantilly lace at the neck and wrists. It is so feminine."

Molly eyes shone with excitement. "Really? I was thinking of wearing the black watch plaid taffeta skirt with my white-lace blouse and a sweater vest. Besides I have a Shetland wool cape that would look smashing with it."

Fern shook her head. "No, men like their ladies to wear more feminine attire."

Molly laughed aloud. "How do you know that? You sound like Lady Pembrooke."

"I didn't have to grow up under the tutelage of some hoity-toity English lady to know what men like," the fifteen-year-old huffed and returned to evaluating the dresses in the wardrobe.

"Sorry! You are right," Molly admitted. "The high, lacy neckline certainly does soften my dark hair and bring out the pink in my complexion. And my snowy-white woolen shawl with my blue bonnet would be a pleasing choice." Molly had come to admire the younger girl's bravery and wise judgment. "So when is your birthday, Fern? You never told me."

"My birthday is in August."

Molly caught a glimpse of herself in the mirror above the walnut dresser. She twirled one curl around her finger. "You must be excited, getting married in less than a year." When the girl didn't reply, Molly glanced her way. "You are excited, aren't you?"

The girl shrugged. "I'm not so sure."

"Why?"

"Mae-Mae reminded me that I will have to leave the Adamses' employ and cleave unto my spouse, whatever that means."

"But if you love him—"

"Yes, and then there's that. What if I can't stand him? What if he's mean and ugly and rude?"

"At least you have prospects of having a real home of your own and having children. Look at me. I can't even consider falling in love for at least two years, and then what? Settle for the likes of Ridgley or Simms? *Eeugh!*"

Fern laughed. "That would be disastrous!"

"Can you imagine kissing Ridgley's dry, paper-thin, puckered-up lips?" She grimaced. The two girls giggled at the thought.

Fern picked up the tortoiseshell brush with the boars' hair bristles from the top of the dresser. "Why don't you change out of your house-dress and slip your best chemise over your head? Then I can begin working on your tangled squirrel's nest head of hair."

By the time Fern shaped the last of Molly's curls around her finger and patted them in place, Mae-Mae called from the bottom of the stairs. "Molly, your young man has arrived." The round and cheery cook didn't suspect the charade in which the young couple was involved. Being a romantic at heart, Mae-Mae would have still believed love was in the air even if she had known.

Molly's face glowed at the thought of seeing Tavis once again. "Oh! Oh!" She grabbed the shawl from the bedpost and headed for the closed door.

"Wait! Don't forget your bonnet and your gloves and your parasol." Fern handed the items to Molly. "I put one of your laciest handkerchiefs in your reticule, just in case."

"Oh! Oh!" Molly paused to take a deep breath. "Slow, deliberate steps. Remember to take slow ladylike steps down the stairs. I would hate to catch my heel on the hem of my dress." She laughed nervously.

"Falling at his feet would certainly be a dramatic enough entrance," Fern chuckled, handing Molly her doeskin purse and opening the door. "You go meet your handsome knight while I run to the barn to help Grandpa Percy. I'll be back in a few minutes to chaperone you wherever you plan to go."

Molly paused at the second landing of the house's main staircase to catch her breath. Carefully, she slipped the white kidskin gloves on her hands, looped the handle to her parasol and the drawstring of her purse over her left wrist. Tilting her head to one side and, with as much dignity as she could muster, slowly descended the stairs to the foyer. As her shoes touched the marble flooring at the base of the stairs, she graciously extended her hand toward the waiting young man, his black beaverskin hat in hand. Slowly, she lifted her gaze to his face and started in surprise.

"Seamus! Seamus Sheridan! What are you doing here? Where is Tavis? I thought you were Tavis Lloyd."

The man shot her a quirky grin. His knee-length black frock coat with a matching waistcoat and high-collar linen dress shirt gave him the air of a fashionable country doctor. All he lacked was a black leather medicine bag. Before replying to her query, he kissed the back of her hand. "Sorry to disappoint you, Mistress Molly. Tavis sends his utmost apology for not keeping his assignation with you."

Miffed, Molly sputtered without thinking before speaking, "Where is he? I can't believe he'd do a thing like this!"

"Unfortunately, Master Lloyd is being detained at the local sheriff's office. I will be his substitute for the afternoon, if you will allow me to do so." Seamus paused and cast an appreciative glance at Molly's outfit. "By the way, you certainly look fetching today, Mistress Molly. But then you looked fetching even when you were retching at sea."

Molly wanted to wipe the smirk off the young doctor's face. "A gentleman would not bring up such a distasteful memory!"

Seamus arched his left brow. "Did I say I was a gentleman, Mistress Molly? I'm only a simple country doctor who says what he thinks, sometimes without thinking."

Molly frowned. "Perhaps I should stay here until Tavis can escort me as he promised."

"As you wish." He gave a sweeping bow. "But I do believe we must carry out the plan, not for our sakes, of course . . ." He left the thought suspended in the air.

Molly signed. She'd already forgotten the purpose of the outing. Some runaway slaves were depending on her cooperation.

"I have asked the attorney groomsman to hitch up two of his finest steeds to an open carriage for our afternoon pleasure." He flashed her a confident smile. "I shall, of course, be leaving my humble medicine wagon in the carriage house until we return." Bowing graciously, Seamus opened the leaded glass and oak front door. "I understand Tavis promised you a rowboat ride on the river this afternoon. I was a master rower during my undergraduate years at Queen's University of Belfast."

Molly eyed him appreciatively. *Perhaps,* she thought, *he isn't the quack doctor I thought when I first met him on board the ship.* The girl glided onto the portico and took his arm. As he assisted her down the granite steps, Molly glanced over her shoulder to see Mistress Julia slip out of the carriage house and disappear into the walled garden. It was the first time Molly had seen the woman outside the confines of the main house and garden.

"It seems my arrival has caused quite a stir." Seamus pointed to one of the windows in the law firm's outer office, where four law clerks wrestled for prime viewing rights. When he waved at the faces in the window, the window's heavy velvet curtain dropped back into place.

Seamus chuckled and led her down the slate pathway toward the carriage house. Harnessed and waiting in the doorway was the shiny black gentleman's carriage and the two handsome sorrels. Behind the waiting carriage was a closed wagon. Painted on the sides were brightly colored flowers and the words "Doc Sheridan's Magic Elixir." Beneath it in smaller lettering, it read, "Guaranteed cure for lumbago, chilblain, miasma, gout, the vapors, dropsy, the grippe, and snakebites."

"That is your wagon?" Molly asked, her voice filled with disbelief.

"Yes, ma'am. Isn't she a beauty?"

Molly gulped. "That's not exactly how I would describe it."

Seamus chortled. "It gets me where I am going and does the job it's supposed to do. Plus I can make a pretty penny hawking my magic elixir."

"Your magic elixir?"

Again he laughed. "Can't give you the recipe, but it is guaranteed to make the customers feel very happy."

"Sounds like it contains a bit of the Irishman's comfort to me!"

He shrugged and cast her a sheepish grin. "It's been known to ease a bloke's loneliness on a stormy winter night."

Molly clicked her tongue in disapproval, but not before he took her arm and helped her into the open carriage. "Where is Fern? Attorney Adams gave strict orders that Fern was to accompany me on these outings."

"Both Percy and Fern are busy at the moment. Mae-Mae will be accompanying us." He tucked in the last of her abundant skirts and closed the carriage's half door.

"Mae-Mae?"

"Yes, she'll be along in a minute."

He dashed to the kitchen door, escorted the family cook to the carriage, and helped her climb in beside Molly. When Seamus climbed on board, the fit was tight. Molly felt uncomfortable with Seamus's leg pressing against hers. She could feel color rising up her neck and into her cheeks. She had always felt safe with Tavis, almost as if he were her brother as she tagged after him back in Ireland. But with Doctor Seamus Sheridan, an air of danger and mystery surrounded him.

Sensing her discomfort, he said, "Don't worry. I've been around good horses since I was a boy. These beauties have been well trained, as have I." He tapped the stiff brim of his shiny top hat and urged the horses down the alleyway and onto the busy cobblestone street.

CHAPTER TEN

SABOTAGE

A HEAVY SILENCE ENSUED DURING the short drive to the teahouse. Even Mae-Mae, who usually talked incessantly, remained strangely silent, her hands folded across her ample middle.

"Are you all right, Mae-Mae?" Seamus glanced around Molly at the older woman.

The woman shot a quick glance at the road behind them. "Yes, Doctor Sheridan. Did you know that a closed carriage has been following us ever since we left the Adamses' place?"

"Good. That mystery man took our bait. Did you recognize the driver?"

"No, sir. His face was in the shadows."

Seamus drove the carriage to the rear of the English cottage and climbed out of the carriage. "Molly, stay here. I'll be back for you in a moment after I introduce Mae-Mae to Nettie, the cook. Nettie is expecting her. And watch for that carriage."

Molly thought she saw the vehicle in question roll passed the front of the teahouse, but she couldn't be sure. To her, one black carriage looked pretty much like the next. A few minutes, later Seamus returned.

When Molly stepped into the foyer of Upton's English Teahouse and Garden, her eyes filed with tears. The building reminded her of the home she'd shared with her parents. A hostess wearing a dust cap and a calico gown patterned after clothing from the American colonial period led them into a small sitting room. The hand-printed pineapple design on the walls lent a quaint aura of friendliness to the room. Soft light filtered through the lacy priscilla curtains at the four small-paned windows.

Creamy-white linen tablecloths draped the six small tables. In the center of each table sat a silver vase holding a bouquet of red and gold maple leaves. In one corner of the room, an elderly couple was eating scones and drinking tea. Two men sat at a table nearest one window.

Seamus gestured toward a green-velvet upholstered love seat at the closest table. "Mistress Molly?"

Numbly, Molly obliged. After she was seated, he slid in beside her. When Seamus reached for the printed menu, his coat sleeve brushed against her arm. Molly's breath caught in her throat.

"I've been told Nettie's wild blueberry jam is unbelievable, as is her apple butter. Do you like apple butter?" His breath caressed her cheek as he spoke. She mumbled a barely audible Yes.

Nothing Lady Pembrooke had taught her about the art of courtship prepared Molly for the strange sensations coursing through her body. She heard Seamus speaking to her, but she couldn't concentrate.

Noting her distraction, Seamus continued, "I've been told that their hemlock tea is exquisite as well."

"That would be fine," she agreed, unable to focus.

Seamus knitted his brow. "Molly, are you OK? Hemlock tea is poisonous. Remember Lady Macbeth? Did you hear what I said?"

She blushed. "Oh, how silly of me."

"Would you like me to order for you?"

"Yes, please," she murmured. "That would be fine."

He leaned closer. "Molly, do you not like this place? Would you prefer to go somewhere else?"

She cast him a startled look. Her lips were within inches from his. "Uh, oh no. This place is lovely."

And it was lovely—the tea, the crumpets, the wild blueberry jam. What a perfect afternoon, except for Molly's topsy-turvy emotions. By the time they finished high tea and left the teahouse, the sun had disappeared behind a bank of gray clouds. Molly eyed the sky. "It looks like it might rain," she warned as Seamus helped her into the carriage. "Perhaps we should postpone our boat ride until another day."

As she adjusted her skirt and layers of petticoats around her legs, Molly caught a glimpse of a pock-faced man lurking beside the teahouse. When their eyes met, he quickly disappeared from view. "That's funny," she commented. "That man." She pointed to the left side of the building. "I think I've seen him somewhere before."

"What man?" Seamus asked as he pretended to adjust the reins on one of the horses. "Will you be all right while I fetch Mae-Mae?"

"Of course." She continued to watch the corner of the building where the man had disappeared. When Seamus returned, he helped Mae-Mae into the carriage.

"There was a man watching us from beside the teahouse. I know I've seen him before, but I can't remember where or when."

"He's probably a driver for one of the teahouse guests." Seamus shook the reins; the carriage began to move. "Norfolk is a relatively small city. So, tell me Mae-Mae, did you have a pleasant afternoon?"

"Did I ever!" The woman chuckled aloud. "Nettie is absolutely delightful. She shared her recipe for crumb cake with me. I can't wait to make it for Master Adams."

Why didn't Seamus take her information seriously? Piqued, Molly folded her arms and remained silent while Seamus lazily flicked the reins. "Are you ladies ready for a rowboat ride on the river?"

"Not me!" Mae-Mae declared. "I get seasick at the thought. Besides you young'uns don't need me along. Have a good time. I'll sit on the grass and feed the ducks."

Molly frowned at the gathering clouds. "I don't think a boat ride is in order. I would hate for it to begin raining while we were out in the middle of the river."

He glanced up at the clouds. "Too bad, but I suppose you're right. Would you ladies prefer I take you home?"

"Yes, I think so," Molly admitted.

As the carriage jounced over the cobblestone street, Seamus and Molly rode in silence as Mae-Mae shared her afternoon adventure with them. Finally, he whispered, "Are you upset with me?"

"Yes, Seamus, I am."

Mae-Mae clamped her mouth shut and pretended to watch the passing scenery.

Molly knew she was being rude, but she didn't care. "When I

96

agreed to be a part of this little charade, my one condition Tavis and Master Adams agreed to was that everyone be completely honest with me. Frankly, your response to my question regarding the stranger watching us from the shadows was dismissive and condescending."

Seamus studied the road ahead of the carriage for several seconds. "Molly, I simply did not want to alarm you. Yes, I saw the man watching us. He's a scout for two bounty hunters from Georgia. I have encountered him many times during the past few months. He is probably the man responsible for the having the sheriff haul Tavis in for questioning this morning."

"The sheriff arrested Tavis? Will he be all right?"

Seamus heaved an expressive sigh. It was obvious that the man found it difficult to share such dangerous information with her, but she insisted. "Please, I have to know!"

Slowly, Seamus relented. "Fortunately, he wasn't caught with a runaway in his possession, so they had nothing on which to hold him. He managed to shift the cargo from his carriage to mine before the sheriff arrived. My guess is that he will be released from custody by this evening."

Relieved, Molly continued questioning him. "And the runaway slave?"

"The young man in question is hiding in a safe house awaiting transport out of the country." Seamus glanced toward the young woman. "And that's as much as you need to know at this time. The success of this program is having no one know more than is necessary to perform his or her part in the escape. That way you can't accidentally or otherwise let slip names and places if you don't know them."

Molly frowned. "I suppose you're right."

"I know I am." A water droplet splattered on the tip of Seamus's nose. "And it looks like you were right as well. It is starting to rain." He flicked the reins, and the horses broke into a trot. Molly's lacy sun parasol did little to keep the raindrops off her and Mae-Mae.

By the time the carriage came to a stop inside the horse barn, the shower had drenched all three of them. The brim of Molly's bonnet drooped around her face; her shawl hung limply on her shoulders.

"Well, that was quite the excursion," he laughed and helped the two women down from the carriage. "A little more adventure than I'd planned."

Like a black Labrador puppy after a bath, water sprayed in all directions as Molly shook the rain from her bonnet and shawl. Seamus eyed the steady downpour from inside the doorway of the carriage house. "It looks like we have two choices. We can either make a dash for the house, or wait here until the rain lets up a bit."

Her blue-and-white dress and knitted shawl hanging limply, Mae-Mae silently eyed the downpour as if trying to make the rain stop by sheer willpower.

Seamus glanced toward the older woman and then back at Molly. "By the way, did either of you see our mysterious watcher after we left the teahouse?"

Molly laughed. "No, I was too busy trying to stay dry to worry—"

A voice from the shadows caught Molly midsentence. "I'm glad you made it safely back." Tavis stepped out of an empty stall and tipped his wide-brimmed brown suede hat toward Molly.

"Tavis!" Molly threw her arms around the young man. "When I heard the county sheriff had detained you, I was so worried. Are you all right? Did he mistreat you?" She remembered hearing tales about county sheriffs in Ireland who sometimes brutalized their prisoners.

Tavis grinned and disentangled himself from her arms. "And hello to you, Mistress Molly, as soggy as it is. I am fine. I hope you had a pleasant afternoon, at least more pleasant than mine. Did you enjoy the teahouse?"

"Oh, yes, it was lovely. And Mae-Mae managed to procure a new recipe or two from the cook. And Seamus was delightful host, though we didn't go for our boat ride on the river, due to the sudden rain shower." The girl knew she was babbling but couldn't stop.

"A wise choice to be sure." Tavis shot a quick glance toward Seamus. "I hope he was not too delightful in my absence."

Molly's face reddened as she recalled her reaction to Seamus's closeness. To hide her discomfort, she swatted Tavis's arm with her folded parasol. "Oh, Tavis, you're such a tease."

Seamus scowled at the easy banter flowing between Molly and his friend. "By the way, we saw our nemesis, or I should say Molly spotted him lurking around the teahouse."

Tavis paused and frowned. "Really? I thought I'd shaken him from my trail this morning."

"I guess we weren't as clever as we thought." Seamus shook his head. "He's like a hound on the scent of a fox. We need to be more careful in the future."

"I'm making a run for it." Mae-Mae dashed toward the house, splashing through puddles as she ran. Molly shuddered as a sudden cool breeze whipped her skirts and sent an unexpected chill up her spine.

Tavis noticed and removed his suede jacket and wrapped the coat around her shoulders. "We'd better get you inside, young lady. Your lips are turning blue. We don't want you to catch a chill."

With one man at each arm, Molly's feet barely touched the brick driveway as they hurried her toward the house. Fern met them at the kitchen door.

"My goodness, Molly, you are soaked. Mae-Mae's upstairs changing. She told me to help you out of your wet clothing and put you to bed. As for you, gentlemen, Mae-Mae said to warm yourselves by the fire; she'll be down in a few minutes to brew you some hot peppermint tea." Fern took charge of Molly and returned Tavis's water-spotted jacket to him. "You white folk don't have enough sense to know when come in out of the rain!"

Molly's teeth chattered as Fern swept her up the stairs. Without a word, Fern helped her shed the rain-drenched clothes. While Molly towel-dried her hair, Fern gathered up Molly's dress and petticoats. Molly had slipped into her warmest flannel nightgown and burrowed under several quilts on the bed by the time Fern returned with a heated bed warmer.

The girl's temperature soared and plummeted as she sneezed, sniffed, and coughed her way through the next two weeks. Mae-Mae, who seemed no worse for wear, refused to allow the girl to leave her room.

With little else to do, Molly spent much of the time reading from her book of Shakespeare's sonnets and from *Pilgrim's Progress* by John Bunyan. Nights were the loneliest. That's when she would try to read her parents' Bible. But try as she might, Molly found it difficult to concentrate on the words. Only the texts her mother had underlined stayed with her.

Her two suitors sent numerous messages. Tavis's letters were sincere and to the point, while Seamus's writings were more flowery and almost poetic at times. Molly was grateful even though their seeming interest in her was but a charade for their cause. And if the truth be known, Molly was glad that she did not have to make a real choice between the two.

During those seemingly endless nights, Molly would often sit in a rocker and stare out the window. Occasionally, she spotted shadowed forms skittering along the garden wall only to disappear into the hedges. In the morning, she realized that she knew what was happening; but how? They seemed to just disappear into the hedge.

After a few weeks, Molly's fevers lifted and her coughing subsided. Mae-Mae granted the girl permission to return to work.

"Mornings only!" Mae-Mae insisted. "You must rest—or your cough will return, or worse yet, develop into consumption!"

On her first morning back to work in the library, Molly first organized the stack of receipts and statements that had come into the office during her illness into categories by date. When she opened the ledger, she frowned. Something was wrong. In several columns, dating all the way back to her first days on the job, many of the threes had been altered into eights. This caused the credit-deficit balance to be incorrect. She was busy analyzing the problem, when Master Adams strode into the room.

"Ah, Mistress Molly, I am so glad you're feeling better. I've been looking over the books during your illness and frankly, I have several questions." He paused and pursed his lips. "Surprising to say, I've found numerous errors in your calculations. These errors add up to several hundreds of dollars."

"I can see that, sir." The girl felt heat rising in her cheeks. Even a whiff of possible duplicity distressed her. "I have several questions myself." She turned the book back two pages and showed her employer. "Look! See this eight. The ink on the left of the number is much thicker than the ink on the right. I've seen the same pattern on several pages. And the smudges and rewriting of the tabulations at the bottom of the pages are not typical of my work. I would never enter such a messy page into the final ledger." She wanted to accuse Ridgley of sabotage but bit her tongue.

Master Adams took the ledger and sat down in his chair by the fire to study the problem. "I'm glad you pointed out the obvious differences in the penmanship. I know how careful you are. I knew there had to be some logical explanation. Now I can see that whoever did this has a heavier handwriting than do you."

"I'll correct the errors, sir. I can't imagine who would do such a thing and why."

His face hardened. "The why is to steal from me and to have you blamed for it. An extra penny here, a dollar there adds up. As to who would likely do such a thing, don't worry. I'll do some digging. Sooner or later, I'll find out." He rose from his chair, walked across the room, and returned the ledger to her. "In the meantime, I would appreciate it if you would check the old receipts against the numbers in the book and make any and all necessary corrections. Then list the names of any clients who might have been cheated so I can make things right. Also look for any bogus statements that might have been issued."

Finding the guilty person became a process of elimination for Molly. Fern would have no reason to do such a thing; neither would Percy. Mae-Mae couldn't read or do simple arithmetic, let alone doctor numbers. One of the four law clerks would be the most logical person since they had easy access to the library, especially during her illness.

In her mind, she eliminated Kerr and Samuels; neither would be aggressive enough to embezzle from their employer. As for Simms, he was about as cunning as a basset hound puppy. Every road led back to Ridgley. As for Master Adams, he said nothing more about the doctored books.

Yet Molly couldn't let it go. In the middle of the night when she couldn't sleep, she would review the situation again and again. She set traps for the culprit; memorizing the position of every item on her desk before leaving the room, and checking that nothing had been disturbed when she returned. Once she found a teacup stain on the page she'd just finished and had to reenter the information. Another time she found ink smudges on a page, obliterating some of the numbers. Again she had to redo her work. She considered reporting the sabotage to Master Adams, but Molly preferred catching the culprit in action. "If I get my hands on the culprit, I'll wring his neck!"

Frustrated, Molly couldn't shake the thought that it was Ridgley. The man held nothing but scorn for her. Every opportunity he got, he belittled her in front of clients or criticized her to the other workers.

He intimated that she was not only inept but also less than honest in her bookkeeping. At every turn, Ridgley had been in great sarcastic form.

Keeping her promise to her mother, Molly opened the Bible and began to read what were to her archaic words strung together with little meaning. If the girl hadn't promised she'd read from it every night, the Book would have long since been collecting dust on the windowsill.

Molly lifted the slim, red grosgrain ribbon from the page where she'd left off the previous night and began to read Jesus' words in Matthew 5:44: "Love your enemies." She could almost hear her father's voice reading aloud the same text at the family's evening worship.

Frustrated, she slammed the Book shut and tossed it onto the nightstand. "Love my enemies? Love my enemies? How can I love the scoundrels who are making my life so miserable?" Molly snarled aloud to the empty room. The girl tried to imagine how she would wreak havoc on the culprit. *Revenge will be sweet,* she decided.

The girl threw herself facedown onto bed and pounded her fists into her pillow. Fearful that someone might hear her cries, she sank her head into her pillow to stifle the sound. Without warning, a flood of hate-filled tears spilled onto her pillow, tears she'd been stifling for months. As illogical as she knew it to be, she shouted aloud to God, "I won't cry! I won't cry! And I won't love the people like Ridgley, and the baron, and anyone else who has tried to destroy—"

A loud knock on her bedroom door caught her midsentence. The door flew open and Fern, wearing a flannel nightgown and stocking cap on her head and brandishing a brass candlestick, rushed to her side. "Mistress Molly! Mistress Molly! Did someone break into your room?" When she realized Molly was safe, Fern said, "Whatever is wrong? Are you sick? Should I call Master Adams?"

Embarrassed, Molly sniffed and lifted her face from the pillow. "No! No! I'm sorry I disturbed you. I'll be fine."

"What happened?"

"I just can't take it anymore. I absolutely hate Ridgley! He does everything to make my life miserable. And I'm sure he's the one who is sabotaging my work!"

Fern sat down on the bed beside her and rubbed her shoulder. "Oh

Molly, *hate* is a very strong word. Grandpa Percy says hate will eat you alive from the inside out." She brushed a tear from her friend's cheek. "I do understand. I've had to fight hate in my heart as well."

Molly rolled over on her back and eyed Fern. "Really?"

"Really. I haven't always live here with the Adams family. I was born on a tobacco plantation in North Carolina. The overseer was very cruel. He enjoyed beating the slaves under his control, 'just to keep them in line' as he would say."

"Were you ever beaten?"

"Once when I was six. I still wear the scars on my back to prove it."

"Why?" Molly couldn't imagine what a six-year-old could do that was deserving of such treatment.

"Only so much food was allotted to the slaves. It was carefully rationed. The male field workers ate first; female field workers ate second. The women, especially the pregnant ones, were fed third, while the children who were too young to work and the old who were too weak to work ate what was left. As a result, I was always hungry. One day while picking strawberries in the kitchen garden, I ate a handful. The cook saw me and reported me to the overseer. After my beating, I was sick in bed for a week."

"How outrageous! How did you manage to survive?"

"I'm truly blessed. When I was ten, our owner sold his plantation and his slaves to a neighbor. Our new owner immediately sold my mother to a plantation owner in Mississippi. Because Grandpa was considered too old to work the fields, the man sold him to Master Adams. When he did, Grandpa Percy begged Master Adams to buy me as well."

Molly shook her head in wonder. With all the hunger and heartache she'd witnessed in Ireland, she never knew there were people being treated so terribly in far-off America.

Fern continued, "I was told later that my mother died on the way to her new home."

"Don't you just hate that man who ruined your life? Do you ever wish for revenge?"

"Oh, no, not anymore. I've been too blessed. When we arrived at our new home, Master Adams handed Grandpa Percy and me our freedom papers. But I confess that even with my freedom purchased,

I was still angry at losing my mother. I would cry myself to sleep every night. If it weren't for Grandpa Percy and for Mae-Mae, I couldn't have made it."

Fresh tears glistened in Molly's eyes—tears, not for her own difficulties, but for Fern's.

"That's how I knew how hurt you were feeling when you arrived here. And that's why I can understand what you are feeling in your heart right now."

"But how did you deal with it? The hate, I mean?"

A wide grin swept across the young girl's face. "Grandpa Percy takes me to meetings each week where he preaches to a small congregation of freed slaves. Week after week, he reminds us that God is love. If we love God, we can't hate His children—and we're all His children. If we hate, we will live out our lives as a slave to the one we hate. The best revenge is forgiving him or her. That's the only way you can be truly free of that person."

She searched Molly's face for understanding. "Hate is a cruel overseer. I didn't want my overseer controlling my life ever again. So one day, during an altar call, I decided I would not allow another human being to enslave my soul."

Molly gazed in wonder at the young girl sitting on the edge of her bed. How mature and confident she seemed. The girl's speech was as eloquent as any Molly's father had used in his sermons. "But aren't there times when remembering makes you angry?"

"Oh yes, but you see, forgiving is for my benefit, not for the benefit of the one who hurt me. They'll never know, but I will." The girl chuckled aloud. "Sometimes I hum the melody to a song I remember my mother singing to me as I fell asleep, 'Nobody Knows the Trouble I've Seen.' "

Molly did remember hearing Fern humming the tune while making beds or folding clothes. "It's as simple as that? You just choose to forgive—and that's it?"

Again the young girl chuckled. "Not always. As Grandpa Percy says, 'God's principles may be simple, but they're not always easy.' "

Later that evening, Molly lay awake recalling Fern's words. When sleep refused to come, she lit her lamp and picked up her mother's Bible. "Where do I start?" she asked the room's four empty walls. "Where do I start?"

CHAPTER ELEVEN

MORE THAN AN ADVENTURE

WITH THE HAUTEUR OF an English butler, Ridgley opened the library door and stepped over the threshold. "Mistress Molly, Master Adams wishes you to come to his office—immediately."

Instantly, Molly wondered whether she'd made a mistake in her accounting. "Should I bring along the ledger?" she asked.

"He didn't tell me what he wants or why he's asking for you. He's just asking!" The clerk tilted his nose higher, seeming to add another inch to his thin form. The hint of a sneer on his upper lip indicated that he, too, thought she'd done something wrong.

Whenever possible, Molly avoided walking past the law clerks in the outer office. The men still resented having a woman working in the office as well as the trust Master Adams had placed in her. The girl sighed, dried the ink on her last entry, and closed the ledger. Before leaving the library she made a quick note of her desktop, memorizing where she'd left everything

"Master Adams is waiting!"

"I'm coming, Ridgley!" She noted that again irritation had crept into her voice. The last thing she wanted was to let Ridgley's attitude fire up her Irish dander.

The young man held the door for her as she gathered her skirts and glided into the hallway. Before she reached the attorney's office entrance, Ridgley pushed past her and knocked on the door.

"Mistress Molly is here, as requested," Ridgley announced and then took a step back to allow the girl and her voluminous skirts to enter the office.

Master Adams, his spectacles perched on the tip of his nose, looked up from behind his desk and gave a stiff smile. "Thank you, Ridgley. That will be all." From the tone in the man's voice, something had upset him.

Standing in front of the man's giant mahogany desk, the girl felt like an errant schoolgirl. Ridgley didn't move from the doorway.

When Adams failed to speak, she asked, "You asked to see me? Is anything wrong?"

"Of course not!" he snapped. "At least, not with you! Why should there be?"

She sighed with relief. "No reason I can think of."

"Ridgley!" Master Adams flicked his hand toward his head clerk as he might wave away a bothersome fly. "Close the door!"

"Yes, sir." Reluctantly, Ridgley obeyed.

When the door latched shut, the attorney gestured toward the wooden straight-backed chair beside her. This was the chair the law clerks referred to as the chair of torture. Whenever he wanted to get the upper hand over an opponent or scold a miscreant, Master Adams would seat the person in that chair. It was just uncomfortable enough to make anyone squirm.

"Yes, sir." Molly lowered herself onto the woven cane seating.

The attorney came around to the front of his desk and leaned against its edge. "Molly, I have a task I need you to do for me. But before I ask, I must be sure you are willing."

"How can I be willing if I don't know what you are asking of me?" Relieved that she was not in trouble for anything, she straightened and threw back her shoulders. "However, I'm sure I can handle whatever the task may be."

"Fair enough." He paused for several seconds before continuing, "As we've indicated before, Master Tavis and Doctor Sheridan operate a spur on Virginia's Underground Railroad, and your outings with the young men are diversions for moving runaways along their route to freedom."

"Yes." The girl stirred in the chair.

106

He cleared his throat and pursed his lips. "Up to this point, we've not asked you to do anything dangerous or illegal, right?"

"That's correct." Molly thought she might explode with curiosity.

"Think seriously when you hear what I'm about to ask of you. The task is both dangerous and illegal," he continued. "If caught, you could get into serious trouble."

Molly blinked in surprise. "I-I-I'm not sure."

"Hmm." A frown deepened on his forehead.

Before he could question her further, she blurted, "Yes, I am willing to do whatever you ask of me."

The man hit the palm of his hand on the desktop. "Good girl! I told Percy you were a real soldier! I need you to conduct a young girl to the next station. The poor little thing is battered and exhausted. Somehow she made her way safely to Norfolk without anyone's help. Fortunately, Percy found her hiding in the woods behind the barn."

Molly frowned. *"Ooh,* the poor thing."

"She's about the same size and age as Fern. So I'm depending on the fact that few white people notice the facial features of colored folk. They've seen you and Fern shopping together each week. Just laugh and chat the way you two do whenever you're together." Master Adams continued, "Look for a sailor sitting on the pier, repairing fishing nets. He will be wearing a blue-and-red jersey shirt and canvas overalls.

"You will ask him if he has any herring to sell. He will answer, 'No, but I have fresh striped bass.' Your answer will be, 'I'll take two.' He'll then tell you to pay the fishwife at the stand across from where he's sitting. You will talk with the woman until she thinks it's safe to slip your cargo behind the wooden stall where a man will be waiting to take the girl to a ship that is departing for Canada this afternoon. Fern will be waiting behind the stand to take the girl's place for your walk home."

"How will Fern get there?"

"That information is not your concern. Just stick to what you need to know. Will you do it?"

Molly's eyes lit up at the idea of being a part of an afternoon adventure instead of working on the end of the month invoices. "Of course, I will."

"You need to realize that if you are stopped by the law at any point, it could get dangerous."

"I understand. Thank you for trusting me." The confident smile on Molly's face didn't match the trepidation in her heart. "Where is she now?"

"She's eating a bowl of stew in the kitchen. Earlier my wife gave the young girl a bath and a clean dress to wear so she won't attract attention in the marketplace. The girl's face will be hidden with a deep brimmed sunbonnet." The attorney frowned. "I hope I'm doing the right thing involving you, Molly. Please be careful."

Fearful, she might change her mind, Molly hopped to her feet. "I guess I'd better fetch my bonnet and cloak while our runaway finishes her meal."

Molly found Ridgley loitering in the hall. "So did the boss fire you yet?"

She shook her head. "Not yet."

Her heart pounded as she rushed through the kitchen and up the stairs to her room. Molly grabbed her gray-felt bonnet and matching cloak from the wardrobe and her leather drawstring purse from the top dresser drawer and then bounded down the stairs to the kitchen.

"Hello, my name is Molly," she told the girl cowering in one corner of the room. "What's your name?"

"Anna," the girl mumbled.

"Nice to meet you, Anna. I used to have a friend named Anne in Ireland." The girl's frightened response worried Molly. If they were going to convince anyone watching that she was Fern, she'd have to relax a little. "I know you don't know me, but you and I need to pretend we're two silly girls on a shopping expedition. Can you do that?"

The girl nodded.

Molly picked up a sunbonnet from the end of the table and handed it to Anna. "Here. Put this on. It will help to hide your face from view. Can you carry the shopping basket?"

The girl nodded.

"Good! See you later, Mae-Mae. Wish us luck." Molly linked her arm in Anna's.

"You will need more than luck, my dear. My prayers will go with you both," the older woman promised.

With Anna in tow, Molly skipped through the kitchen door and onto the pathway toward town. "Isn't it a perfectly glorious day to go shopping? Brisk and cold! The truth is any day is a good day to shop, right?"

Anna ducked her chin and allowed Molly to drag her along the cobblestone street. All the while, Molly chattered on about the weather, about Mae-Mae, and about working at the Adamses'. "So what is your favorite color, Anna? Mine is green—vivid emerald green."

"Pink," the girl turned toward Molly and whispered. "I like pink."

"Oh, yes, I like pink too—especially pink tulips. So where are you from? I'm originally from Ireland. Do you know where Ireland is?"

The girl shook her head.

"It's way across the ocean. Sometimes I miss it. Don't get me wrong. I like living here in America, but I left a part of my heart in the old country." Molly continued her lively banter despite Anna's reluctance to respond. When they passed one of her and Fern's favorite shops that sold ribbons and sewing supplies, Molly waved at the hunched-over proprietor. "Hi, Granny Ninon. It's a beautiful day, isn't it?"

Hoping to lure the girls to the stall, the woman called, "I have a new supply of Christmas ribbons, straight from New York City."

"Fern and I will stop by to take a look on our way back home, I promise." Molly tugged on Anna's arm to hurry her along. The girls passed several townspeople who called out to Molly. "Sorry, Fern and I are in a hurry today," she explained. "Mae-Mae wants her groceries in time to fix dinner." She gave a cheerful laugh before whispering in Anna's ear, "It would be so much easier if I didn't have to do all the talking!"

"I'm sorry," Anna sniffed.

"I'm sorry, too, for scolding you. Don't worry; I'll talk enough for both of us."

Afternoon shoppers crowded the boardwalk by the pier. Molly and Anna weaved in and out of the milling crowds, all the while on the alert for a sailor in the blue-and-red shirt with canvas overalls. When she spotted the man hunched over a worn net spread out on the deck, Molly's heart raced. She told herself, "Slow down. Act as if he's no different from the other fishermen in port."

Molly stopped directly in front of him. He squinted up at her.

"Hello!" The girl cocked her head to one side. "Did you catch any herring this morning?"

For a moment, the sailor cast a suspicious glance at her and then up and down the wharf. When satisfied no one was listening or following them, he said, "Nope, sure didn't. But I have couple of fresh-caught, striped bass. My wife has two left at the fish stand over there."

Molly and Anna strolled over to the fish stand. When Anna disappeared behind the stand and Fern emerged, Molly fought an urge to throw her arms around her friend. The fishwife wrapped the bass in yesterday's paper and handed the package to Fern while Molly paid for the fish. "Tell your cook that for the best flavor, sauté them in olive oil." The woman blew on her hands to warm them.

"I will do that. Thank you." Molly linked her arm in Fern's. "Let's go home, shall we?"

"Yes, let's!" The girls giggled with relief and skipped down the boardwalk as if their shopping adventure were like any other of their trips to town. They paused to examine Grandma Ninon's array of colorful ribbons. "I love this one. How about you, Fern? Wouldn't it look lovely tied in a bow around the neck of my baby-blue calico?"

Grandma Ninon looked up from the ribbons and gasped a second before Molly felt a heavy hand tap her on the shoulder and heard, "Excuse me, miss."

Molly whirled about to find herself face to face with a shiny tin star pinned to a massive blue woolen jacket. She lifted her gaze to the frowning face of a beefy, six-foot, five-inch tall officer of the law. Her eyes widened. All the color drained from her cheeks. "Yes?"

"It's been reported to me that you aided and abetted a known runaway slave. Is this the girl?"

Molly shook her head. "No, sir. I am but a simple servant girl indentured to Attorney Adams, and Fern here is the Adamses' chambermaid."

The sheriff scratched his three-day growth of a beard on his neck. "I smell something fishy here. It's pretty cold out today for shopping. Just what were you two doing at the wharf?"

Molly sniffed the air. "Me too. It stinks, doesn't it." She glanced toward Fern.

Fern lifted the wrapped fish closer to the man's nose. "This must be what you're smelling, Sheriff."

The man grimaced at the aroma and turned toward Molly. "How do I know you're telling me the "truth?"

Molly shrugged her shoulders. "Unwrap it. It's a fish all right."

He grunted in irritation. "Your companion here could be the runaway the bounty hunters are looking for."

"She could be, but she's not," Molly quipped, innocently batting her eyelashes at the man. "Fern is the granddaughter of Percy Adams, both freed by the attorney."

"Young lady," the man directed his coldest of glares at Molly. "You do know it's against the law to harbor or aid a runaway slave escape?"

Molly gave him her best puppy-dog stare. "Yes, sir."

"You should know that for some time I've suspected Attorney Adams of being involved in the Underground Railroad link to the coast. But I didn't know he was employing young ladies like yourself to conduct his illegal activities." The sheriff snorted. "I don't much cotton to lawyers from up north, especially ones who break the laws of my county and my state."

Don't show that you're afraid, Molly thought to herself as she continued to look the man straight in the eye. *Smile! That will disarm him.*

The sheriff pointed a finger at her nose. "You think this is funny, young lady?"

"No, sir." Molly struggled to keep her voice from revealing the quiver of fear she felt in her stomach. "What I do think is Mae-Mae's fish is growing older the longer we stand here. We need to get it home in time for supper. Perhaps you could let us leave."

Again his eyes narrowed. "Don't get mouthy with me, lassie."

"No, sir." Molly shook her head emphatically. "I would never speak disrespectfully to an officer of the law."

Hmmph! He grunted. "I don't like it. I still think you were involved in the aiding and abetting the reported runaway, but I guess I'll have to let you go with a warning. But know that I will be watching you both. If you are involved with the theft of another man's rightfully purchased property, sooner or later, you will be caught and arrested!"

"Yes, sir." Molly nodded, her eyes wide.

"And you, too, girl." He poked his finger inches from Fern's face. "Freed slave or not, you'd better watch out—or someday someone might kidnap you, tote you out of the state, and sell you to a Southern plantation owner."

Molly took a deep breath. "May we go?"

"Yeah, git on home! But remember, I have my eye on you both."

He took a step back to allow the girls to pass on the narrow wooden walkway. "Don't forget," he called.

Molly sensed the threat in his voice. Instinct told her to get as far away from the man as quickly as possible. Common sense told her not to run. She slipped her arm in Fern's and took slow, measured steps. "Don't look back," she whispered. "And whatever you do, don't run!"

Later, gathered in the family parlor with Mae-Mae, Mistress Julia, and Percy, Master Adams insisted the girls repeat their story several times. "Words are important. They have different meanings in how they're said. So tell me again exactly what the sheriff said."

When the story had been retold to Master Adams's satisfaction, he turned to Percy. "Obviously, sending Molly and Fern on this mission was a bad idea. Sheriff Fox means what he says. Now that he suspects them, he will be watching the girls with eagle eyes." The attorney turned to the girls. "I don't want either of you leaving the property without a male escort, at least until spring. Do you understand?"

Molly nodded, this time in earnest.

* * * * *

Tavis visited the Adamses' home two more time before Christmas. On his last visit, he brought a handmade blue-velvet purse on which Enid had embroidered white daisies. "Your mom wishes you a Merry Christmas," he told her. "She made this for you."

Molly's eyes filled with tears as she ran her finger over the tiny stitches. "Thank you," she whispered.

"Here's something from me, too, for you hair." Tavis placed a small white package in her hand. "Open it."

Molly smiled and removed the wrapper. A rainbow of satin ribbons slipped out and onto the floor before she could catch them.

"Oh!" She bent to pick them up at the same moment as Tavis reached for them. A sharp crack was followed by cries of pain. Molly rose, holding the side of her head. "I didn't know you had such a hard head, Tavis Lloyd."

"You either!" he laughed.

* * * * *

Christmas passed and the new year began. All traffic on the Underground Railroad slowed to barely one delivery a month, in which Molly wasn't involved.

The icy winds of January and February whipped through the costal town of Norfolk. By mid-March Mistress Julia was in her garden once more, and the night shadows had returned, beginning with a trickle and growing into a steady stream. Observing her, Molly was eager to, once again, become involved.

CHAPTER TWELVE

SUMMERTIME ROMANCE

WITH THE ARRIVAL OF June, the gentle beauty of Virginia's flowering dogwood and redbud trees changed overnight into a verdant green canopy, ideal for romance. It was the season for afternoon picnics in the park, carriage rides along the shore, rowboat excursions on the river, and Sunday strolls in town.

And with the arrival of the milder weather, activity on the Underground Railroad increased, making Molly's outings with either Seamus or Tavis more frequent. At least once a week, a footman would deliver a note to the Adamses' offices, informing Molly of a delightful afternoon or evening planned by one of her two beaus.

The young woman would have never imagined her life could be so rich. Returning home at the conclusion of each idyllic outing, Molly would twirl in her tiny room and thank Lady Pembrooke once again for all the hours she invested in teaching Molly social graces. In her quieter moments, the girl questioned the heightened excitement she experienced with both of the men. *Should I respond to* both *men in such a manner?* she wondered. *Is it normal?* The touch of a hand on her waist, a brush of a sleeve against her arm, the thrill of a shared glance—the strength of the sensations she felt confused her. *If only Mama were here.*

Whenever the couple's destination allowed a person of color to accompany them, Fern would chaperone. Otherwise Mae-Mae chaperoned them. It became a habit on each outing, to allow Molly and her date a few private moments in which to flirt and to chat. Molly could almost fool her heart into believing the lovely dream she was living was real, that Tavis and Seamus were actually trying to win her love. But she never forgot that strangers would inevitably be watching from the shadows.

With the arrival of August, both Molly and Fern celebrated their birthdays. Molly turned nineteen on the twelfth; Fern turned sixteen. That evening Fern and Norwood Washington announced their pre-arranged engagement. Norwood Washington was a quiet young man. Behind the mask he maintained around strangers, a deeply intense thinker lurked. The quote about Cassius in Shakespeare's *Julius Caesar* described the man well. "Yond Cassius has a lean and hungry look; he thinks too much: such men are dangerous."

While Molly tried to be happy for her friend, she wondered what it must be like for Fern, planning to marry a man she'd never before met. Molly's passionate Irish nature recoiled at the idea of a marriage without love.

One evening Molly retired early. Before hopping into bed, the girl opened her bedroom window to enjoy the aroma of the rambling roses climbing on the garden wall. As she picked up her mother's Bible for her nightly reading, something outside crashed to the ground, followed by a stifled cry of pain. Molly rushed to her window in time to see two women and a man disappear through an iron gate at the back left corner of the garden. *Where have they gone? How did they get into the garden?*

So many times Molly had explored the exterior of the moss covered wall and the gray stone garden shed. Peering through the cracks in the shack's bolted wooden door, she saw shelves of empty clay pots and several garden tools. There was hardly enough room to hold three people, let alone several.

The following morning, Molly asked Fern about the shed. In response, the girl shook her head and warned, "Stay away from Mistress Julia's gardening shed. She becomes very agitated when anyone goes anywhere near it."

Molly grinned. "How can you tell she's angry? The woman never speaks."

Fern eyes grew round and fearful. "Oh, Mistress Julia doesn't need words to let you feel her displeasure, believe me! Plus she has Mae-Mae to do her talking! And you know what happens when that woman gives you a piece of her mind."

The mystery of the disappearing runaways plagued Molly. She believed that if she could get inside the shed, her curiosity would be satiated. One morning, the library grew stuffy from the summer's heat. The girl walked to the French doors and gazed at the back wall and shed. She knew it was too hot for Mistress Julia to work in the garden during the heat of the day. Appreciating the cool refreshing breezes on her face, the girl strolled to one dark corner of the garden and sat down beside a marble fountain.

As Molly dragged her fingers through the water, she let her mind dabble in what-ifs. What if Tavis were somehow in a position to court her? What if Seamus's attentions toward her were real? Which man would she choose? Of course, she realized it was only conjecture, but she found pleasure in toying with a string of what-ifs. The girl turned her face toward a patch of sunlight peeking through the tree leaves when she heard the gentle tap, tap, tap of approaching footsteps on the brick walkway. Almost silently, Mistress Julia, carrying a wicker basket draped with a red-and-white checked tablecloth, glided more than walked to the tool shed, unlocked and open the door, and stepped inside, closing the door behind her. A few minutes later, Mistress Julie emerged from the shed without the basket. Once Mistress Julie had left the garden, Molly returned to the library. As she crossed the threshold, Simms popped up from behind her desk. Startled almost as much as she, the man grinned sheepishly. "Oh, Mistress Molly, a letter arrived for you this afternoon."

She glanced toward the open ledger and the stack of receipts she'd been posting. Everything looked to be the way she'd left it. "Why are you behind my desk?" she snapped.

"Ridgley asked me to give you this letter. And when I tossed the envelope on your desk, it slid across the desktop and onto the floor. I went to pick I up." He waved the white envelope in question. "Here! See? I'm sorry."

Molly frowned. "Next time, please be more careful!"

"Yes, Mistress Molly," the young man replied as he scurried from the room.

Molly strode to the desk and removed the envelope's wax seal. She wondered why Simms had acted so nervous. Was he the culprit, sabotaging her work? Not likely. The poor young man was barely old enough to shave, let alone concoct a devious scheme against her. Eagerly, Molly opened the note.

Dearest Mistress Molly:

I have acquired tickets to a concert performed by the world-renowned Swedish vocalist Jenny Lind this evening. I would be honored if you would accompany me.

Because I will be driving my employer's closed carriage and the concert will end late in the evening, please invite Mae-Mae to chaperone us. I look forward to sharing a delightful dinner with you and Mae-Mae at the East Little Creek Inn, a restaurant of distinction and class in north Norfolk. Then rounding out our evening, we will attend the performance. I will arrive for you tonight at 6 P.M.

Your devoted servant,

Tavis Lloyd

"A concert by the famous Jenny Lind? How utterly marvelous!" Molly clasped the letter to her chest for a moment. She'd read in the newspaper all about the famous soloist's sold-out concerts from New York City to Baltimore and Washington, D.C. The girl leaped from the desk and bounded out of the library into the garden where Mistress Julia was now removing the dead roses from her ramblers. "Good afternoon, Mistress Julia."

Mistress Julia started in surprise.

"Isn't it an incredibly beautiful day?" Molly twirled in circles like a schoolgirl, her skirts billowing in the breeze. The girl's feet barely touched the brick walkway as she skipped to the kitchen door where she found Mae-Mae dozing in her rocker.

"Mae-Mae! Wake up! We're going to a Jenny Lind concert tonight!"

The woman blinked in surprise.

"Put on your fanciest gown. Tavis will be here at six." She shot a quick glance toward the kitchen clock on the fireplace mantel. "Oh, no! That's less than three hours from now. I've so much to do! If you see Fern, tell her I need her to help me choose what to wear."

Molly darted up the kitchen stairs to her room. Finally, she had a reason to wear her most elegant ball gown, the impractical one of emerald silk with the ten-inch-long lace on the sleeves and a rounded neckline that revealed her ivory shoulders.

Lady Pembrooke had insisted on buying the garment even though Molly had no grand occasion at which to wear it. "Someday, child, you will wear this dress in front of royalty," the woman had promised. Jenny Lind wasn't exactly of royal birth, but the Swedish Nightingale, as the newspapers called her, was probably the closest to royalty Molly would ever meet in America.

The girl burst into her room and flung open the doors to her wardrobe. Behind her, Fern appeared with a broom and dustpan in hand. "What has happened?"

When told about the planned evening, Fern squealed with delight.

"If only you and Norwood could go with us. You could borrow my yellow damask gown with the embroidered bodice," Molly offered. "My yellow-and-orange feather hairpiece would look incredible in your hair."

Fern laughed as she pulled the silk garment out of the wardrobe and gave it a smart shake. "Thank you for the generous thought, dear friend, but you and I both know a man and a woman of color will never be welcomed in white society."

"Someday, you will; you'll see."

Fern chuckled as she held the dress up for inspection. "Looks like it needs a bit of ironing."

"Oh, do be careful. That fabric was imported from the Orient and is extremely delicate. But, of course, you know that." Molly paused. "I think tonight is the perfect occasion to wear Lady Pembrooke's beautiful brooch as well, don't you think?"

"Brooch?" Fern wrinkled her brow. "What brooch?"

"Oh, wait until you see it. Lady Pembrooke gave it to me before we left Ireland. I think I'll wear it around my neck on a black velvet ribbon." Molly threw open the lid of her trunk. "I can't believe I've never shown you the brooch. But then most of the time, I forget I even have it." She reached the bottom of the trunk, slipped her hand into the narrow slit in the lining and held up the brooch for Fern's inspection. The diamonds and the silver filigree sparkled in the afternoon sunlight. "Or would it be more dramatic if I wore it on the bodice of my white silk one dress—you know the one with the lace overskirt?"

"*Ooh!*" Fern admired the exquisite detail in the grand lady's profile and cascade of curls carved in the ivory cameo. "I've never seen anything so beautiful. Your Lady Pembrooke must have really loved you."

Molly thought for a moment. "Yes! I guess she did. For a while after my father's death—I told you how he died saving her—I hated her for living when he had to die, even with all the nice things she insisted on doing for me. Maybe she was trying to make it up to me for Dad's sacrifice."

"Molly! And maybe she genuinely loved you. Isn't that possible? She may have thought of you as the daughter she never had." Fern clicked her tongue in irritation. "People don't always have to have an ulterior motive for being nice, you know."

Molly cast her a sheepish grin. "Yes, I guess you're right. Though Ridgley, if he does anything nice, I immediately suspect he has something up his sleeve."

Fern lifted one eyebrow and shot her a warning look. "Be careful. When people always think evil of others, they may become evil themselves."

The afternoon disappeared in a flurry of ruffles, crinolines, and curling irons heated on Mae-Mae's iron stove. As a finishing touch, Fern pinned the brooch on the neckline of Molly's gown. "You are going to outshine the Swedish Nightingale tonight. Master Tavis won't be able to take his eyes off of you."

One glance in the mirror and Molly knew Lady Pembrooke would approve. The green and gold-feathered hairpiece perfectly accented the cascade of ebony curls tumbling down the back of her neck. As Molly wrapped her silver lace shawl around her shoulders, a pebble hit the dormer window.

Fern placed a hurried kiss on Molly's cheek. "Have fun tonight, dear friend." And then she fled from the room. Intent on her evening, Molly tucked a lace-edged linen handkerchief into the palm of her glove, gathered up her Spanish lace fan, and exited her room. The girl paused at the top of the second-story floor staircase landing. Below she could hear Tavis and Master Adams speaking to each other in anxious whispers.

If only this evening could be unencumbered by runaways and politics, she mused. And then quickly she stifled her thoughts of romance by picturing real, live human beings quaking in the darkness, fearful that at any moment they would be recaptured and returned to face an unbelievable punishment for running away from their owners.

Her voluminous silk skirt swished as she took the first steps down the stairs. As she came into view, the men stopped talking. The appreciative glint in Tavis's eyes told her that the efforts of her afternoon had not been wasted. Master Adams appeared equally transfixed.

"I'll tell Mae-Mae that you're ready to leave," Master Adams finally said, but neither Tavis nor Molly saw nor heard him leave.

Without taking his gaze from her face, Tavis stepped forward. He took her gloved hand and placed a gentle kiss on it. As he straightened, he didn't release her hand.

"Somehow calling you 'little pigeon' the way I did when you were a child no longer seems appropriate. You've become an exquisite young woman right before my eyes. How did I miss seeing it happen?" Tavis whispered.

Molly executed a graceful curtsy. As she straightened, she cast him a coy smile similar to the one she'd tested on him several years back in Ireland. This time the smile had the desired effect.

"Why, thank you, kind sir. And you look quite dashing as well in your cutaway suit."

Uncomfortable, Tavis shifted from one foot to the other and tugged at his striped silk cravat with his free hand. "To be honest, I feel sort of silly. Master Taylor insisted that my buckskins would not be appropriate for the occasion."

She giggled at his discomfort, but silently hoped he would never release her hand. She tapped the satin lapel of his coat with the end of her fan. "Well, I am certainly impressed. You look like one of the London 'dandies' Lady Pembrooke described."

"I admit that, at first, I fought the idea." He rolled his tongue around in his left cheek and grinned. "But after seeing you, I'm glad I relented."

The arrival of Master Adams and Mae-Mae, dressed in the black crepe gown she kept for funerals, weddings, and other important occasions, broke the spell. Tavis suddenly released Molly's hand as if he'd suddenly touched a hot burner on the stove. The look in Master Adams's face told Molly that he'd seen the gesture, and it didn't look approving.

Tavis quickly recovered. He kissed Mae-Mae's gloved hand, turned toward Master Adams, and nodded. "We'd better be going. Our dinner reservations are for seven o'clock. Fortunately, it's but a short stroll from the inn to the concert hall and tonight, the air is balmy."

At dinner the couple sat side by side while Mae-Mae sat across from them. When familiar emotions coursed through her at the touch of his hand on hers, Molly's cheeks flamed. His appreciative glance her way sent chills down her spine. When the waitress placed a platter of baked shad, buttered turnips, greens, and corn bread on the table, Molly doubted she'd be able to eat any of her dinner. She could barely concentrate on what Tavis and Mae-Mae were saying. Experiencing these strange emotions when in the company of two different men frightened her.

"Personally, I prepare my shad fried in butter with a dash of vinegar," Mae-Mae admonished. "The fish has a much richer flavor."

"Have you tried the corn bread?" Tavis asked.

The woman bit into the yellow bread. "Yes indeedy, it's quite good, though I sometimes add a dollop of molasses to mine. *Mmm,* it melts in your mouth."

While the woman closed her eyes enjoying the moment, Tavis glanced toward Molly. Their eyes met. He gave her a slight grin and a wink. The girl's heart skipped a beat. She could hardly catch her breath.

"Molly, aren't you going to eat your meal?" Mae-Mae asked.

"It's delicious, especially the corn bread, but I'm afraid I'm not too hungry tonight."

"You should eat something," Tavis insisted, buttering a square of the corn bread and touching it to her lips.

Trapped by his beguiling gaze, she opened her mouth and took a small bite, and then nervously licked the crumbs from her lips.

"You missed a crumb." He touched his finger to one corner of her lips. They both froze for an instant. This time Molly knew by the startled look on his face that he'd experienced a similar jolt of emotion.

Attempting to recover, he asked Mae-Mae, "Did you save room for dessert? Master Taylor said we must try the inn's specialty, strawberries with whipping cream."

Mae-Mae's eyes lit up at the mention of the culinary delight. After finishing her dessert, the woman admitted she would have licked her bowl clean if she'd been home in her own kitchen. Even Molly managed to eat most of the uncommonly delicious confection.

Tavis laid down his spoon, removed his watch fob from his vest pocket, and groaned. "I am too full! I ate too much! The time is going by quickly. We'd better be heading toward the concert hall."

Tavis held her chair as Molly rose to her feet and then helped Mae-Mae with her chair. "It's such a lovely evening I arranged with the innkeeper to leave Master Adams' carriage here so we could walk to the concert hall."

"What a lovely idea." The idea of walking arm in arm with Tavis delighted Molly. Along the way, the girl didn't fail to notice the appreciative glances as the three of them strolled along the gaslit avenue. To the girl, the moment was like a scene straight out of one of Lady Pembrooke's French novels. She gazed up at the stars as Tavis regaled them with interesting facts about Jenny Lind.

"Miss Jenny Lind began singing opera as a child in Sweden. To please a wider audience, she added folk songs to her repertoire. In a very short time, she became an instant hit in Europe. They say the author Hans Christian Andersen fell madly in love with her and begged her to become his wife, but she refused."

Molly possessively pressed against Tavis's arm. "What a lovely idea you had to take us to hear her sing."

"To be honest, it wasn't my idea. I'd never heard of the woman until Master Taylor suggested it. He'd purchased the tickets and discovered he wouldn't be able to use them. So here we are."

He returned to the subject of Jenny Lind. "We're very fortunate to have her tour America. When P. T. Barnum heard her sing in Europe, he begged her to come to America. She agreed. The man was trying to elevate his reputation from the Wild West shows he'd been sponsoring in order to appeal to a higher class of attendees. It is reported that Miss Lind donates a portion of every concert to the poor."

Molly idly glanced over her shoulder in time to see a man dart into the shadows. She frowned. She knew she'd seen the man before on several of their summer outings. The girl considered telling Tavis, but in the excitement of joining the line of concertgoers entering the building, it slipped her mind.

Once inside, Tavis handed the tickets to an usher. Instead of following the crowd through the main doors into the concert hall, the usher handed each of the three a program, led them up a grand staircase and down a corridor, where he opened a gilded door and bade them enter. The darkened enclosure overlooked the main auditorium and the rows of seats filling with concertgoers. Along the mahogany walls of the theater, gaslights twinkled in gilded sconces. Deep crimson velvet draperies covered the stage. Matching velvet swags edged with thick gold fringe swooshed dramatically across the top of the draperies. In the front of the theater, musicians warming up their instruments filled the air with discordant sounds, which added to the buzz of the excited crowd.

"I hope they can play their instruments better than that!" Mae-Mae grunted. *Hmmph!* "And why are we a-way up here? Aren't we good enough to sit with all of those folk down there?"

"These are what they call box seats," Tavis explained. "Master Taylor says box seats are the best seats in the place."

"Well, goodness me!" Mae-Mae lowered herself into the upholstered theater seat nearest the stage. "I would have thought the exact opposite was true!"

"Oh, no," Tavis hastened to explain. "Master Taylor buys only the best, I assure you." He guided Molly to a front seat, and then sat down beside her. The back row of seats remained empty.

Molly's eyes twinkled as she gazed about the auditorium. When an elegantly clad couple entered the box beside them, Molly smiled and gave them a nervous wave. Both frowned and glanced away.

The house seats quickly filled, as did the other five boxes overlooking the theater. Molly's excitement mounted as the gaslights dimmed; the orchestra played a fanfare worthy of English royalty; and the curtains opened to reveal a woman in a baby-blue satin gown, her blond hair parted in the middle, braided, and wrapped around each side of her head. Before the singer opened her mouth, the crowd broke into thunderous applause.

Jenny Lind gave an appreciative bow. The orchestra played an introduction and she opened her mouth. Sweet, lilting notes filled the auditorium.

All in the merry month of May,
When green buds were swellin',
Young Jeremy Grove on his deathbed lay,
For love of Barbara Allen.

Tears sprang into Molly's eyes. Leaning closer to Tavis, she whispered, "My mama used to sing me to sleep with this song."

He smiled, took her gloved hand, and kissed her fingertips; then he placed their joined hands on the armrest of her chair. Ballad after ballad, Molly recognized tunes sung to her by her mother or played by Lady Pembrooke on her fortepiano.

When the Swedish Nightingale sang a peppy rendition of "The Fox" and Molly tapped her toes to the music, Tavis squeezed her hand and grinned at her. She smiled back. The girl had never heard a voice so beautiful.

Miss Lind concluded the concert with "Lavender's Blue" and then exited the stage. The crowd rose in one thunderous ovation. No one wanted the evening to end. They continued applauding until the singer returned for a second and a third bow. And then, to satisfy the audience, Miss Lind returned one last time to sing an encore, "Amazing Grace." The audience remained hushed after her last notes faded into the night. And then they leaped to their feet, clapped, screamed, and whistled. After taking three more bows, the woman exited the stage for the final time.

CHAPTER THIRTEEN

TERROR BY NIGHT

OLLY'S EYES SPARKLED WITH stardust as she clutched her program and scanned the auditorium. She vowed never to forget the magical evening. When Tavis placed an arm about her waist and drew her closer to his side, the girl felt a delightful mixture of pleasure and surprise until he leaned his lips close to her ear. "It seems we have company," he whispered.

"What? Where?"

"*Ssh, ssh, ssh!* Smile. Act normal." He gestured toward the theater box directly across from theirs. "We are being watched."

She pasted the requested smile on her face and whispered, "You're right. That is the same guy who was following us earlier this evening."

"You didn't say anything."

"I've gotten so accustomed to seeing him lurking behind every bush and shrub during our outings that I didn't want his presence to ruin our evening."

Tavis wrapped her shawl around her shoulders as he glanced both directions. "If we hurry, we can mingle with the crowd and possibly lose him." He took Molly's elbow and pushed through the departing crowd. Poor Mae-Mae struggled to keep up with them.

Outside the theater, the sheriff and a six-man posse appeared to be waiting for someone. Tavis placed his arm around her shoulders and nuzzled her neck. By this time, Mae-Mae had caught up with the couple. "Tell me Mae-Mae, how did you enjoy Miss Lind's concert?"

Because the older woman always had a better recipe for food prepared by any other cook, Molly expected her to reply in like manner about the music. Instead, Mae-Mae's eyes glistened; her face glowed. In a emotion-choked voice, she admitted, "I have never heard anyone sing so beautifully, even in church."

Molly smiled to herself. The girl had attended Mae-Mae's church several times where she heard the church's lead soprano warble painfully off-key and loudly enough to frighten away any nesting songbirds out of their trees.

"What a beautiful evening! Thank you, ladies, for making it truly memorable." Tavis placed Molly's hand in the crook of his arm, and Mae-Mae's in the other and set a fast pace toward the inn. Weaving in and out of the milling crowd of concertgoers, they quickly arrived at the inn.

The groom at the inn led the horses and carriage out of the barn. When Tavis dropped a few coins in the boy's hand, he brightened and tipped his hat. "Thank you, sir. Have a pleasant ride home."

The groom helped the women into the carriage. Tavis climbed on board next to Molly. "I think we'd better head back to the Adamses' place as quickly as possible. I am sensing something's wrong."

As Tavis flicked the horses' reins, the carriage leaped forward. Molly grabbed the edge of the seat with both hands as they bounced over the cobblestones.

No one spoke during the ride home, including Mae-Mae. Molly's anxiety grew when she spotted a police wagon along with several horses tethered to the hitching post in front of Adamses' offices.

"I don't like it!" Tavis turned the carriage around and drove back in the direction from which they came. They'd barely ridden a couple of carriage lengths when a man on horseback passed them. The man's hat partially hid his face, but Molly recognized him as the one who'd been stalking them all evening. Tavis recognized him as well. He glanced past Molly to speak to their chaperone. "I think it's a perfect night for a ride in the moonlight, don't you Mae-Mae?"

"Absolutely!" The older woman gritted her teeth and set her jaw.

Once he was sure the rider hadn't followed them, Tavis slowed the animals to a comfortable pace. The tiny oil lanterns mounted on each side of the carriage illuminated the roadway. The *clip-clop* of the horses' hooves and the rolling of the carriage wheels filled the air. Under normal circumstance, it was a perfect night for romance.

After several minutes, Tavis guided the horses along a deserted, rutted road used by farmers to take their produce to market. At the crest of a small ridge, Tavis halted the horses and climbed down from the carriage. Using his top hat, Tavis shaded the left lamp from view, then lifted the hat and hid the flame three more times.

"What are you—" Mae-Mae started to ask.

Ssh, ssh, ssh, he whispered. "Watch the horizon." Waiting ten seconds, Tavis repeated the exercise. Following the third try, Molly spotted a pinpoint of light answering Tavis's message—one, two, three.

"There!" she whispered, her voice carrying much farther than she'd intended it to. "Look to your right."

A second series of lights flashed in the night, and then a third.

"Good!" Tavis hopped back into the driver's seat. "That's Percy telling us it's safe to return. Let me know immediately if you see any more lights." The horses moved forward slowly. They'd gone around the first curve when a man holding a lantern stepped out of the shadows. Molly inhaled sharply. Tavis's muscles tensed as if he were poised to whip the horses into a run.

The man, his face hidden in the shadows, called, "Who goes there?"

"Percy? Where's Percy?" Tavis hissed. "Who are you? What have you done with Percy?"

"Seamus! Seamus Sheridan." The man lifted the lantern to reveal his face.

Relieved to hear a familiar voice, Molly felt as weak as a rag doll.

"What's happening? What are you doing here?" Tavis halted the team. "You should be halfway to Richmond by now."

"There's been a shooting. The county sheriff, his posse, and half a dozen bounty hunters were here at the Adamses' tonight."

Upon hearing there'd been a shooting, Mae-Mae threatened to leap from the carriage.

"Stay put! Who's been shot?" Tavis asked.

"I don't know. One of Master Adams's law clerks met me as I was coming into town. He sent me to warn you against returning to the house."

Tavis frowned. "After the concert, there was a commotion in front of the opera house. That's why we came home a different route. Tell me, did our three passengers make it to the next safe house?"

"Sort of, I think."

"What do you mean, 'sort of'?" Tavis demanded. "That little mother and her nursing baby were exhausted when I brought them here earlier this afternoon. They'd come all the way from South Carolina!"

"I know. I know. I don't like the way the authorities were on top of this one—much too fast."

Tavis heaved a giant sigh. "I think we have leak in our organization. Perhaps our entire spur has been compromised. My suspicions point to one of Master Adams's law clerks.

"Which one do you suspect?" Seamus drilled the toe of his boot into the dirt."

"I don't know. And we won't know until you or I can assess the damage."

"You're right. In the meantime, take the ladies through the rear door of the carriage house. I'll take them to Miss Julia. If, for some reason, you need to make a quick escape, my team is hitched to my wagon a half mile down the road. In the meantime, I'm going to the Adamses' house to find out what's happening."

For Molly, all lingering thoughts of the delightful dinner they'd shared, the splendid concert, and the romantic ride in the moonlight faded.

The horses seemed to understand the need for stealth as Tavis urged them on the alternate route to the back of the stables. Without a word, he helped the women from the carriage. He'd already begun removing the horses' harnesses when Mistress Julia silently stepped out of the shadows behind Molly. Startled, the girl jumped. Mae-Mae, her eyes wide with fright, whirled about as if to hit her employer.

Ssh, ssh, ssh. Mistress Julia placed her finger to her lips.

Taking Mae-Mae by the hand, Mistress Julia gestured for Molly to follow. The three women slipped silently around the edge of the carriage house and darted into a patch of dogwood trees along the back of the property. In the open area between the house and the barn, a group of rough-looking men sat in a circle on the ground, smoking pipes and laughing.

Mistress Julia led Molly and Mae-Mae past two redbud trees at the edge of the well house. The three of them inched along the outside of the moss-covered garden wall to the locked wooden gate. The woman withdrew a large iron key from her apron pocket. She then inserted it into the lock on the gate. Without a squeak, the gate swung open on heavy leather hinges.

Molly and Mae-Mae followed Mistress Julia into the garden and along the wall to the tool shed. Once there, she inserted a second key into another lock. Despite the door's rickety look, it opened silently. As she entered, Molly eyed the tiny shed and wondered how three grown women, two wearing multiple petticoats under their voluminous skirts, would fit inside the tiny shed. Musty odors of chicken fertilizer and moist soil accosted her nose. To keep from coughing and gagging, she held her handkerchief firmly over her face.

Mistress Julia backed the two women to one side of the shed; bent down and removed a large burlap bag from the stone floor, revealing a trap door. Lifting the wooden cover, she gestured for Molly and Mae-Mae to descend into the darkness.

Taking a deep breath, Molly led the way. Halfway down the ladder, two strong hands grasped her about waist and lowered her to the earthen floor of a small darkened cellar.

A small oil lantern was mounted on one of the walls. The light shone on the face of a woman holding a bundle that Molly suspected contained a baby. When the bundle whimpered, his mother nestled him against her shoulder. Moving out of the way so Mae-Mae could climb down the ladder, Molly made her way to a pile of folded blankets on the far side of the room and sat down.

The man who'd helped Molly down the steps of the ladder then patiently guided Mae-Mae from rung to rung until the woman stood on the hard-pressed earthen floor. It was obvious to Molly that Mae-Mae, who knew everything about everybody in the household, didn't know about Mistress Julia's clandestine activities.

The trap door dropped into place. Silence descended on the room, except for an occasional whimper from the infant. For the first time, the customarily undaunted Mae-Mae appeared overwhelmed. Finally, the disappearing shadows Molly had seen made sense. That silent Mistress Julia would be brave enough to play such an active part in helping runaways astounded the girl. Molly leaned her head back against the wall and closed her eyes. Her head throbbed with pain and confusion. *Isn't anyone at the Adamses' place who he pretends to be?* she wondered. *And what's happening with Percy and Fern? Are they hiding somewhere as well?*

Time passed slowly. Before long, the events of the evening caught up with Mae-Mae. Only the cook's gently snoring could be heard. The baby had fallen asleep as well. Occasionally, Molly heard whispered exchanges between the runaways, but she couldn't make out what they were saying.

After what seemed like an eternity to Molly, the trap door opened, and she heard Seamus call softly, "Molly! Mae-Mae! It's safe to come out now."

Molly climbed out of the cellar and took a deep breath of the fresh, clean morning air. It felt so good to be free once more. She had dozens of questions to ask Seamus. But before she could begin, Mistress Julia appeared and hurried the runaways out of the cellar and through the garden gate. Mae-Mae leaned on Seamus as they made their way to the kitchen.

As to Molly's questions, Mae-Mae beat her to it. "What is going on? We were told that someone got shot last night. Who shot who? And is Master Adams all right?"

In the cool, practiced voice of a calm country doctor, he explained, "It's true. Master Adams was injured in the skirmish last night, but he's resting comfortably this morning. Mae-Mae, he asked me to tell you not to worry about fixing breakfast. Just go to your room and take a nap. Mistress Julie prepared a batch of oatmeal for everyone."

Seamus took Molly's hands in his and brushed away a smudge of dirt on her nose. "Listen carefully, Molly. Master Adams wants you to go to your room and pack your belongings as quickly as possible. You must be ready to leave whenever Tavis returns from delivering the runaways to their next station."

"What?" Terror washed over the girl. "Where am I going?"

Seamus planted a kiss on the back of each of her hands. "When you finish packing, come to the parlor, and Master Adams will explain."

She started to resist. He shook his head. "Molly, you need to go now! I'm sure you're hungry by now. Mistress Julia packed a basket of food to take with you." The sharp edge in his voice spurred the girl to action.

Molly dashed up the three flights of stairs and threw open the door of her room. At the threshold, she froze. Her belongings covered every surface in the room: dresser drawers, the gowns in the wardrobe, even her personal undergarments lay strewn across the floor. Her trunk had been turned upside down; its contents spread out on the carpet. Her mattress had been turned; the sheets and bedding heaped in the middle of the floor.

"What happened here?" Tears burst from her eyes. "Where's Fern?" Molly's voice echoed down the empty hallway, but no one responded. Now totally on her own, the girl leaped into action. After righting her trunk, she checked the slit in the trunk lining. Her treasured copy of Shakespeare's sonnets was gone. Her hand flew to the cameo brooch attached to the neck of her dress. If she hadn't been wearing the brooch, she knew it, too, would have been taken. Her mother's Bible had been tossed onto the bare mattress. Grateful to find it intact, she clutched the Book to her chest. And then, like a little whirlwind, Molly whipped into action. She shed the fancy gown she'd worn to the concert and donned a lightweight cotton dress her mother had made for her. After tying a sash about her waist, Molly stuffed dresses, petticoats, pantaloons, and shoes into the trunk at record speed, leaving out only a gray woolen shawl, her matching bonnet, and her purse. Before closing the lid of the trunk, she placed the Bible on top of her clothing.

Before leaving the room, she tossed the bedding onto the mattress and closed the empty drawers in the bureau. A moment of sadness overwhelmed her as she gazed about the room that had been her home, her fortress against loneliness for more than a year. Where was she going? Would she return? Molly didn't know.

Before closing the bedroom door for the last time, Molly remembered that her mother's letters were still in the drawer of the nightstand. She found the treasured letters untouched and stuffed them into her purse.

In the parlor, she found Master Adams on the sofa, his right leg bandaged and elevated. Mistress Julia sat calmly on a horsehair footstool beside him.

"Come in. Come in," he called. His voice lacked its usual jovial tone. "Are you packed and ready to travel?" he asked.

"Yes, I am, but why? Where am I going? Please help me understand what is happening."

"I'm so sorry." Master Adams shook his head sadly. "After you left for the concert last night, things got lively around here. Last evening a scout for a gang of bounty hunters from Mississippi spotted Seamus as he was loading the three runaways—the ones you met in Julia's cubbyhole. When he hurried back to tell his employers, it gave Julia time to hide them." He patted his wife's hand.

"Without warning, six bounty hunters burst into the parlor. Two of the men stayed behind with Ridgley and me while the other four searched the house for the runaways. Percy came in from the garden and tried to stop them. One of the bounty hunters threatened to shoot him.

"When I tried to defend Percy, the second bounty hunter hit my kneecap with the fireplace poker. Plucky little Fern came up behind him and smashed him over the head with my favorite Chinese porcelain planter. She knocked him out cold, she did.

"In all the confusion, the man with the gun began shooting wildly about the room. Fortunately, his aim was as poor as his judgment. The thug put bullet holes in the mahogany paneling." Master Adams chuckled. "We had a genuine Irish donnybrook going on around here!"

Molly gently touched Master Adams's forearm. "Are you all right? How about Percy? Is he all right?"

"The bounty hunters threatened to take Percy with them to Mississippi. I tried to tell them he is a freed slave, but they were in no mood to listen to reason. If it weren't for the timely arrival of the sheriff, Percy would be on his way south. Wisely, they skedaddled. But before they left, the wounded man's brother vowed to come back for Fern. He said he'd chase her to her death, if necessary. Fortunately, she hid in the barn until they left."

"Poor Fern! She must be terrified. Where is she now?"

"Upstairs packing her things."

"What about Percy?"

"He's packing as well. The sheriff warned me that the bounty hunters would probably return and carry out their threats." Master Adams winced from the pain in his knee. "Fortunately for me, Seamus arrived immediately after the sheriff left. He did a good job of wrapping my knee, don't you think? Maybe the man's not a quack after all."

Molly bit her lower lip. "But I don't understand why you are sending me away too. Will I be coming back?"

He shook his head. "Because both the sheriff and the bounty hunters are looking for you, too, I can't take the chance. They know you're a part of the organization. They would as likely snatch you off the street as look at you. I can no longer risk the safety of the people I love. This entire spur of the Underground Railroad is closed down for a time."

"But I have eight months left on my contract," she reminded him. "Are you selling my contract to someone else?"

"Oh no, I wouldn't do that to you, Molly. I am canceling it. Julia and I talked about it, and we asked Seamus to get you, Fern, and Percy out of the commonwealth and away from the threat. His medicine wagon will be a perfect cover. The floor of the wagon has a false bottom where you can hide if anyone comes sniffing around. To passersby Seamus will look like a traveling quack, selling his magic potions to unsuspecting settlers."

"And he's agreed to do this?" Molly eyed her employer with grave concern. "What about Tavis? Is he coming too?"

The attorney shrugged. "I do not carry his papers. He still has eight months to serve Taylor, as does your mother."

Suddenly, parting took on a deeper meaning. Tavis had always been there for her, he was her confidant when her father had died, her solace when they had left Ireland, and her . . . Molly paused for a moment, uncertain of the role he now played in her life. Their outings together had created much stronger bonds than she'd ever imagined possible. Not knowing how to explain her confusion, she blurted, "But, Master Adams, I don't want to leave you and Mistress Julia. This has become home to me. Isn't there another way?"

"I'm afraid not. Letting you, Percy, and Fern go, knowing I'll probably never see any of you again, pains me greatly. Can you ever forgive me?" He removed a sealed envelope from his pocket. "If you reach Independence, Missouri, this is the letter of introduction to a classmate of mine from law school who will help you get started.

Sam's a good man. He sacrificed his home and a promising political career in upstate New York for the cause."

"Thank you. You've been an inspiration to me." Molly glanced toward his wife. "And you, too, Mistress Julia. You have helped so many people in your own quiet way."

The woman smiled sadly and placed a small leather pouch in Molly's hand. The girl looked down at the pouch. By the pouch's weight she knew it contained coins.

"Julia insisted we give you seed money. We can't have you depending on other people's charity. We are doing the same for Percy and for Fern." He paused and wiped his eyes. "The journey is rough and long. But you're strong; you'll make it."

Tears slid down Molly's face. She recalled the fear and the anger she'd felt the day Master Adams brought her to his home. Yet she adjusted and had come to think of it as her home. The words her mother whispered as they parted popped into Molly's mind. " 'Have I not seen the righteous forsaken, nor his seed begging for bread.' I am trusting you to our Father's care."

Taking Mistress Julia's hands in hers, Molly whispered, "Thank you so much. I will never forget you."

The woman smiled and in a soft voice said, "I will miss you too. Here." She handed Molly a small piece of monogrammed notepaper with a penned message. "This is my prayer for you."

> May you always have a sunbeam to warm you;
> a moonbeam to charm you;
> and a sheltering angel,
> so nothing can harm you.
> —An Irish prayer

CHAPTER FOURTEEN

INTO THE UNKNOWN

O N THE FOURTH DAY of her journey, Molly stared silently at the passing scenery. Words seemed inadequate. She'd been up-rooted again. *Will I ever have a home to call my own,* she won-dered. As the brightly painted medicine wagon bounced over the rut-ted road to Richmond, her childhood dream of living the rest of her life in a lovely Irish cottage seemed almost laughable.

"Molly!" Seamus shook the girl by the arm. "Wake up! You're going to fall off the wagon seat if you're not careful."

"*Hmm?* Oh, I guess I dozed off for a minute or two. Is it safe yet for Fern to be outside the wagon? I'd be glad to spell her or Percy for a while." A body quickly tired of riding on the wooden sleeping cot in-side the wagon. The first day out of Norfolk had been more difficult, having to hide beneath the wagon's floorboards whenever they en-countered other travelers.

"I don't know. I kind of like having you all to myself." The young doctor cocked his head to one side and shot her a roguish grin.

"You are indeed an Irishman with a silver tongue, Seamus Sheri-dan!" She teased in her best Irish brogue.

The late August sun beat down mercilessly on her bonnet and shoul-ders. Sweat streaked down her face and her armpits. Her nose and cheeks glowed a sunburned red. Occasionally, a breeze across her face eased the discomfort, but not for long. Maintaining a sweet temper after three days on the trail was as trying as the nagging backache and persistent headache she had since leaving Norfolk. "I think I'll ask."

Before he could object, she opened the small escape door in the wagon's interior, swung her legs over the back of the seat and dropped into the darkened box. With no air stirring, the space inside the wagon felt as hot as Mae-Mae's oven on bread baking day. As the grateful Fern climbed out onto the wagon seat, Molly asked herself why she'd decided to be so generous.

Percy sat with his feet dangling out the back door of the wagon. Molly could hear him humming a familiar tune that seemed mightily appropriate at the moment: "Nobody Knows the Trouble I've Seen."

Hoping to catch a short nap, Molly curled up on the wooden cot. "It won't be long, Mama," she muttered as she drifted into a troublous sleep. Saying goodbye to Mae-Mae and Master and Mistress Adams had hurt, but knowing that she would soon be reunited with her mother made it less painful.

Though the girl would never admit to it, her unspoken wish was that Master Taylor would be as generous as Master Adams had been with her, that the plantation owner would release her mother and Tavis from their indentured contract, and they all would travel happily together into the great American West.

Mentally, she concocted this rosy ending to her fantasy, but Molly knew all too well that life seldom had storybook endings, despite her mother's claim that " 'we know that all things work together for good to them that love God, to them who are the called according to his purpose.' "

How can she believe that? How much good has Mama experienced since Dad's death? Molly asked herself. *Certainly, Mama loves God. She's a good woman and a faithful believer. Maybe she hasn't been called according to God's purpose. If that's true, God's not fair!* Her hip grew sore from lying on the hard surface. She rolled over and curled up on her other side, but not before wiping the sweat from her brow onto her sleeve. *When I see her, I'm gonna ask her to explain that one!*

Molly had barely closed her eyes when the wagon rolled to a stop and she heard a familiar voice call her name. "Molly! Molly!" Enid shouted as she ran toward the wagon. "Where are you, Molly?"

The girl hopped down from the back of the wagon and into her mother's waiting arms. Enid used her apron to wipe the sweat from

Molly's face. "Oh poppet, my little poppet, I've missed you so much. When I heard you were coming, I just had to praise God. He's answered my prayer."

Tears quickly replaced the perspiration on both of their faces. "Oh, Mother, I missed you so much."

"And I missed you too. Isn't this an unexpected blessing? But wait, you must be thirsty. Come, I have apple cider from the cold cellar for everyone. Just go make yourselves comfortable on the veranda. I'll be back with cold drinks in no time."

Percy, Seamus, and Fern could wait on the veranda for her mother to return but not Molly. The girl matched her mother step for step to the cold cellar and back around the side of the house to the veranda. A light breeze stirred the leaves of three giant hickory trees that shaded the veranda. They found Seamus stretched out on a chaise longue. Percy and Fern sat on the steps below.

An elegant blond woman, wearing a dress of white eyelet with a light-blue satin sash appeared at the screen door of the plantation house. The woman's hoopskirt swooshed through the door way as she glided out onto the veranda. Seamus leaped to his feet.

"My, my, what do we have here, Enid? No one told me we were throwing a party," the woman simpered.

"Mistress Blanche, meet Doctor Sheridan. He made the crossing on the same ship as I. And this is my darling daughter, Molly." The note of pride in her mother's voice made the girl wish she'd dressed more appropriately for the occasion. Enid glanced toward Percy and Fern. "Molly, you'll have to introduce your two friends. I don't know their names."

"Of course, Mama. This is Percy and his granddaughter."

Having lost interest, the woman asked Enid to bring her a cold drink too.

Enid gave a tiny bow. "Yes, of course, Mistress Blanche. Take mine. I'll get another."

A broad smile flashed onto the woman's face as she switched her attention to Seamus. "So you're a doctor? I am so happy to meet you, Doctor Sheridan. Most of the people my husband brings into my home out here in the Virginia wilderness are illiterate bumpkins who can barely put two sentences together." She frowned in Percy's and

Fern's direction. "And so, tell me, how long will you be staying with us?"

At the woman's undivided attention, Seamus employed his silver tongue. "Why Mistress Blanche, you are so beautiful. How difficult it must be for a lovely flower like you to waste away in such seclusion. As to our time with you, however long we stay will not be long enough to satisfy me."

Blanche Taylor giggled. "Oh, you naughty, naughty man. How you flatter me, Doctor Sheridan." The woman flipped open a lacy white fan and fluttered it in front of her face. Recognizing the flirting technique Lady Pembrooke had taught her, Molly fought to hide her smile.

Seamus leaned closer to her. "Oh, madam, please call me Seamus."

She giggled again. "Only if you'll call me Blanche."

"All right. Blanche." A devilish grin crossed his face.

"But doctor, your arrival here is fortuitous. I've been having a painful kink in my left shoulder. I don't know what is causing it. Do you think you could massage it away, or perhaps recommend a salve that might ease my discomfort?"

Seamus stepped behind Blanche and began gently kneading the woman's shoulders when Molly's mother returned. "Mistress Blanche, would you mind if Percy and Fern cooled off in the stream while I take Molly to my room?"

A flash of irritation flitted across the woman's face that was immediately replaced by a brilliant smile. "I think that's a lovely idea, Enid."

The afternoon passed much too quickly for Molly and her mother. They had so many things to share. Molly's first question was, "Do you like it here?"

Enid shrugged a shoulder. "Master Taylor has been good to me. And Tavis is always here for me." Molly caught her message. Dealing with Mistress Blanche was no cause for joy.

Then it was Enid's turn. "Are you reading the Word every day like you promised?"

"Yes, Mama." Molly averted her eyes.

"Good! Your father would be very pleased. He spent most evenings reading the Good Book by candlelight. Do you remember?"

"Yes, I do."

When the two returned to the kitchen to prepare supper, the girl was pleasantly surprised to find Tavis seated at a heavy oak table with Master Taylor, the owner of the plantation. Tall and lanky, the man wore leather breeches and a matching shirt, much like Tavis's. A dark curl spiraled in the middle of his forehead.

As the women entered, the men rose to their feet. Master Taylor bowed and kissed Molly's hand. "So this is the talented young lady my friend Angus Adams tells me so much about. It is good to finally meet you."

"And you, sir, as well." Molly bowed gracefully. "My mother tells me you are a good employer."

"Why thank you for saying so. And I sure do enjoy her blackberry cobbler, as well as her pumpkin pies. I hope I can talk her into staying with us after her contract is finished."

Molly sent a questioning glance toward her mother. Enid glanced toward the dry sink. *No,* Molly thought, *I can't lose her again!*

Taylor folded his arms across his chest. He'd caught Molly's look of surprise and disappointment. "Tavis and Mr. Percy have been telling me about your little adventure. I'm certainly thankful no one was seriously hurt, or worse."

"Where are Percy and Fern?" the girl asked.

"We have them settled into the annex for the night."

"The annex?" Molly questioned.

"Our servant's quarters behind the main house. Don't worry. Effie will take good care of them. So tell me, Molly, are you as good with numbers as old Angus claims?"

Before Molly could answer, a servant girl a couple of years younger than Molly entered the room. "Mistress Blanche would like supper served on the veranda. And she's requesting a plate of cucumber finger sandwiches be brought to her immediately, along with a pitcher of sweet tea."

Molly watched in horror as her mother dashed about the kitchen to fulfill Mistress Blanche's instructions. The girl clicked her tongue in disgust and hissed, "Doesn't she realize you were already working on the food for tonight's main meal? Is she always this demanding?"

With her forearm, Enid brushed a stray lock of graying hair from her forehead. "Pretty much."

Molly's eyes narrowed; her lips tightened. "Oh, Mama, are you strong enough to endure another eight more months of this?"

Before she could answer, the two men excused themselves and left the kitchen. Enid tenderly touched the side of her daughter's cheek with the back of her hand. " 'I can do all things through Christ which strengtheneth me.' The promise works, even on the busiest of days." She paused and then added, "So tell me, where are you heading after you leave here? I want to be able to find you in a few months."

Relief flooded Molly to know her mother wasn't considering staying on with the Taylors. "Master Adams wrote a letter of introduction to a lawyer friend of his in Independence, Missouri. I will stay there until you arrive next summer. Seamus promised Master Adams that he'd take me that far. After that, I don't know."

Her mother frowned and pursed her lips. "I am thankful that Percy and Fern will be traveling with you. I don't want to speak ill of the man after he's been so kind as to bring you to me, but I don't particularly trust him. He seems like a real ladies' man."

The girl laughed. "That he is, a real chip off of the Blarney stone. But don't worry, as charming as he is, I've given my heart to no man."

Enid stared into her daughter's eyes for several seconds. "Are you sure? Just be careful, my poppet. I'd feel a lot better if you were traveling with Tavis instead."

"Me too," Molly admitted. "Sometimes I'm so confused, Mama. I don't understand how the touch of Seamus's hand on mine can give me the same sensations as when Tavis holds my hand."

Molly's mother gave her daughter a compassionate smile. "Honey, what you are feeling is natural. It's God's way of preparing your mind and body for the delightful experience you'll find in giving your heart to the man who will become your husband. Just don't let passing pleasant emotions you might have rule your head." Enid gave her a silly grin and then added, "Did you know that even after being married to your father for twelve years, I felt downright giddy whenever he took my hand?"

"Really?" Molly frowned. "Seamus and I have had some fun outings together. He keeps me laughing even when I don't feel much like laughing. But, with Tavis, we can have a lovely afternoon together even when we hardly speak a word. He's comfortable to be with. I feel safe."

The older woman nodded knowingly. "Remember, all that glitters is not gold. As my mother used to say, 'Winter 'em and summer 'em before you marry 'em. And never settle for less than the best."

Molly tucked her mother's advice away in her heart. While Tavis and Seamus dined with the Taylors, she and Enid ate their evening meal at the kitchen table. The girl tried to memorize each word coming from her mother's mouth. Questions tumbled from Molly's mouth faster than Enid could answer them. Both were determined to enjoy every moment they had together.

"I will treasure this day always," her mother said as they prepared for bed that evening.

"Me too." Molly's eyes glistened with tears. "I don't want tomorrow to come."

"I know." Enid patted her daughter's hand.

Molly asked, "You do still have the coin from Lord Pembrooke, don't you?"

"Absolutely. Perhaps you should take it back. You may need it."

The look of concern on the older woman's face touched the girl's heart once more because she had the same concern for her mother. "No, you may need to pay for your move to Independence. The Adamses have taken care of my financial needs very well."

The night grew silent as the two women looked into each other's eyes. Enid took her daughter's hands in hers. "Our separation is but a comma in our time together. It's not a period and certainly not an exclamation point, merely a comma."

Enid's words comforted the girl as she attempted to fall asleep. But after the day's excitement, sleep refused to come. Molly tossed and turned in the hot and humid air in the tiny room. When she heard her mother snoring softly beside her, the girl longed to awaken her so they could spend more time together, but she knew her mother was exhausted and needed to sleep. So she wouldn't disturb her, the girl slipped out of bed, put her mother's cotton plissé robe over her muslin nightgown and wrapped the tie about her waist. As she tiptoed from the room, Molly grabbed her hairbrush.

With the cook's living quarters immediately off the kitchen, Molly found her way to the summer kitchen. There she filled a glass with water from the well and ambled outside to a small stone patio behind the house.

A mosquito buzzed around her head as Molly breathed in the sultry summer air. A cool nighttime breeze wafted from a nearby river toward the plantation house. Reluctant to return to her mother' stifling bedroom, Molly strolled out onto the lawn. There she untied her sleeping braid and brushed through her long, wavy locks. When finished, she lay the brush on the grass, wrapped her arms about her knees, and gazed at the fireflies dancing above the grass. She listened as the frogs by the river serenaded their mates. A host of crickets added their rhythm to the night song.

For a time, she tracked the moon across the sky. *Believing in a God who keeps the world in motion is easy on a summer night like this,* she decided. But to think He could possibly care about her and her problems, Molly still found hard to accept. *Even if the promises in Mama's Bible are true, the perfection of tonight will fade into the coming sadness of tomorrow,* she reminded herself.

The girl leaned back on her elbows and followed the path of three shooting stars across the sky. Before long, her eyes grew heavy. She drifted into a stupor only to awaken to the sound of approaching footsteps. Hoping the interloper would not become aware of her presence, she froze.

A man passed within ten feet of where she sat. She watched him amble toward the riverbank, where he dropped to his knees and splashed his hand in the water. Thinking she'd found an opportunity to escape undetected back to the house, Molly rose to her feet.

Suddenly, the man whirled about to face her. "Who goes there?" he challenged. Then she saw his face in the moonlight. It was Tavis.

To describe her feelings at that moment would have been impossible. Fearful, embarrassed, awkward, and pleased—she wrapped her arms about her body to protect it from the strange emotions playing tug-of-war in her brain.

"It's just me," she called. "Sorry, I didn't mean to startle you." A playful breeze whipped several loose curls about her shoulders.

"What are you doing out here?" He strode over to where she stood. "Don't you know that it's not safe being alone out here at night? All kinds of critters, both the four legged and two legged, abound in these parts."

She attempted an explanation. "The room was so hot; I had to get some air."

Shadows covered his face as he stared down at her. He stuffed his hands into his pockets. "Molly, I fear for you. You are so innocent, so trusting, and so unprepared to face the real world. Remember, you are no longer in the Adamses' safe, enclosed garden. There are real dangers out here." He paused. "You can't imagine how much I hate letting you leave here tomorrow without me."

Sensing the agony in his voice, she replied, "Don't worry. I'll be fine. Seamus and Percy will protect me."

"If only life were that simple, little pigeon. Percy, yes, he would sacrifice his life to protect you and Fern, but Seamus is cut from different cloth."

"What do you mean? He's been nothing but a gentleman around me!" Why she was defending the man, Molly didn't understand.

"That's good to know." Tavis paused a second time. "Molly, I want you to make a promise to me that before you retire each evening, you will place a small iron skillet beside your pillow."

"A skillet? Whatever for?"

He heaved a troubled sigh. "As protection. And if you ever have to use it, make the first blow count."

Molly laughed aloud. "Tavis, you are so silly. I would never hit someone over the head with a frying pan!"

His voice grew gruff. "Just promise me you'll do as I ask."

The girl rose to her feet. Standing toe to toe, she placed a hand on his forearm. "Tavis, you worry too much about me—but I must confess I like knowing you care."

"Oh, I care, little pigeon. Never doubt that I care."

Her heart skipped a beat when, for a moment, he dipped his face toward her. She licked her lips in anticipation of receiving what would be her first kiss. But without any warning, he straightened and almost snarled, "It's time you go back inside. Morning will be here soon."

Taken aback by the sudden change in his attitude, Molly retrieved her brush from where she'd been sitting and turned toward the summer kitchen and her mother's bedroom.

For the next few hours, she tossed and turned in the bed. What had she done wrong? Molly hadn't a clue. Whatever it was she'd done must have irked him, or why would he have sent her away so abruptly?

As dawn broke in the eastern sky, Molly sensed her mother slip out of the bed to wash and dress. Before leaving the room, Enid bent down and kissed her daughter on the forehead and whispered, "Sleep a little longer, child. From what I hear, it's probably the last comfortable sleep you'll have for a while."

Enid was right. The girl had barely dragged her body out of the bed, when Percy knocked on the door. "Mistress Molly," he called. "Are you packed and ready to go? Is your satchel ready to be loaded in the wagon?"

Snapping awake, she leaped from the bed and threw on her traveling dress. So many of her dresses were unsuited for the rigors of the road.

Packed, fed, and ready to roll, Seamus urged Molly and Fern to hurry. "We have a long way to travel today. We don't want to lose anymore daylight hours than necessary."

Tavis waited nearby as Enid kissed her daughter goodbye a second and a third time. The woman took Molly's face in her hands and reminded her of her promise. "Remember to read your Bible every day."

The girl smiled. "This is really important to you, isn't it?"

"More important that you can possibly know. Consider it our special time together each evening." Enid rubbed her nose against her daughter's as she had when Molly was a young child.

Tears sprang in the girl's eyes. "I will, Mama." She threw herself into her mother's arms and sobbed, "I am going to miss you so badly."

"And I'll miss you too. But don't worry; I'll see you in Missouri come summer."

Percy and Fern watched from the rear of the wagon. Impatient to hit the road, Seamus waited in the driver's seat. Finally, Tavis led Molly to the wagon. He placed his hands about her waist to lift her onto the wagon bench and whispered, "Do you have your iron skillet ready like you promised?"

Molly grinned. "I sure do. And it's a heavy one!" Before he removed his hands from her waist, she asked, "Tell me, did I do or say something wrong last night?"

He planted a brotherly kiss on the end of her nose. "No, little pigeon, you did absolutely nothing wrong." When a tear trickled down her cheek, he brushed it away with the back of his hand. "Whatever happens, wait for me. I promise I'll come to you next summer."

* * * * *

How strange they must have looked to the rare passersby as the brightly colored wagon, decorated with an advertisement for "Doctor Sheridan's Miracle Elixir: A Cure for Any Pain That Ails You" rolled away from the plantation and north toward the border with the Commonwealth of Pennsylvania.

Molly wept all morning. She wept all afternoon. She wept that evening as she and Fern fixed supper. She wept throughout the night. The next morning, as they resumed their travels, Molly continued to weep until Seamus finally growled, "Are you going to do that all the way to Missouri?"

"Do what?" she sobbed.

"Cry!"

"Yes."

Before the end of their first week on the rail, the dust blowing in her face had given her a headache; sitting for hours on the hard wooden wagon seat had given her a backache; and for so many reasons she couldn't even begin to count, her heart continued to ache. Molly knew that so much could happen between August and the following June.

"Hey!" Seamus jangled the horses' reins. Eager to please, the animals responded. "You'll see your mom in a few months."

"I hope so."

"Oh, blarney! Molly, you possess the luck of the Irish. Look how you've landed on your feet at each turn in your life. You'll do the same in Independence."

Molly sniffed into her handkerchief. "My mom doesn't believe in luck. She believes that a Divine Being watches over us."

"Really?" Seamus's tone of voice contained sarcasm. "And just what do you believe?"

"I don't know. I'm still searching." The girl heaved a deep sigh. "Do you believe in a God who watches over you and cares for you?"

The man snorted. "Not likely. As I see it, a man makes his own good luck. He's got to stay at least one move ahead of the next guy, or he'll be stomped into the ground."

His reply hit Molly between the eyes. "That's pretty cynical, don't you think?"

Seamus shrugged. "That's what life has taught me so far."

When they stopped that night in a grove of saplings on the Pennsylvania border, Molly helped Fern make a batch of pancakes. All enjoyed some of the blueberry jam Mistress Blanche had insisted that Seamus take. Later, as Molly prepared to sleep, she read from her Bible by oil lamp as promised. And to keep her word to Tavis, she placed a medium-sized iron skillet at the edge of her pillow.

Boredom set in as one day followed the next—eating a breakfast of oatmeal with the applesauce Mae-Mae had packed; hitting the road before dawn; traveling all day with only jerky for lunch; stopping again at night; eating, sleeping, and doing it all over again the next day. The only break in their routine came whenever Percy and Seamus switched driving or Molly and Fern traded places.

Relief came whenever they passed through a small town or by a farm along the way. Seamus would stop and peddle his elixir. The colorful wagon with its windup calliope player never failed to draw a curious crowd. Dogs barked and children ran alongside, eager to view the expected sideshow. For most people living in the small towns, Seamus's arrival was the most exciting event since the three-legged race on Founders' Day.

Fern and Molly would draw the flashy gold curtains across back of the wagon to shield their living quarters from public while Percy assembled a stage at the rear of the wagon and Seamus donned his silk morning coat, French cravat, and top hat. When a crowd had gathered, Seamus would make a dramatic entrance onto the stage and spout his claims to heal "whatever ails you" and sell as many bottles of his questionable medicine as the townspeople could purchase. The night would follow with Seamus slipping away to a saloon, if the town had one, and not returning until daylight.

This bothered Molly. Later while watching him mix the ingredients to his concoctions, she challenged him, "How can you claim this stuff heals anyone? It's just water, ginger, camphor, and cheap alcohol."

"I am surprised at you. Can't you see the service I provide?" Putting on his best expression of disappointment in her pity for those he duped, he said, "The people in most of these towns have no doctor to cure their aches and pains. They live a life of boredom and exhaustion. My elixir gives them hope and comfort, and—for some—healing." Unconvinced, she refused to help him hawk his wares, though he asked several times. However, after each sale, he would buy fresh produce and canned goods that would add variety to their meals for the next few days. He would also surprise her with a small trinket he'd purchased at a local mercantile store.

The summer days grew shorter as their wagon rolled west. The towns became fewer and farther between. The nights turned cooler and mornings more brisk. All too soon the woods changed from their seasonal green to hues of yellow, brown, and orange, and then the leaves began to fall. Each night Seamus made camp near a farmhouse, where he would arrange with the owner for them to sleep in the barn in exchange for the price of a bottle of his elixir.

One morning the ground outside the barn where they stayed the night was covered with frost. Molly blew on her hands to warm them enough to start a fire while Fern drew water from the farmer's well.

As Molly bent over to stir the fire, Seamus sneaked up behind her. "Hey, look what I have. Eggs! Fresh milk too. The farmer's wife insisted on sharing with us."

The idea of having fresh eggs for breakfast set the girl's taste buds spinning. When Fern returned, she, too, was excited at the prospect of eating something other than oatmeal or corn bread for breakfast.

When they gathered round the fire to eat their scrambled eggs, Seamus announced, "The farmer says we should see the Mississippi River before noon!"

The prospect of finally reaching the mighty Mississippi after so many weeks of travel buoyed Molly's spirits throughout the morning. As she and Seamus rode side by side on the wagon, she even indulged in a little playful flirting. Whenever their conversation lulled, she'd slyly glance his way. Their eyes would meet, and they'd exchange smiles. She realized how much she liked him when he was being his charming self and not the hawker of questionable wares. It was at these times as he shared stories about surviving on the streets of Cork as an orphan, that she began to understand why he did some of the things he did.

The farmer's prediction proved to be accurate. The wagon rolled into the narrow strip of a shantytown along the river just before noon—the perfect time of day to attract a crowd and their money, as Seamus had said so many times before.

CHAPTER FIFTEEN

OUT IN THE COLD

THE CONSTANT HUM OF the paddlewheel churning through the muddy water replaced the creaking of wagon wheels. On deck, Molly and Fern gazed at the water flowing by as the *Mississippi Princess* inched northward past tiny hamlets, large plantations, and clusters of fishing shacks.

Molly lifted her face to enjoy the cool breeze sweeping up from the water. "I surely don't miss riding in that creaky wagon all day!"

"Me either. If I never had to travel another mile in the stuffy box, I would be a very happy girl." Fern's good nature had returned since they boarded the riverboat. So had Molly's.

The luxury of strolling around the deck instead of the riding blind in the back of the wagon, of dining at linen-draped tables and sitting in real chairs instead of perching on a wooden box or sitting on the ground, and of sleeping between clean sheets instead of under a smelly horse blanket, had a calming effect on the travelers. Bathing and putting on fresh underclothing refreshed the ladies as much as anything. Molly dreaded the day the ride up the river would end and she would be forced to return to the painful inconveniences of wagon travel.

The girl most enjoyed the evenings aboard the riverboat when she could put aside her calicos for the recently neglected brocade, satin, and silk gowns in her wardrobe like several of the grand Southern ladies on board wore.

"Let's stroll around the deck again." Molly gathered her gray wool shawl about her shoulders. The skirts of her midnight-blue taffeta gown swooshed as she walked. She knew she drew favorable attention from the men and envy from the female passengers on board.

"All right, if we must." Fern, wearing a gold satin gown borrowed from Molly, struggled to keep up with her friend. The gown, over layer upon layer of starched petticoats, would, with each step, wrap itself about her legs.

Molly, more than Fern, relished the attention she garnered when walking past the gaming salon in the evening. In the dimly lit room beyond the open door, impeccably dressed gentlemen with gold-tipped canes played cards at dark oak tables while dapper young men lingered near the entrance, admiring the ladies strolling past. Two or three women, with layers of makeup caked on their pocked faces and wearing cheap satin knee-length dresses and black net stockings, sashayed from table to table, serving drinks to the customers.

Leaning against the brass railing outside the establishment, a well-dressed man in his midthirties tipped his hat toward Molly. "Good evening, lovely lady. Are you enjoying your evening constitutional?"

"Why, yes, we are, thank you." The girl batted her eyes, smiled, and attempted to step around him. Fern cowered behind her.

"It's a lovely evening for a stroll. Would you mind if I joined you?" He extended the crook of his arm toward her. Molly liked the laughing smile on his face and the hint of a dimple in the man's chin.

"Actually, she would!" a gruff voice from behind her snarled. Seamus pushed between Molly and the stranger. "She's with me!"

Mildly irked at him, she snapped, "Seamus, I thought you were in the saloon drinking."

The stranger paused. A frown gathered on his lips as if he was considering throwing a punch at Seamus. Instead, he slowly backed away. The stranger touched the brim of his top hat and threw Seamus a tight-lipped smile. "Sorry, sir, I didn't mean to intrude. A word of advice—you need to keep a better watch over your woman." He tipped his hat a second time and disappeared inside the saloon.

"Your woman?" Molly demanded. "What is he talking about?"

"Forget him! Why aren't you reading a book in your stateroom?" Seamus grabbed Molly by the upper arm and gave her an abrupt shake. "Don't you know you ladies should be retiring at this hour?"

"Let go of me, sir!" Angry tears sprang into Molly's eyes. She shook her arm free of his grasp. "You're hurting me!"

"If you were my woman, I'd—" He bit his lip. "Someone needs to teach you a lesson!" His eyes flashed with fury.

"What do you mean, 'your woman'? I'm nobody's woman!" Toe to toe, she matched him glare for glare. Exasperated, he clutched and unclutched his fists and suddenly stormed into the saloon.

"Of all the nerve. Who does he think he is?" Molly had never before been so angry. She could feel her cheeks becoming hot. A tear slid down her cheek.

"Come!" Fern gently took her friend by the hand. "I think it's a good idea for us to return to our cabin."

"Well, I don't!" She shook Fern's hand away. "I have half a mind to walk into that saloon and ask for a sarsaparilla."

"Please, Mistress Molly, I wouldn't do that—"

"Since when do you call me 'Mistress Molly'?" The girl snapped.

Fern ignored her question. "Sorry, if you are going into that room, you are doing so alone." The girl held her ground with a defiance Molly had never before seen.

Molly blinked in surprise. Fern had always been the most compliant of companions. She'd never said a cross word or even objected to Molly's most outrageous suggestions.

"Fine!" Tears of embarrassment filled her eyes as Molly stormed down the corridor to their stateroom.

Too proud to ask Fern for help with her tightly bound corset, Molly struggled out of her garments and slung them over the only chair in the cabin. Determined to be certain Fern understood how insulted she felt, Molly silently threw on her nightgown and climbed into her bunk. Her head had barely hit the pillow when she remembered she hadn't kept her promise to her mother to read from the Bible. Molly heaved a dramatic sigh, sat up, and snatched the Book from the shelf over her bed while Fern undressed and climbed into her own bunk. In minutes, Molly heard the girl snoring softly.

The girl mumbled under breath as she fingered through the pages to find the spot where she'd left off the night before. "Proverbs twenty-nine, verse twenty-two," she muttered. Finding the desired book, chapter, and verse, Molly began to read. " 'An angry man stirreth up strife, and a furious man aboundeth in transgression. A man's pride shall bring him low; but honour shall uphold the humble in spirit.' Obviously, Seamus should read that verse!" she growled, turning off the flame on the oil lantern next to her bed. Scooting under her covers, Molly's fingers touched the handle of the iron skillet she'd hidden between the mattress and the wall. Immediately, she thought of Tavis and sighed.

Drifting between consciousness and sleep, Molly heard the metal hinges on the cabin door squeak. The gentle rhythm of Fern's snore didn't change. The soft light from the hall fell across the stateroom's wooden floor as the shadow of a man crossed her bed. Suddenly alert, Molly's fingers wrapped around the skillet's handle.

Who could be standing in our cabin? What did he want? Can it be Percy? she wondered. *No, he would have knocked before entering. But who else would dare enter our cabin in the middle of the night uninvited? Maybe the man has mistaken our cabin for his. It's possible, but not likely,* she thought.

The interloper drew near. Watching through half-closed eyes, the girl sensed rather than saw the intruder pause beside her bunk. As he leaned closer, she inhaled a nauseating wave of alcohol. Terrified but undaunted, Molly tightened her grip on the skillet handle. With one swing, she delivered a perfect backhand to the side of the man's head. "Take that, you cad!" she shouted. "Now, get out of here before I give you more!"

The loud *bong* followed by a startled yelp awakened Fern. Fern screamed a sustained high C. She pulled the blankets up about her neck as the injured man tumbled to the floor. The man groaned. Still holding the skillet by the handle, Molly leaped from her bed and bounded to the cabin door. "Help! Help!" she shouted in the corridor.

Yells from passengers sleeping in nearby cabins shattered the quiet of the night. Doors flew open up and down the corridor. From inside the staterooms, women screamed while men of all ages and sizes burst forth, brandishing canes, umbrellas, and shotguns.

"What's wrong, lady?" Ready for battle, the man in the room next door asked. Molly's face reddened at the size of the crowd assembling in the corridor.

"Molly," Seamus's weak voice came from inside her cabin. "Please close the door. I can explain."

She glanced over her shoulder at the man sitting on the floor, holding his head and leaning against the bunk. "Seamus, you're drunk!"

A beefy man, wearing a knee-length flannel nightshirt and wielding a brass candleholder, stepped toward her. "Lady, are you all right?"

Molly raised her hand to stop him from coming closer. "I am so sorry, sir. I thought I saw a snake, but I guess I was dreaming." Without further explanation, she closed the door and lit the oil lamp.

A whimper came from Fern, who still clutched the bedding to her neck and cowered in the corner of her bunk.

Molly planted her hands on her hips and stared at the man on the floor in the middle of her stateroom. "Seamus, what are you doing in Fern's and my room, especially at this hour?"

"You could have killed me, woman!" A more sober Seamus rubbed the goose egg on his forehead.

"You realize no sheriff would have arrested me." Molly cast him a withering glare. "I would have been within my rights!"

The man struggled to his knees.

"Stay right where you are, mister!" She raised the skillet over her head. "I'll hit you again if you come near me or Fern!"

Seamus sat back down. "You sleep with that thing?"

"I certainly do. I keep it in my bed to ward off predators like you! You still haven't explained why you entered our room."

His face flooded with shame. "Thank you for lying for me. I would have been kicked off the boat at the next port—or even worse if I'd been arrested!"

"Just desserts, don't you think? By the way, I didn't lie. I did see a snake! You! And I wish I'd been dreaming." Molly planted the chair in front of the door, sat down, and placed the skillet in her lap. "You haven't yet explained yourself, Seamus Sheridan!"

The man bowed his head. "I don't know what came over me. It must have been the liquor."

"You can't blame the liquor! You've been drinking every night since we boarded this boat. And every morning you've been hung over. Did you think no one would notice?"

Seamus didn't answer.

"Why did you come here?" she insisted.

He grew agitated as she pressed him for an answer.

"It's really your fault! You and your flirty ways! How do you think I feel when you sashay up and down the deck of the ship, dressed in your finest, and sending come-hither looks toward every Joe and Tom?"

Seamus's eyes grew cold. "Little lady, I've treated you with respect throughout our journey west because I hoped your flirting would lead us somewhere. Well, tonight you were ready to go who knows where with that guy outside the salon. After more drinks than I can count, I decided it was time to teach you a lesson or mark my claim! That's why I was here!"

Molly stared in horror at the man she thought she knew. "Get out! Get out of here, you, you cad, you bounder!" Blinded by sudden tears, she leaped off the chair and swung open the door. "Don't you ever dare come near me again! Ever! Next time I'll aim to kill!"

Seamus struggled to his feet and staggered into the hallway. "Don't worry, lady. There are plenty of other fish in the sea!"

"Fine. Fish on the other side of the boat!" Molly slammed the door and threw her body onto her bunk. Her cries of humiliation drowned out the shouts of anger coming from nearby staterooms.

At breakfast the next morning, Seamus approached her and Fern's table in the breakfast room. "Molly," he began, "I want to apologize for last night."

The girl glanced toward Fern. "Did you hear something, Fern?" Molly paused and pretended to listen. "No, I guess not." She bit into her slice of toast and slowly chewed the bread as if Seamus wasn't standing beside her table. "*Mmm,* don't you just adore the apple butter? I can taste a hint of cinnamon in it, can't you?"

Trapped in the middle of an embarrassing situation, Fern studied the raisins on the top of her oatmeal.

The awkward silence between Seamus and Molly continued throughout the rest of the journey to St. Louis and in the wagon trip across Missouri. As uncomfortable it was to ride in the back of the wagon, Molly avoided, whenever possible, sitting on the bench beside Seamus. Instead, Fern and Percy took turns riding in the coveted seat.

In the back of the wagon, Molly spent her days brooding over the event on the paddleboat. Whenever she thought about Seamus, her mind raced to the baron's despicable behavior in the Pembrooke library and on to Ridgley's attempt to discredit her in front of Master Adams. The more she mulled, the angrier she became.

Molly knew she needed someone to talk with, someone to comfort her for the injuries she'd experienced. Before speaking, she eyed Percy for several hours. The old man sat at the far end of the opposite bunk, scraping dried mud from his boots with his pocketknife.

The girl heaved a dramatic sigh. "Did Fern tell you what Seamus did on the boat?"

"Yes, Mistress Molly." Percy's lips tightened.

Molly folded her legs under her voluminous skirts and leaned forward on her elbows. "Then you understand why I can't forgive him."

A chunk of dried Missouri mud popped out of the seam of his boot and onto the floor. "If you say so, Mistress Molly."

Irked at failing to get the desired response, the girl pressed further. "Then you must admit that Seamus is a drunken cad to do what he did!"

"If you say so." The man's expression hadn't change.

Frustrated, she snapped. "Is that all you're going to say, 'If you say so'?"

"If you say so."

"But surely you can't approve of Seamus's behavior! What if he'd broken in the room to molest Fern? How would you feel then?" she growled.

"Wouldn't like it, I presume." The old man wiped the dried soil off the blade and onto his pant leg.

"What would you do? Defend her honor?"

"Probably." He rolled his tongue around on the inside of his left cheek for several seconds. "But I'd also threatened to tan her bottom for leading him on."

"What?" How could Percy say such a thing? Indignant, she shot to her feet. As she did so the left wheels of the wagon hit a rut in the road. The girl lost her balance and sat down with a thud on the hard wooden bunk.

Percy's face remained devoid of emotion. "You asked me what I'd do, Mistress Molly, and I told you."

"But I don't understand."

Percy spoke in softer tone. "My granddaughter knows better than to trifle with men's emotions just for fun."

"But, but, but I don't . . ." Molly's face reddened.

He shrugged a shoulder and tipped his head to one side. "If you say so."

The sting of his words haunted the girl for the rest of the journey. She'd mutter under her breath as she stirred each pot of stew heating over the open fire or when she scrubbed clean a kettle. "I don't care what Grandpa Percy says," she told herself. "I refuse to take any of the blame for Seamus's bad behavior. I did nothing wrong! And I will never forgive him! Never!"

Percy's reaction to her query affected her friendship with Fern. Molly no longer felt comfortable talking with her about it, especially if Fern felt the same way as her grandfather did. Dark depression replaced the girl's natural ebullience. When they stopped in towns to sell the elixir, Molly sulked in the wagon. She emerged only to help with the cooking and after-dinner cleanup.

One day's travel from Independence, Seamus made camp. A stream, covered with a thin crust of ice, flowed near where he parked the wagon. Fern had to break the ice for drinking water and for washing the dishes. After the two girls cleaned and stowed away the remains of supper, Fern hung her wet dishtowel to dry on their portable clothesline to dry. "Just think Molly, tomorrow night we may be sleeping in real beds and eating supper at a real table."

Molly only grunted.

"Molly, why are you mad at me? Why won't you talk to me anymore?"

The girl couldn't explain. She shook her head and disappeared inside the vehicle. Fern climbed in behind her and closed the curtain, plunging the interior into darkness. "I miss you. You must know I'm not going to give up until you speak to me!"

"Leave me alone!" Molly mumbled, kicking off her boots and shedding her cotton dress.

A flash of pain swept across Fern's face. "Is this the way things will stay between us?"

"Probably so!" Molly appreciated the irony of answering Fern with the same retort Grandpa Percy had given her. The girl knew it was unreasonable to blame Fern for anything that had happened, but

Molly didn't feel particularly reasonable toward anyone at the moment.

Fern placed her hand on Molly's knee. "Whatever is wrong, I love you and I want to help."

When Molly didn't reply, Fern continued, "You're the only friend I've ever had, so I don't want to lose you."

Fern's confession almost broke Molly's heart because the same wasn't true for her. In Ireland, Anne had been Molly's friend. *But friends come and go,* she mused. Yet Molly regretted the pain she was causing Fern. Placing her hand on Fern's, the girl whispered, "Please give me time. I need time to work things out."

After the sun set that night, Molly lit the oil lamp and opened her Bible to one of the texts her mother had underlined. Molly could see her breath in the air as she mouthed the words. " 'Trust in the LORD with all thine heart; and lean not unto thine own understanding. In all thy ways acknowledge him, and he shall direct thy paths.' "

I know what I'm doing and where I'm going, Molly thought. *I don't need someone, even if He's God, to tell me what to do and where to go!* She skimmed the words of the next verse and blanched. " 'Be not wise in thine own eyes; fear the LORD, and depart from evil.' "

Irritated, she placed the Bible on the head of her bed and extinguished the lamp. Instantly, the room darkened. The wagon became bone-chilling cold.

Fern, huddled under her stack of blankets, said, "Imagine! Tomorrow we finally see Independence. Isn't it exciting?"

"Yes, it is," Molly admitted, snuggling deeper under her bedding.

"Seamus calls Independence 'the city on the edge of the American frontier.' Seems fitting that it is called Independence, isn't it?"

"Yes, I suppose so."

"The name itself is magical. Independence. Independence. It rolls so sweetly off the tongue, doesn't it?"

"Yes, it does. Good night, Fern." Their short exchange soothed the girl's conscience for being so hateful. Determined to fall asleep quickly, Molly tugged her blankets over her head to conserve every bit of warmth she could. That Percy and Seamus were bedded down beneath the wagon and might be even colder than she was didn't cross her mind.

* * * * *

The sun shimmered above a cloudbank on the western horizon as Seamus stopped the wagon on the outskirts of the city the next afternoon. Molly poked her head out of the wagon. "Why are we stopping? Are we there yet?"

Seamus glanced over his shoulder. "I need to change into my Doc Sheridan garb before we hit the town. No doubt you ladies may want to freshen up as well."

Molly sniffed her woolen shawl and eyed the faded skirt she'd worn every day since the weather had turned colder. "Good idea!"

"Percy, how about you? Do you to want to change?"

"Into what?" the man chortled. "Not much else left that is clean other than my Sabbath-go-to-meeting overalls. Seamus, the ladies and I'll watch the horses while you change. That will give Molly and Fern time to primp before we reach the town's business district."

"Good idea." Seamus hopped down from the wagon while Percy and Molly switched to the wagon bench with Fern. Minutes later, icy shivers skittered up and down Molly's spine as she tossed her trail-worn coat and dusty bonnet onto the bunk and opened her trunk.

"Here's a bucket of water for you," Seamus called from outside the back door of the vehicle. "Sorry, it's cold."

"Thank you." Fern opened the door a crack, took the bucket from his hand and quickly shut the door once again.

Molly dipped her hands in the cold water and splashed some on her face, arms, and neck. Feeling refreshed, Molly opened her trunk. She knew which garment she would wear—her gray linsey-woolsey dress with its white linen collar. The girl eyed the wrinkles in the skirt and sighed. "Oh well! It can't be helped." She dropped the garment over her head and began fastening the tiny buttons on the bodice.

"Here, let me help you re-braid your hair." Fern unfastened the one long braid down Molly's back and began brushing the snarls out of Molly's hair. "Isn't this exciting? You're fortunate to know where you're going. I have no idea if Grandpa Percy will decide to stay in Independence or move farther west. I'm not worried, just excited." Fern's face flushed with high color.

Molly smiled. She'd never before seen Fern so excited. "Doesn't it bother you not knowing your future, what with Norwood back in Virginia?"

"Not really. Are you sure you know yours? I believe God will direct us to the place where He needs us to be."

Molly wondered how Fern could be so trusting, first of her grandfather, and then, of a God she'd never seen. As Molly thought about the frightening unknown, she wished she had Fern's trust and assurance.

Molly planted her best gray woolen bonnet on her head and wrapped her heavy woolen shawl about her shoulders. "There! I think I'm ready to face this brave new world."

CHAPTER SIXTEEN

SERENITY INN

THE TWO GIRLS CLIMBED onto the buckboard seat while Seamus and Percy switched seats. Too curious to remain inside the wagon, Percy crawled into the space between the wagon and the buckboard. As Seamus flicked the reins, he glanced toward Molly and smiled. "Good to see you again, Mistress Molly."

"And you, Doctor Sheridan." She gave him a polite nod.

"Mighty cold last night." He gave the reins a second shake.

The taller buildings in town towered above the treetops along the riverbank. "The city looks much bigger than I had imagined," Molly admitted.

"Mr. French, the farmer I talked with during our dinner break last night, said that Independence is the second largest city in the state even during the off season. Come spring, more than five thousand people will pass through the town on their way west."

Molly recalled the throng in Liverpool. Did the crowd on the docks where they boarded the ship for America number five thousand? She didn't think so.

Seamus continued, "At that time the roads are so clogged with covered wagons, farm wagons, and every other mode of transportation imaginable, that getting through the town to the jumping off spot takes hours."

Beyond the curtain of trees, their branches barren of leaves, the town stretched out before them. Buildings of various sizes and importance quickly came into view. Two- and three-story brick homes stood side by side with one-room log cabins. A few white clapboard edifices rivaled the opulence of the plantations houses she had seen in Virginia. In contrast to Virginian plantations expansive lawns, small white picket fences edged many of the properties here.

Delighted that Molly would listen to him, Seamus had assumed the role of guide. "The town stretches from the Methodist church spire you barely see above buildings to your right, all the way to the Congregational church spire to the south. Independence has thirty dry goods stores, two hotels, five boardinghouses, and more than thirty drinking establishments, as well as several other places of business where ladies of questionable character ply their trade."

Having heard her father speak of the goings-on in the pubs and on the streets of Ireland, Molly grunted her displeasure. "I suppose that's where you'll be spending much of your time, Doctor Sheridan."

Seamus's eyes narrowed; he jammed his hat further onto his head. The expression on his face hardened. "Probably so, Mistress Molly, probably so! After the last few days of this journey, I need to get plastered! For that matter, I might not see the light of day for weeks!"

Determined to ignore Molly, he glanced over his shoulder at Percy. "That massive building to our left is the largest builder of freight wagons west of the Mississippi. You might be interested to know Hiram Young, a freed slave, owns and operates the establishment. You might check whether he's hiring," Seamus suggested.

"We're only a few blocks from the section of town where you and Fern will be able to find lodging and from the hotel where I'll be staying. I can keep Fern with me until you return."

"I'd like that." Percy's eyes brightened. "Imagine living in a place where a freed slave can do so well."

"Before you get too excited, my friend. Missouri is not that friendly to people of color. While it sits at the crossroads for runaways traveling to Canada, it's also the place where bounty hunters, slave owners, and abolitionists have been known to collide. And thanks to the Missouri Compromise, things won't change anytime soon."

"Well, I guess I didn't really expect otherwise. And I guess there's no time like the present to look for a job." Percy hopped off the wagon and strode toward the main door of the factory building.

Seamus signaled the horses to keep moving. As the wagon drew closer to the center of town, wooden sidewalks appeared on each side of the road. The larger homes at the edge of town changed to the familiar red-brick row houses similar to the ones in the city of Norfolk.

A smattering of shoppers watched the brightly colored wagon, with its advertisement for magic elixir on the side, bounce over the ruts and potholes in the unpaved street. Seamus stopped the wagon in front of the Pierson House Hotel. "If you ladies will excuse me, I am going inside to book a room for the night. Should I reserve one for you as well, Molly?"

The girl hesitated. Reading the uncertainty on Molly's face, the man added, "Don't worry. You will be forever safe from me, Mistress Molly."

Her face reddened. "I don't know. I'd like to meet Attorney Pownell before making any arrangements for the night. He might have other suggestions for me."

"Fine." Seamus walked up the steps of the hotel and through the double doors. A short time later, he emerged from the building, climbed onto the wagon, and without a word urged the horses forward. Ahead, the rows of buildings ended abruptly; and in their place was a large fenced-in square. An impressive three-story, red-brick building occupied the center.

"That's the Jackson County Courthouse," Seamus explained. "It was built in 1836. The hotel clerk told me that in the spring, a long line of trader caravans heading for Santa Fe will completely circle the square before heading south to Liberty Street, the jumping off point for the American frontier." His eyes looked wistful. "Sure makes traveling west sound mighty appealing."

"Not to me!" Molly stated and shook her head. "I don't want to move another inch! I intend to plant my feet firmly in Independence soil and never travel more than ten miles east or west in a wagon of any kind!"

Fern nodded in agreement. "The way my body aches right now, I may do the same. Let men explore the unknown West to their hearts' content; we women will stay here and keep the home fires burning!"

Just past the town square, wooden stores replaced the brick townhouses. Signs advertising doctors and dentists, cobblers and apothecaries lined the street. Molly spotted a black-and-white sign with a painting of a raised gavel. It read, "Samuel Pownell, Ltd. Attorney-at-Law."

"Stop the wagon!" Excited, Molly leaped to her feet, lost her balance when the wagon lurched, and fell back against the seat with a thud.

"Are you all right?" Fern asked.

"Yes, thank you!" She straightened her bonnet and glared at Seamus, who slowed the horses to a stop, climbed down from the wagon, tied their reins to a wooden hitching post, and strode away, leaving Molly to maneuver off the wagon without any help. Two men watched as the girl hiked her skirt to her knees and jumped down. Molly wrapped the drawstrings of her leather purse around her gloved hand and brushed a free hand across the most visible wrinkles in her skirt. She paused to take a deep breath before entering the establishment. As she pushed open the door, a bell announced her arrival. Molly couldn't help but compare the small dusty law office with Master Adams's opulent establishment.

A striking, lovely middle-aged woman, her blond hair pilled high on her head, glanced up from a magazine she'd been reading and smiled broadly. The woman looked totally out of place with her surroundings. "Welcome to the Pownell law offices. How may I help you, miss?"

Molly gripped her purse tightly with both hands. "I'm here to see Attorney Pownell. Is he in?"

The woman smiled and rose to her feet. "Yes, he is. What may I say is the purpose of your visit?"

Molly fumbled with her leather drawstrings as she extricated Master Adams's precious letter from her purse. "I have a letter for Attorney Pownell from a classmate of his."

"Oh?" the woman brightened and extended her hand. "If you'll take a seat over there, I'll give him your letter."

Molly shook her head. "If it is all right with you, ma'am, I'd prefer to hand it to him myself."

"As you wish. And who may I say is calling?" Though the woman continued to smile, the girl realized that the moment had come when she would need to impress this total stranger. Always before she'd been moved from place to place in the presence of her mother or Lady Pembrooke or Tavis. She never before had to operate on her own. She cleared her throat, "Molly, Molly Maguire."

Detecting the girl's nervousness, the woman's eyes twinkled. "Well, Molly Maguire, if you'll make yourself comfortable in one of those chairs, I'll tell Attorney Pownell you are waiting to see him. He's with a client at the moment."

Molly warmed her hands over the pot-bellied stove in the center of the room for a moment, and then reluctantly, she left the stove's warmth to sit in the first of the five wooden chairs against the wall. Gazing about the room, the girl wondered where the lawyer's law clerks worked. Perhaps in a second room off of the main reception room, she decided. As Molly studied the wall opposite from her, she could make out a rough outline of England and Europe in the cracks in the wall. But when she squinted, she could see the outline of her beloved Ireland. Intent on her observation, Molly failed to hear the woman return.

"Miss Maguire, my husband will see you now."

Husband? Molly blinked in surprise. The girl couldn't imagine Mistress Julia ever working in her husband's office. She followed the woman into a small dark office crowded with oversized furniture and towering stacks of law books, some on shelves and many others on the floor. Out of the corner of her eye, she spotted a man dart out the rear door of the office.

At the sound of a chair scraping against the wooden floor, she turned to face the man she supposed was Attorney Pownell. Almost as tall and as thin as Master Adams, sporting a snowy-white mustache and a matching pointed beard, the attorney rounded the corner of a massive oak desk. A curious smile tipped the ends of his mustache upward. He extended his hand toward the girl. "Miss Maguire, it is a pleasure to meet you. How may I help you today?"

"I was told to give you this." With the palms of her hands Molly smoothed out a deep crease in the envelope before placing it in his hands.

Attorney Pownell took it from her, broke the wax seal, and withdrew the letter. His lips moved as he scanned the message. As he read, a smile filled his face. "My, my, fancy hearing from my old Harvard roommate after all these years. And how is the old shyster? Still cheating penniless widows out of their life savings?"

Molly bristled. "Sir, Master Adams is a fair and just attorney. He would never—"

The four walls vibrated with the man's thunderous laughter. "Sorry, Miss Maguire, I was just joshing you. That is a long-standing joke between old Angus and me. Of course, the old man would be as honest as the day is long. On that you can depend." He paused and scanned the letter a second time. "And now about you. Angus says you are a top-notch accountant and that I'd be a fool not to snatch you up before some other trickster in town hires you away from me. So is my friend accurate? Are you good at keeping books?"

Molly tilted her chin a trifle. "Yes, sir. I believe I am."

"Good answer. I like that you didn't simper a reply." He strode to the office door and called, "Josephine! Your savior might have arrived."

From the woman's immediate appearance, both Molly and the lawyer knew the woman had been listening to all they'd said. "Molly Maguire, meet Josephine, my wife and all-round office assistant who hates her job to the bitter core. There's nothing more that dear Josie would like to do than stay at home taking care of our little boy, Wesley James, making quilts, and spoiling our grandbabies." Again the man's laughter filled the room.

Josephine squealed with delight. "Oh, praise God! Sam, do you mean it?"

"Absolutely, that is if Miss Molly Maguire will come to work for us. How about it, Miss Maguire?" Both the lawyer and his wife focused on Molly, waiting on her answer.

"I think I'd like that very much." A smile spread across Molly's face. "What would I be doing besides keeping the books?"

"Just about everything!" Josephine quipped. "I'm sure my husband will give you more than enough instruction tomorrow when you come for your first day of work." The woman beamed with happiness. "So how long have you been in Independence, and where are you staying?"

"I arrived this afternoon by wagon. And, as yet, I'm not sure where I'll be staying," the girl admitted.

"Are you traveling with family?" Josephine asked.

"No. My mother, my only relative, is an indentured servant at a plantation in Virginia. She'll be coming here next summer, when she completes her contract."

Attorney Pownell turned to his wife. "There's no establishment in town where I'd want a daughter of mine to stay. Honey, do you know if Serenity has a room available at the inn?"

"I'm sure she does. It is the off season." Josephine turned to Molly, "Our daughter and her husband, Caleb, converted a Christian mission into a boardinghouse a few years back. Since it's more Serenity's project than Caleb's, they named it Serenity Inn. Caleb is a blacksmith by trade. Families who'd prefer a quiet and relaxing atmosphere to the more, er, should I say, exciting life a frontier town offers, stay with them until they continue their journey westward."

"Yes! Molly could ride to and from work each day with Preacher Earle. The preacher is a part-time handyman at the lumberyard and part-time pastor at a small church on the edge of town," Sam explained.

"Good idea." The woman slipped her arm through Molly's as if the problem had been solved. "Now, my dear, if you agree, Sam will take care of everything for you. I presume you have luggage with you?"

The girl felt overwhelmed by the pair. "Yes, Mistress Josephine. My trunk is on Doctor Sheridan's wagon."

"Doctor Sheridan?" Sam frowned.

Molly smiled. "Trust me, you won't miss him. He and his wagon will be causing a traffic jam near the center of town."

The woman chuckled. "Mistress Josephine? How quaint. Molly, you will find people more casual out here on the prairie. Please call me Josephine, and I will call you Molly. Is that acceptable to you? Do we have a deal?"

The girl nodded.

"And as my husband often tells people, you can call him anything as long as you don't call him late for meals, but to look at him, you'd never think he eats that much."

"Stealing my thunder, dear?" The man gave his wife a squeeze around the waist. "Actually, when around clients, Mister Pownell will do. Otherwise, call me Sam. All right then! It's settled. If you agree, I'll have your trunk delivered the Serenity Inn."

While Sam left to retrieve her trunk from Seamus, Josephine swept Molly into a carriage and transported her to a charming home surrounded with a white picket fence on the western edge of town. Once inside the kitchen, the aroma of freshly baked molasses cookies stimulated Molly's senses. Until that moment, the girl had forgotten she hadn't eaten since morning.

"Come, my dear, let me take your wrap and bonnet. You must be starving and tired. I remember how exhausting it was, traveling across country." Josephine led her to a pristine white kitchen.

The yellow-and-white gingham café curtains at the windows and matching tablecloth lent a cheery, springlike air to the room. The woman gestured for her visitor to sit to the table. "I've found that a taste of home cooking rejuvenates one's spirits." She placed a plate of cookies and a pitcher of milk on the table. "Let's have a moment of prayer before you start. We won't wait for Sam. He'll be along shortly."

Overwhelmed by Josephine's buoyant personality, Molly bowed her head as her hostess prayed aloud, "Dearest Father, I thank You for this most amazing day. I especially thank You for bringing Molly to our family. You answered my prayer; I am so grateful. Now, as we break bread together, I thank You for Your abundance that You shower on us daily. Bless every mouthful we take. May it strengthen us to better live our lives for You. Amen."

Molly had barely eaten one molasses cookie when Sam burst through the kitchen door. He assured her that her trunk was on its way to the inn. "Your companion, Doctor Sheridan, was reluctant to release it to me until Sheriff Mason vouched for me. Interesting character, your Doctor Sheridan."

Not ready to explain her connection to Seamus, Molly gulped, "Yes, he is."

Though obviously curious, Sam didn't press the subject. "I found him parked in front of Pringle's Mercantile Store, where he was selling his elixir." Upon mentioning the elixir, Sam cleared his throat. "Your friend Fern gathered your belongings together for you. She sends her love to you and hopes to see you again soon."

Molly's eyes misted. "Fern's a good friend."

Sam nodded. "I could tell. Don't worry. Independence isn't so large but that you'll see her soon."

Molly had to force herself to keep from wolfing down the entire plate of cookies. After sharing some banter about the town, Sam pushed away from the table. "You must be exhausted. I need to get you to Serenity's so you can take a long, hot bath and finally sleep in a comfortable bed once more."

"What do you mean, you are taking her? I'm going too! Do you think I would miss the opportunity to hold Caleb and Serenity's beautiful babies, if only for a minute or two? *Hmm,* think I'll take along a plate of cookies for them. We grandmas have to do our best to spoil those precious little creatures. Wesley will miss out on the fun. But he is spending the afternoon and evening with one of his little friends."

When Molly began gathering the dishes from the table to carry to the sink, Josephine waved her hands in the air like a butterfly in flight. "Leave the dishes, Molly. Sam and I will take care of them later this evening. Won't we, Sam?"

The man uttered a groan of mock dismay. Josephine leaped from the table. "Let me get my wrap and my bonnet, and I'll be ready to go."

As she watched the Pownells interact with each another, Molly was baffled. She'd never met anyone who made her feel at home so quickly. And yet a part of her was skeptical of their overtures of friendship.

* * * * *

From a distance, Molly spotted the lights of the inn shining in the twilight. Sam halted the carriage in front of a sprawling one-story building, but not before a huge black dog ran from behind the barn and began to bark.

"Quiet, Onyx," Sam shouted, hopping out of the carriage and tying the reins to the wooden hitching post. "It's only us."

"Don't be afraid of Onyx." Josephine patted the gentle giant on the head. "He's a good dog, the best. Serenity and Caleb brought him all the way from western New York State. Imagine, the poor thing coming the entire distance."

Nestled against a small rise in the open prairie, Serenity Inn looked welcoming and homey. Even before entering the inn, the girl realized that to turn a sod mission into a warm, inviting place took the unique touch of a gifted woman.

Serenity and Caleb Cunard welcomed her at the door as if they'd anticipated her arrival. "Daddy! Mama! What a delightful surprise! Sammy, look who's here," the diminutive woman called over her shoulder. "It's your grandmama."

"Grandmama! Grandmama!" A towheaded boy of four appeared out of nowhere. He squealed and leaped into Josephine's waiting arms.

"Grandmama, come see the new train engine Daddy bought me for my birthday. It's green, my favorite color."

"*Ssh!* I know you're excited, Sammy, but try not to waken your little sister," Serenity called after the two disappeared down a narrow hallway.

After a short explanation by Sam, Serenity said Molly's trunk had already been delivered. "Bert just left." She led Molly to the room that would be hers during her stay. While Sam and Caleb relaxed in the parlor, Serenity led Molly to the room that would be hers during her stay,

"We are so glad to have you here, Molly. Consider this your home while you're here, and stay with us for as long as you like." Serenity's brilliant smile unnerved Molly. *What is it with these people?* the girl wondered. *They seem too nice to be real.*

Later, after Josephine put her grandson to bed for the night, Serenity invited Molly to join the family in the kitchen for slices of fresh homemade bread and hot chamomile tea.

A fire roared in a large river-rock fireplace. A red-and-gold crazy quilt lay casually across the arm of a tall Windsor rocker beside the fireplace. And a red rag rug covered the wooden floor in front of the hearth. Several shiny copper pots hung on hooks above a long oak trestle table in the center of the room.

Molly ran her hand along the smooth tabletop. "This is a lovely table."

"Yes, it is, isn't it?" Serenity poured tea into her guest's cup. "The missionary who built Serenity Inn crafted it for his wife's wedding anniversary. Isn't that utterly romantic?"

"So how is little Seri doing?" Josephine asked. "Is she over her bout with croup?"

"She seems to be." Serenity passed Molly another slice of bread. "At least she's sleeping through the night now. And that's a blessing!"

"It certainly is!" Caleb interjected. "For a while, the child had either Serenity or me up almost every night."

"You were two when you had croup, Serenity. Your mother wouldn't leave your side, day or night," Sam reminisced.

"Your mother." That sounds strange, Molly noted. Josephine caught the puzzled look on Molly's face and laughed. "Sorry, Molly, I'm sure

what I said made no sense to you. I am Sam's second wife. He married me after Charity, Sam's first wife and my best friend, died. By that time Serenity was almost out of her teens."

"I would never have guessed," Molly admitted. "You all get along so well. You seem like the perfect family."

Josephine rolled her eyes and grinned. "The getting along part took time for Serenity and me."

Serenity patted the other woman's hand. "But now I can't imagine life without her. And she's been so good for the children and for my dad. And what joy to have a little half brother."

Josephine's eyes misted. "Why, thank you, sweetie."

"Really!" Serenity continued. "My father would be incorrigible if Josephine weren't around to soften the edges." The two women exchanged tender glances.

"Hey, watch it!" Sam retorted. "Molly will discover my rough edges soon enough."

Caleb dropped two sugar cubes into his teacup. "As if our wives have no rough edges of their own."

Josephine stuck out her tongue at her son-in-law. Everyone laughed.

Later as Molly unpacked her clothing and hung her dresses in the wardrobe, she marveled at how quickly she'd been accepted into their circle, as if she were a long-lost relative. *No wonder travelers enjoy staying at the inn,* Molly mused. Snug in bed, in the darkness of the night, the girl thought about her own parents' marriage. As happy as she remembered them to be, Molly couldn't imagine they would ever openly welcome a stranger into their home. *If I ever I marry, I want to be like these people,* she decided.

CHAPTER SEVENTEEN

A NEW LIFE

OLLY'S LIFE EVOLVED INTO a comfortable pattern, working in Sam Pownell's quiet law office during the day, and at night, enjoying a quiet home life with the Cunards. Except for also being the office receptionist and deciphering and recording Sam's daily notes, she could have been back in Norfolk. From the town mayor to the county sheriff, from the banker to a variety of wagon masters and scouts, she'd developed an easy rapport with each.

Occasionally, Fern would drop by the office to say hello. She and Percy had found a one-room cottage in the colored section of town. While Percy worked at the wagon factory, Fern cared for several babies of mothers who had to work at the factory or as maids for the wealthy families of Independence.

One afternoon Fern brought a young man named Charley Lee by to meet Molly. The short, wiry man had an easy smile and an engaging laugh. Charley taught elementary school for the children of the colored community. Happy to see Fern making a new friend after losing Norwood, Molly also secretly envied the girl. During one visit, Fern told her that Seamus was taking his act to the southern part of the state.

Good, Molly thought. *If I never see him again it will be too soon.* Yet alone in her room at night when she mulled the list of injuries she'd suffered throughout her life, loneliness and her old list of resentments would build within her heart, keeping her awake, plotting of ways she could get even. The obligatory reading of her mother's Bible each evening did little to ease her pain.

The week before Christmas, Serenity suggested that Molly invite Percy, Fern, and Charley to Christmas dinner. "Everyone needs someone special with whom to celebrate the blessed day."

Molly appreciated Serenity's thoughtfulness. "Is there anything I can do or contribute to the meal?" Molly asked.

Serenity laughed. "Are you kidding? I'm going to put you to work in the kitchen, I assure you. At Christmas everyone contributes!"

On the day before Christmas, another blizzard hit—the third for the season. A strong wind whipped the snow about the corners of the inn. For the most part, Josephine stayed in the children's room to keep Sammy, Wesley, and Seri from being underfoot. Molly was in the kitchen, rolling the dough for the pumpkin pies while Serenity stood at the opposite end of the trestle table, humming softly as she kneaded the bread dough.

Molly knew she'd heard the tune before, but couldn't remember where. "What is that tune you're humming?" she asked.

"It's called 'Amazing Grace.' There's an interesting story attached. A former English slave trader wrote the words after inviting Jesus Christ into his life. Some believe the tune is one the slaves would sing aboard ship on their way to England. I don't know. But I do know the words tug at my heartstrings every week when we sing it at church."

Molly's emotions overwhelmed her when she remembered where she'd last heard the tune. Jenny Lind sang it at the concert she had attended with Tavis. "Would you sing the words for me?" she asked.

"Sure." Serenity's sweet soprano voice filled the kitchen.

"Amazing grace! how sweet the sound, that saved a wretch like me!
I once was lost, but now I am found, was blind, but now I see.
'Twas grace that taught my heart to fear, and grace my fears relieved;
How precious did that grace appear the hour I first believed!"

"It's very beautiful," Molly admitted. "But what does it mean? I don't understand."

Serenity placed the giant lump of bread dough in a large pottery bowl, covered it with a dishtowel, and set it on the back of the stove to rise. "When the man who'd done despicably cruel and inhumane things to the slaves came face to face with the love of a forgiving God, only then he realized how hopeless he truly was. His only salvation, his only escape from his past, was to cast his sins at the feet of Jesus and accept the divine grace granted him at the Cross."

The Cross. Divine grace. Being lost and then found. To Molly, they were mere words. She had no idea what it all meant. Serenity adjusted the dust cap protecting her curls. "Understanding the depth of God's grace takes a lifetime, I think. You should attend church with us on Christmas Day. It may help you understand. For that matter, you're welcome to attend with us any time you'd like."

Serenity had invited Molly to attend church with the family when she first arrived, but the girl had declined. Instead, she'd stay in her room and brood over her past. The only light in her life came when she remembered Tavis's promise to come to her in the spring. To that promise she held on for dear life.

On Christmas Day, twenty people gathered around the Cunard table, people of every hue and color, including Caleb's best friend and his wife from a neighboring Indian village. As the abundant bowls of mashed potatoes, gravy, sweet potatoes, and string beans were passed, Molly marveled at the strange gathering. She thought of her father's heart for people; she knew he'd be pleased. After the meal, the children played on the parlor floor with their new toys while Serenity heated water on the stove, and the men cleared the table.

"To me, this is the best part, after the men retire to the barn to chat." Josephine's face beamed with joy. "I was born into a wealthy family, so I never experienced the friendship a bunch of women can enjoy when they gather in the kitchen after a big meal to do the dishes. It's so much fun!"

Molly had never thought of doing dishes as being fun, but the girl had to admit, she almost felt sad when the last pot was dried and the last kitchen towel hung on the rack beside the sink to dry.

Sharing memories of Christmases past, singing carols around Serenity's piano, and laughing at the humorous experiences shared completed a truly unforgettable day. The Pownells had brought the people from town in their sleigh. When it was time to leave, Fern pulled Molly aside.

"Thank you so much for inviting us to share today with you." She paused. "I didn't think white folk ever had so much fun."

Onyx stood beside Molly as she waved until the sled could no longer be seen and the jangle of the bells, no longer heard in the night. Molly and the irrepressibly friendly dog had become good friends since her arrival at the inn. It wasn't that Serenity hadn't invited Molly to join them for their evening vespers; she just felt awkward intruding on their family time. So each evening when the Cunard family gathered in the parlor for worship, Molly would don her heaviest clothing, and she and Onyx would hike to the top of the rise behind the house. The girl would stare into the blackness where the prairie met the sky and wonder if her mother or if Tavis were gazing up at the same stars and missing her as much as she did them.

After several invitations, Molly reluctantly attended church with the family. The girl loved the music. She loved the way the tiny congregation welcomed her. And she enjoyed the weekly potlucks that followed the morning service. But the sermons made her uncomfortable. To Molly, it seemed Preacher Earle's every sermon, from the origin of sin to the second coming of Jesus, included the subjects of forgiveness and grace. And during the following week, she couldn't get the man's words out of her mind. Because she rode to and from town with him every day, Molly had plenty of opportunities to ask the preacher for clarifications, but the girl feared the man would ask her too many questions. *No,* she decided, *I have to work this out myself.*

Winter lingered long on the plains that year. January, February, March, and April brought blizzards and bitter winds swirling off the prairie. As she would bundle up in her warmest clothing for the short morning ride to town, the girl missed the milder temperatures of Norfolk and of her home in Ireland. As she checked the days off the office calendar, Molly dreamed of the day when Tavis would come for her.

But the green fields of spring turned golden with the arrival of summer. Day after day, she'd glance to the east as she left the office at the end of a working day, hoping to see a familiar face. Conestoga wagons filled with excited pioneers, eager to venture into the unknown, continued to roll through town. She'd heard the stories of hardship, sickness, and death that awaited them, but they continued to come and leave. Long wagon trains trailed through town only to be swallowed up by the vast rolls and heaves of a green ocean of waving prairie grass.

During her lunch break, Molly would stroll to her favorite mercantile store to examine the storekeeper's newest supply of trinkets and sewing notions. And then, after purchasing a giant dill pickle from the pickle barrel to eat, she'd head back to the office.

One day Molly lingered longer than she'd intended. Not wanting to be late from her lunch break, the girl rushed out of the double doors and was face to face with her redheaded, freckle-faced nemesis—Seamus.

"Molly Maguire! Fancy meeting you here." He tipped his wide-brimmed black felt hat toward her. "I was hoping to run into you, but not quite like this."

"Seamus! I didn't expect to see you here. I heard you had left town."

He flashed her his usual grin. "I did. I spent the winter in Arkansas."

"How nice for you." Her reply dripped with sarcasm.

He grimaced. "Molly, could we go somewhere to talk? I've so much to tell you." He tried to take her arm, but she shook free of his grasp. Her lips tightened into a thin, determined line.

"We have nothing to say to one another—now or ever!"

Two customers brushed past them and out onto the boardwalk. The man insisted, "Actually, we do. Many things have changed since I last saw you." He switched approaches, "Fern tells me you're working for a lawyer. Could we talk in his office?"

Several more customers arrived on the boardwalk, wanting to enter the store. Molly heaved an exasperated sigh. The last thing she wanted was to be alone with Seamus in the office or anywhere.

She glanced at the face of the watch she wore on a chain around her neck. "Mr. Pownell will be back from court by three. You may stop by at that time if you wish."

"All right. I'll see you then." He tipped his hat a second time and disappeared in the crowd of shoppers.

The familiar medicine wagon pulled up in front of the law office exactly at three, and Molly was waiting. The girl had forewarned Sam about Seamus's appointment and asked the lawyer to keep his office door open. "We parted on awkward terms. I don't know what the man might do if he finds me alone." Sam agreed to be alert.

When Molly saw Seamus climb down from the wagon, she dashed to her desk and pretended to be working. Before he arrived, she'd placed one of the stiff wooden chairs opposite her desk. When he opened the door and strode inside, the girl looked up from the file she'd been pretending to read. "Oh? Is it three o'clock already? Please come in and sit down. I'll be with you in one moment."

She folded her hands in front of her on the desk and asked, "And now, Seamus, what can I do for you?"

He glanced down at his hands for a moment and then at her. "Molly, I've come to ask your forgiveness for my bad behavior last year on the paddleboat."

"Bad behavior on the paddleboat? Oh, yes, now I remember. The night you stumbled into my stateroom drunk and tried to molest me."

"Molly, no games, all right?" His blue eyes pleaded for understanding. "I've had a long time to regret what I did. I know you said you'd never forgive me, but I have to ask you one last time. Will you, can you, find it in your heart to forgive me?"

"Why is my opinion of you important?"

"Probably because I once believed you might come to love me."

"Oh, come, come. That will never happen," she scoffed.

He nodded sadly. "I know that now."

Molly leaned forward, placing her chin in her cupped hands. "Why should I forgive you? Has anything changed between us in the last year?"

"Not between us, but a lot has changed for me. Remember I told you I spent the winter in Arkansas? Well, I stayed at the home of Spencer Finch. He's a carpenter who led me to Christ. Since then, my entire life has changed. I no longer sell phony cure-alls to gullible customers. Now I travel around Arkansas and southern Missouri as a visiting physician. People rely on me. They respect me."

Molly tried to hide her surprise with sarcasm. "How very nice for you, and for them."

"Because I am a Christian, I want to make amends to those I've hurt, beginning with you. Obviously, I can't apologize to every person I deceived over the years, but I can ask for your forgiveness."

The girl cleared her throat. "Tell me, is my forgiveness necessary for you to enjoy this new life of yours?"

"No, not really. My Lord tells me to just ask for forgiveness. What the injured party does with my apology is up to him or her."

"Then you've done your part. You've completed your half of the requirement." She leaned back in her chair. "Will that be all?"

Seamus rose to his feet. "Not quite. Please stay right here, I have some-one I want you to meet." He ran to the door and waved. Within seconds, a lovely young woman with red hair brighter than Seamus's shyly entered the office. "This is my wife Kate. She's carrying our first child." He helped the woman sit down in the empty chair. Seamus straightened, his eyes filled with tears. "Molly, with my firstborn child on the way, I wanted this child to be cradled in the arms of a father who has nothing to hide, loved by a daddy with clean hands and a pure heart."

Molly blinked back the tears that threatened to escape her eyes. And while her heart cried out "Yes! Yes," the resentment she'd held for so long resisted.

As the pendulum on the wall clock swung back and forth, ticking away the seconds, Seamus hung his head. His wife struggled to her feet and wrapped her arms protectively about her husband. "Come, honey, you've done what you came to do."

Seamus gave Molly a sad but genuine smile. "It's all right, Molly, I understand. And someday I know you will as well. Christ works with each of us in His own time. May God bless you. And I promise not to bother you again, Molly Maguire."

As the couple left the office, Molly buried her face in her hands. Sud-denly, she didn't much like Molly Maguire. Whatever held her back from granting Seamus forgiveness, she did not know. Surely, the man's apology had been sincere.

The door to Sam's office opened further. She heard but did not see Sam place a file on her desk. "Here, Molly, will you please record this court document for the files?" Without a word, he returned to his office and closed the door.

The rest of the afternoon Molly moved unseeing through her tasks. At quitting time, when Pastor Earle arrived to take her back to Serenity Inn, she knocked on Sam's door before leaving. "If you have nothing more for me, I'll be going now."

"Fine," he called. "See you tomorrow."

* * * * *

The days of August came to an end. Evenings sitting on the hilltop with Onyx demanded Molly wear a jacket instead of her shawl. The girl withdrew more and more from those around her. Her heart grew heavy. Her easy smiles had disappeared behind a mask of determination. Sam and Serenity worried about her but said nothing. At church, the minister continued to preach on the freedom that comes from forgiveness, but Molly determinedly closed her mind to his message.

One night as Molly and Onyx strolled out onto the knoll, a cool north wind whipped her skirt about her ankles and her bonnet off her hair onto her shoulders. The girl sat down on her favorite rock, folded her knees up under her arms and stared across the darkened prairie. Onyx stretched out on the ground beside her. She listened to the hiss of the wind rustling through the prairie grass. In the distance, a wolf howled. An owl hooted.

Molly resented Seamus's and Kate's relationship. She wondered if they would be parents of a boy or a girl. She tried to be happy for Fern and her new fiancé as well, but the girl felt so lonely. She'd been outside for almost an hour when Onyx gave a low growl.

"Molly?" It was Serenity. "Caleb and I have been worried about you. Are you all right?"

"I'm fine. Thank you for asking." That anyone cared or noticed meant a lot to the girl. In the nine months she had been living at Serenity Inn, Molly felt as close to Serenity as she might a sister.

Serenity sat down on the rock beside her. "You know, when Caleb and I were first married I would come out to this rock sometimes to think. Occasionally, I needed time alone. Newlyweds have a lot of growing to do, I assure you."

Molly only half listened. To her the Cunards' marriage seemed perfect. The couple truly enjoyed one another. With her hopes for Tavis growing as cold as the north wind, Molly wondered if she'd ever find someone to love.

Serenity continued, "I brought a lot of anger into our marriage. Unfortunately, that anger would spill out onto my husband at the strangest moments. Sometimes I would fly into a rage if he tracked mud in from the blacksmith shop or if he let Onyx onto my clean floor." She chuckled aloud. "And I would fume if he forgot to kiss me goodnight."

Molly leaned her chin on her elbows but continued to listen.

"It wasn't until I learned to forgive and let go of the hurts from my past that I was free to truly express my love for Caleb. That's what's exciting about forgiveness. It sets you free."

Molly wanted to know more but didn't want to pry.

"Forgiving Josephine wasn't an easy thing to do. I always considered myself a Christian. After all, my parents were Christian, so what else would I be? I went to church, I prayed, I read the Bible, but I couldn't find joy or the release from resentment that I craved. Finally my hatred became too heavy to carry."

Molly turned her face away. She wasn't sure she wanted to hear any more.

"One morning at church, the pastor told the story of the Cross—you know where Jesus said, 'Father, forgive them; for they know not what they do.' He told us that the entire message of the Cross could be narrowed down to two concepts: love and forgiveness. They cannot be separated. One cannot say he or she loves God and not forgive." Serenity cleared her throat. "I've learned that the greatest revenge against those who hurt you is found in forgiving them. The extra benefit is your enemy is no longer an enemy. Sorry! I didn't come out here to preach a sermon."

Molly stared out into the darkness. "No, it's all right. I don't mind. I'm enjoying your company."

"Thanks. I enjoy yours too. Having you here at the inn has been a true blessing for Caleb and me. You've helped with household chores and babysat the children during the inn's busy season. I don't know what I'll do when you finally leave us."

"Well, by the looks of things, that won't be anytime soon. You know, I believed Tavis when he said he and my mother would be here before summer passed. Unfortunately, autumn is here, and winter isn't far behind!" The girl picked up a stone and threw it at a nearby shrub. "You are so lucky to love a man you can trust. I haven't met too many of those during my life!"

"I don't attribute our love to luck. It has more to do with God's guidance and His love."

Tears welled up in Molly's eyes. Her voice broke. How many times had she heard her mother say the same thing? "Tell me, if it's true, when does God stop talking about love and start blessing someone like me?"

"Oh, honey," Serenity wrapped her arms around Molly's shoulders and drew her close. "He already is loving you. The good Lord brought you to us and to my father's law firm. My dad raves about your work, and Josephine, she loves being free to stay home with Wesley and to enjoy her sewing circles. She hated office work. The way Dad tells it, she wasn't very good at it either." The woman chuckled and gave Molly an extra squeeze.

The girl heaved a ragged sigh. "I cannot imagine Josephine not being exceptional at anything she's set her mind to."

Serenity's laugh came from deep within her body. "I know what you mean. Perhaps that's the reason I hated her so much—especially after my mother's death. I resented having her usurp my mother's place in my father's heart and in our home."

"Really?" Molly started in surprise. Serenity and Josephine appeared to care deeply for one another.

"I was at a finishing school outside of Boston when I learned of my mother's death. My father was an assemblyman for the state of New York. By the time I returned home to Union Springs after my mother's death, Josephine had completely moved in on my father. I hated her so much. Even now, I can't put my fury into words."

"What did you do?"

"At the time I wasn't aware that my father was an abolitionist and that he and our neighbor Caleb, operated a well-traveled branch of the Underground Railroad. One night, a fire broke out in our home. Whether it was caused by bounty hunters, by officers of the law, by runaways hiding in our attic, or by sheer accident, I'll never know. The only thing saved from being totally destroyed was my mother's Bible, thanks to my best friend Annie." Serenity grew pensive for several seconds. "My father was forced into hiding. Onyx and I joined Caleb and his family's move west."

"So when did you and Josephine become friends?"

"It took a long time after she and my father arrived here in Independence. Caleb and I had already married and purchased the inn by then. You know, as much as I knew how it hurt my dad for me to harbor such a strong hatred for his new wife, I couldn't let it go. I blamed her for everything wrong in my life—my mother's death, the fire, having to move west, the latest argument between Caleb and me."

"I know what you mean," Molly mused. "While everyone called my dad a hero for saving Lady Pembrooke's life, I resented him for dying. Isn't that silly? As if he could help it."

Serenity shook her head. "Oh no, I completely understand. Hatred is seldom reasonable. It's a disease that consumes its host from the inside out. Worse yet, the person who you hate controls you because he takes ownership of your thoughts."

Now it was Molly's turn to laugh. She pictured Seamus and Lord Pembrooke wrestling over her mind. "I never thought of it that way, but you may be right."

The two women gazed out into the night for several minutes until Serenity asked, "So tell me, how did you get from Ireland to Independence, Missouri?"

"Huh!" Molly patted Onyx's head. "It was a long journey, thanks to the heels and scalawags I've met along the way. But wait, you didn't say how you and Josephine buried the hatchet."

Serenity giggled aloud. "That's what I wanted to do, bury the hatchet in that pretty blond head of hers. Actually, she had nothing to do with my decision. As I began to tell you, one morning the pastor retold the story of the Cross and the importance of God's forgiveness and for us, in turn, to forgive others. At the end of one sermon, he gave an altar call."

Molly stirred. Altar calls made her uncomfortable. Preacher Earle ended many of his sermons with altar calls. It bothered her that occasionally she felt the urge to go forward, but to this point, she had successfully resisted the temptation.

"I believed going forward was but an emotional release for weaker individuals. I held out as long as I could. But that week, the pieces to the puzzle fell into place for me. Imagine how God's unlimited grace pours down on His children so they can pour out the same grace on others. What an honor!"

A cold shiver traveled the length of her spine. Molly had heard enough about forgiveness, about God's love, about God's grace. She started to rise to her feet when Serenity continued. "My heart melted. Unexplainable warmth washed through me. I began to weep and I couldn't stop weeping." She laughed. "Poor Caleb didn't know what was wrong with me. For the first time, I realized I needed, no I wanted, to beg for Josephine's forgiveness." The woman's voice filled with emotion. She took a deep breath. "Needless to say, many tears were shed that afternoon. But you know, they were cleansing tears of redemption and joy." Serenity grew silent.

Molly's heart had been touched. "If you don't mind, I need to be alone for a few minutes. Go back to the house. I'll be in soon."

"Sure, honey. Always remember that the gift of forgiveness is a gift you give yourself. We've all been hurt. We've all sinned and need God's forgiveness." She gave Molly a quick squeeze, rose to her feet, and headed down the hill toward the inn.

Exhausted, unable to fight any longer, Molly dropped to her knees. "Oh, God, why You would love a hateful character like me enough to send Your Son to die so I could be forgiven, I don't understand. But I know now that I need Your forgiveness." Her voice echoed into the night as she collapsed facedown on the ground. "I am so unworthy! I've fought You every step of the way."

Thinking something was wrong with her, Onyx licked her face, hands, and neck. "Please forgive me for not forgiving Seamus, and for my unrelenting anger toward Lord Pembrooke, and lately, my frustration with Tavis. He isn't even here to speak for himself." Her breath came in ragged gasps. "Take away the demons controlling me. I want to leave them all at the foot of Your cross." Molly lay still for several minutes. Feeling Onyx's cold nose nudging her, she rolled over onto her back and stared at the myriad of stars. For some reason, the girl felt as free as a ten-year-old playing under the stars. "Dear God, You said to call You Father. I do need a Daddy so badly."

* * * * *

It wasn't easy. During the weeks that followed, the temptation to recall the past plagued her. Determined, she devised a plan that whenever a negative thought popped into her mind, Molly would repeat the words of "Amazing Grace." And for the first time, she approached her promise to her mother to read the Bible every night with eagerness. Texts that had made no sense to her before became clear, as if she was wearing spiritual spectacles. Though she still missed her mom dearly, Molly determined to turn her loneliness over to her new Father.

At work, Sam commented on the new effervescent Molly. At the inn, Molly joined the family's evening vespers. At church, she sang the hymns with enthusiasm. She became the chatty, effervescent girl she'd been before. Molly also celebrated the changing colors of autumn. The girl felt as if she had wakened from a deep sleep.

A few weeks later, Molly sat at her desk to record a stack of receipts when the main office door swung open. A shaft of sunlight silhouetted the forms of a stocky man of medium height and a slight woman standing beside him in the doorway.

"Molly." The woman's voice broke with emotion.

Startled, the girl's head popped up from the ledger on her desk. "Mama?"

Forgetting all grace and proper decorum, Enid tore across the room. Molly met her halfway. As she clung to her mother, the girl couldn't believe her senses. Neither of them wanted to let the other go.

"You've finally come!" Molly swiped at her tears.

Enid wiped her nose on a linen handkerchief. "At last! There was delay after delay."

Molly forgot about the man left standing in the doorway. "How did you find me?" she asked. "Where's Tavis? Is he all right? Did he come with you?"

"He surely did. As to finding you, Tavis stopped your sheriff on the street and asked for you. The man immediately knew who you were."

Molly laughed. "Yes, I'm sure Sheriff Masou would know who I am. He and Mr. Pownell play checkers every Thursday afternoon. So where is Tavis?" Molly glanced over her mother's shoulder at the man waiting patiently in the doorway. "Who's that?" she whispered. "Is he with you?"

Her mother blushed and giggled like a schoolgirl. "Yes, you could say George is with me." She turned and gestured toward the man. He strode up to her side.

"Don't be angry with me, darling, until you hear the whole story. George Reade is a merchant I met in Richmond. I spent a lot of time purchasing supplies for the plantation kitchen from his store," the woman explained.

Molly stiffened, not at all sure she liked where her mother's tale might be heading. She shot the man a look of suspicion.

"George's wife died of pneumonia a few years back. He was lonely; I was lonely. And before either of us knew it, we were in love. Did I tell you he was a deacon in the church I attended?" Enid gave her daughter a sheepish grin. "In May, George bought my indentured servant papers from the Taylors so we could marry. When I told him about wanting to see you again, he voluntarily sold his store and his home so we could come to Independence. Isn't he absolutely marvelous?" Enid slipped her arm around the man's generous waist and gave him a squeeze.

The news hit Molly like a lightning bolt. How could another man have taken her father's place in her mother's heart? The girl had never imagined such a thing could happen. The temptation to let Enid and her new husband know exactly how she felt waged war with the new person she was becoming.

"I wouldn't have imagined I could ever love again." Her mother's eyes begged the girl to understand. "But I do, not in the same way as I loved your father, but in a new and exciting way I can't explain."

The man placed a tender kiss on his wife's cheek. "Molly, I love your mother with all my heart. I will do anything to make her happy."

Enid extended her free hand to her daughter. "Please be happy for me."

At the sight of her mother's pleading look, Molly's heart melted. Her eyes brimmed with tears. The muscles on her face softened. "Of course, Mama. I wish you both wonderful happiness." To the man her mother had taken into her heart, the girl warned, "My mother is a very special person, George. She deserves happiness. You'd better be all she claims you are, or you'll have one feisty Irish lass ready to do battle!"

The massively built man gazed down at the sprightly girl with fire in her eyes and laughed. "I promise I will love, honor, and cherish your mom 'till death us do part." He immediately wrapped his big muscular arm around her shoulders.

From the open door, they heard, "Well, what is this? May I get in on the affection?"

Molly immediately recognized the voice. "Tavis!" she squealed and ran to him. "I am so glad to see you! Where have you been? I missed you so much! You said you'd come in the summer. When you didn't, I was so worried you might have changed your mind about coming west." As she babbled, he touched his finger to her lips to silence her.

"One question at a time, little pigeon. I'm glad to see you too. As for where I've been, I had to get the lay of the land from your sheriff. He thinks a lot of you, more than I might like," Tavis teased. "And yes, I missed you, too, more than you can possibly imagine. And no, I didn't change my mind for one minute. Circumstance changed it for me, but I'll tell you about that later. Right now, let me take a good look at you." He held her at arm's length and gazed into her eyes. "Oh yes, you look even better than I remembered. For that matter, you are absolutely glowing." A grin washed across his face.

Eager to feel his arms around her once more, she said, "Tavis, so much has happened. I've so much to tell you."

The man paused; his expression darkened. His hands maintained a firm grip on her upper arms. "Please tell me our news doesn't include Doctor Seamus Sheridan."

"It does in a way, but not directly," she hastened to assure him.

"My biggest fear was that I'd get here and find you had married the man," Tavis explained.

"Marry Seamus?" Molly threw back her head and laughed. "Could never happen! But I'll tell you about it later."

"Good!" He glanced about the office. "How long do you have to stay here this afternoon? I don't want to let you out of my sight, but I need to find a room for the night."

Molly brightened. "That's no problem. You can stay where I stay, at the Serenity Inn. Let me ask my boss for the rest of the afternoon off, and I'll take you there."

"Are you sure he won't mind?" Enid asked. "I wouldn't want to get you in trouble."

Molly shook her head. "Don't worry. Sam will understand. But wait, you need to meet him. He's in his office."

She hadn't noticed Tavis's limp until she led the other three to Attorney Pownell's office. As much as she longed to hear all about it, she knew it would have to wait.

CHAPTER EIGHTEEN

ALL ABOUT TAVIS

I AM SO BLESSED, MOLLY reminded herself as she exchanged glances with Tavis from across Serenity's supper table.

"So, tell me Tavis, how long have you worked with horses?" Caleb asked.

"Since Molly's father trained me as a groom. He had a gentle way with horses. They'd do anything for him. After I injured my leg last spring, I realized being a horse trainer would be difficult. So, for me, the next best thing would be to learn blacksmithing."

Caleb nodded his head. "Well, I could use a man talented with horses here at the inn. I'd be willing to give you a small stipend while I train you to become a smithy."

Molly's eyes danced as she listened to the men's conversation. Could everything in her life be working out as she'd hoped? She glanced toward her mother at the other end of the table. She, too, was smiling.

When Caleb asked what prompted their leaving Norfolk and Richmond, Tavis told about Attorney Adams and the Underground Railroad. "We shipped Molly, Percy, and Fern out of town as soon as we recognized the danger they were in. One of Adams's law clerks set the sheriff on our trail."

"Ridgley?" Molly asked.

"Oh no, not Ridgley. It was Simms. Ridgley was the one who spirited me away from the Adamses' place. We had to detour north of the city to avoid detection."

Molly blinked in surprise. "Ridgley? I thought . . ."

"As Attorney Adams always said, Ridgley was unbelievably loyal to his employer and to the cause."

How could I have been so wrong about Ridgley, Molly wondered? *And about Simms, as well.*

The conversion shifted to the possibility of George opening a new mercantile store in town. Molly only half listened as she toyed with her silverware. Her desire to spend time alone with Tavis intensified. They had so much to tell one another.

As delicious as the mound of mashed potatoes looked, Molly couldn't eat a bite. Even Serenity's berry pie with whipped cream on top didn't tempt her. What she wanted most was for everyone to finish eating, for the women to clean the kitchen after the meal, and for the family to gather in the parlor for family vespers so she could steal Tavis away.

During the course of the meal, Enid told of their trip to Independence. "We left Richmond in late spring. But in Ohio, when Tavis and George stopped to help another traveler replace a broken wheel on his wagon, a garter snake slithered out of the underbrush and spooked the man's horses. The vehicle lurched forward, rolling over Tavis's leg and breaking it in three places. For a time, the doctor wasn't sure he'd walk again." She sent a compassionate glance Tavis's way. "But Tavis is tough and determine, and George and I were loath to continue on without him."

After dessert, Serenity gathered a handful of used silverware and placed them on her soiled plate. "Molly, I would like to get better acquainted with your mother, so why don't you take Tavis up to your favorite boulder?" Turning toward her husband, she added, "As for you, Caleb, I am sure George would love to see your pride and joy—the blacksmith shop."

Having dreamed of this evening for so long, Molly's hands quivered as she put her bonnet on her head and handed Tavis her cloak. Gently, he draped the soft woolen garment over her shoulders and led her out the kitchen door.

Onyx met them at the doorway. Uncertain of this stranger who had usurped his favorite person's attention, the dog tried to nose in between the couple. When that failed, he trotted as close to Molly's other side as he could get.

Hand in hand, Molly and Tavis ambled toward the base of the hill. "So a broken leg is your only excuse for not arriving sooner, as you promised?" she teased, giving his hand a gentle squeeze.

"Afraid so."

A cold November breeze whipped about the edge of the house. Chills not related to the dropping temperature scampered up Molly's spine as she studied Tavis's profile in the moonlight. "Does your leg still hurt when you walk? We don't have to climb the hill. We can sit on the back stoop and talk."

Despite Tavis's limp, his steps were sure. "Molly, I wouldn't miss our walk tonight for all the clover in Ireland."

Heady with emotion, Molly reveled in the feel of Tavis's callused hand holding hers. She thrilled at the sound of his voice. "Huh? Oh, yes. Me neither."

"How do you feel about my apprenticing with Caleb? Should I accept his offer?"

Pleased he would ask, she demurred, "If that's what you want to do."

"Molly, your opinion means everything to me. It's our future I'm talking about."

Without warning, a rabbit popped up in front of Onyx. The dog gave chase. Startled, Molly stepped into the rabbit's hole. She screamed and fell forward. Before her knees hit the ground Tavis caught her by the elbows and scooped her into his arms. Shaken, her breath caught in her throat. The girl could feel his warm breath on her forehead. Even though Molly couldn't see his eyes in the shadows, she couldn't bear to look away.

For an instant, Tavis didn't move. With tantalizing deliberation, he untied the bow on her bonnet and tossed it to the ground. In the process, the combs that held her hair in a bun gave way, freeing her long dark tresses. As if suddenly fascinated by her hair, he wrapped a curl around one of his fingers. "Molly," he whispered.

Gently, he slid a hand under the cascading curls and onto the nape of her neck. Then, slowly and deliberately, he lowered his lips to hers. A thrill like none she'd ever experienced coursed through her as his lips first brushed hers and then pressed against hers with a hunger she'd never before experienced. For what seemed like an eternity and yet a mere instant, Tavis's lips lingered on hers as if not wanting to break the spell of the moment. With great reluctance, he withdrew his lips from hers, but returned to kiss her a second time. Catching his breath, he planted a playful kiss on the tip of her nose and straightened.

Feeling as though her legs would give out from under her, Molly hungered for more. "Did I do something wrong?" she whispered.

"My goodness no!" Tavis laughed nervously; his normally deep voice was husky with emotion. "If I'd known a kiss like that was waiting for me, I would have crawled on my hand and knees to Missouri."

For Molly, the kiss had been a lesson in love that Lady Pembrooke had never taught her. Lacking the words to express her feelings, Molly caressed the side of his face.

Holding her face between his hands, he studied her eyes for several seconds. "Molly Maguire, I hope I haven't misread your signals, but I've waited all evening to tell you how very much I love you."

"Oh, I love you, too, Tavis." The words came from her heart before she considered the consequences. "Since I left Richmond, I haven't thought of much else but you. After our moonlight encounter at the Taylor plantation, I knew I loved you, but I was afraid I was nothing more to you than a pesky little sister."

"You, my dear, have long since stopped being my little sister." She heard the rumble of a laugh from deep within his chest. "That happened the moment I saw you on the Adamses' staircase in that emerald green gown. You were a vision of elegance. I was so enamored with your beauty that I barely heard Jenny Lind."

He buried his face in her neck and planted a string of kisses from her ear lobe to her shoulder. "And this afternoon, when I saw you again in Mr. Pownell's office—you took my breath away."

"I don't know what to say." She might not have known what to say, but Onyx certainly did. Returning from his unsuccessful rabbit chase, he saw the couple embracing and thought Tavis was harming Molly. Running in excited circles around them, his barks echoed through the cold night air.

"*Sssh!*" Molly ordered. "Stop barking!" But the dog ignored her command. "Onyx! Be quiet!"

When they saw the kitchen door fly open and the light from a lantern appear, Tavis loosened his hold on her and took a step backward. Molly immediately felt bereft of his touch.

They heard Caleb call, "Is everyone all right?"

Tavis laughed and assured the man all was well. "I guess that could be debated. It's time to take you home, Molly, my girl. We don't want to set the neighbors gossiping."

The girl's voice quivered, "Tavis, the Cunards' closest neighbor is in an Indian village, several miles away."

"Exactly." He playfully captured her hands in his.

"But we haven't reached the top of the hill yet."

"In time, I promise." Releasing one hand, he took the other in his and led her down the pathway to the inn. Once inside the inn, no one mentioned Onyx's barking or Molly's flushed face.

* * * * *

Something old—the antique white lace wedding dress her mother refashioned from one of Molly's ball gowns.

Something new—the ribbon bouquet Josephine designed for her.

Something borrowed—a lace handkerchief of Fern's.

Something blue—a snippet off of one of the satin ribbons Tavis gave to her in Norfolk.

And the coin that Lord Pembrooke gave her in her shoe.

Butterflies fluttered in Molly's stomach as she waited beside Samuel Pownell in the foyer of the tiny chapel, waiting to hear the pump organ's first wheezing notes of Mendelssohn's "Wedding March." Molly chose Sam to give her away as he was the closest she had to an earthly father.

"I am marrying Tavis Lloyd, the love of my life." Her eyes brimmed with tears of joy. It was almost too good to be true. This had been Molly's dream since she was a child. When she discovered her own father had brought Tavis to Christ, her joy seemed complete.

Molly wondered why she had ever doubted God's leading in her life as she recited under her breath the verse Serenity shared with her the previous night. "Delight thyself also in the Lord: and he shall give thee the desires of thine heart."

Sam withdrew a sheet of parchment paper from his coat pocket and handed it to her. "This is Josephine's and my prayer for you, Molly." The church deacon opened the chapel's double doors. "Shall we go? You don't want to keep your young man waiting."

Once glimpse of her intended, and Molly's nervousness subsided. Confident and unencumbered by guilt, anger, or sorrow, Molly glided down the aisle beside Sam. Her entire being was focused on her beloved.

It wasn't until the couple was alone in their bridal chamber that Molly remembered Sam and Josephine's note.

> May you always have a sunbeam to warm you;
> a moonbeam to charm you;
> and a sheltering angel, so nothing can harm you.
> —An Irish prayer

Tears glistened in Molly's eyes as she reread the words of the very same Irish prayer that Mistress Julia had given her when leaving Norfolk. Like a gentle spring rain, the faces of those she'd met along the way, those who helped her become the woman Tavis would choose as his bride washed over her.

"Today is not a time for tears, my love, but for joy." Tavis extended his arms toward her. Without hesitation, she melted into his warm embrace.

"Darling, mine are tears of joy, not sorrow! All along God wanted to grant me the desires of my heart, but I wouldn't let Him. It's taken me a very long time to learn that releasing bad memories would free me to treasure the good ones that will always be a part of our future."

THE SERENITY INN

KAY D. RIZZO

*Don't miss any of the inspirational adventures
in this heartwarming saga of the old West.*

These time-worn tales of seven young women struggling to build a life on the edge of the American frontier will not disappoint. You will laugh and cry with Serenity, Josephine, Lilia, Abigail, Annie, and Molly as they learn the hard lessons of life. And you will discover, along with each of them, the importance of a deep and trusting relationship with your Lord. Join Serenity and her friends each step of the way in this uplifting saga. You won't want to miss even one!

Serenity's Desire,
Book 1
Paperback, 224 pages
ISBN 13: 978-0-8163-2388-3
ISBN 10: 0-8163-2388-7

Serenity's Quest,
Book 2
Paperback, 224 pages
ISBN 13: 978-0-8163-2389-0
ISBN 10: 0-8163-2389-5

Josephine's Fortune,
Book 3
Paperback, 192 pages
ISBN 13: 978-0-8163-2421-7
ISBN 10: 0-8163-2421-2

Lilia's Haven,
Book 4
Paperback, 224 pages
ISBN 13: 978-0-8163-2423-1
ISBN 10: 0-8163-2423-9

Abigail's Dream,
Book 5
Paperback, 224 pages
ISBN 13: 978-0-8163-2422-4
ISBN 10: 0-8163-2422-0

Annie's Trust,
Book 6
Paperback, 192 pages
ISBN 13: 978-0-8163-2420-0
ISBN 10: 0-8163-2420-4

Pacific Press®
Publishing Association

"Where the Word Is Life"

Three ways to order:

1 Local	Adventist Book Center®
2 Call	1-800-765-6955
3 Shop	AdventistBookCenter.com